Moonlight Bleu

By

Renee Rearden

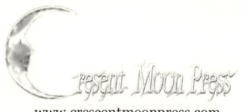

www.crescentmoonpress.com

Moonlight Bleu
Renee Rearden

ISBN: 978-0-9823065-6-7; 0-9823065-6-3
E-ISBN: 978-0-9823065-7-4; 0-9823065-7-1
© Copyright Renee Rearden. All rights reserved
Cover Art: Ash Arceneaux
Editor: Heather Howland
Layout/Typesetting: jimandzetta.com

Crescent Moon Press
1385 Highway 35
Box 269
Middletown, NJ 07748

Ebooks/Books are not transferable. They cannot be sold, shared or given away as it is an infringement on the copyright of this work.

All Rights Are Reserved. No part of this book may be used or reproduced in any manner whatsoever without written permission, except in the case of brief quotations embodied in critical articles and reviews.

This book is a work of fiction. The names, characters, places and incidents are products of the writer's imagination or have been used fictitiously and are not to be construed as real. Any resemblance to persons, living or dead, actual events, locale or organizations is entirely coincidental.

Crescent Moon Press electronic publication/print publication: July 2010 www.crescentmoonpress.com

To Jon, for the happiness I see in your gaze, the joy I hear in your laughter, and the love I find in your arms.

Chapter One

Late Afternoon, Thursday, May 22, 2032–New Angeles

Everything changes, whether you want it to or not. The world changes. People change. Relationships change. Change lurks below the surface, waiting for you to be at your weakest. And the moment you least expect it, change destroys everything you've ever known.

After five hundred years, Saari Mitchell knew that better than anybody.

"Okay, boys and girls. Caller nine gets a shot at two back-stage passes to the 'Rock The Earth' concert," the disk jockey chirped.

Saari snorted and turned off the stereo. "No thanks. Was way too up close and personal during the original one, buddy."

All Saari had to do was glance out her window at the ocean lapping at the Nevada coastline to remember the last time the earth was rocked. The massive quake that liquefied most of the United States' western coastline hit on June 18, 2012—not exactly what the Mayan "end of the world" hoopla had predicted, but catastrophic all the same. With California underwater, Nevada's population exploded as New Angeles, with its resurrected Hollywood, became the place to live.

This year marked the twentieth anniversary of The Great Quake.

Saari propped her elbow on the open window and grabbed a handful of her windswept hair. And she'd be another year older tomorrow. No big deal, really—not when she'd been born May 23, *1499*. That she'd been cursed with immortality on her birthday in 1522 was the real kicker.

The lyrics to "Love Potion Number 9" played in her ear. Powering the windows of her Ford Explorer shut, she tapped her ear bud and answered her cell. "You better not be calling to cancel on dinner tonight."

Nisa's laughter bubbled through the phone. "You're kidding, right? Tonight's *the* night of the year. I wouldn't bail on you."

Saari smiled, despite her present mood. Only a handful of close friends knew she was immortal, and none of them were human in the strictest sense of the word. Some were vampires, a few were werewolves, and then there was the odd collection of those in between human and preternatural, like her.

Nisa fell into the last category. The two women shared a special bond—they were both immortal, though for different reasons and under very different circumstances. Saari had been cursed. Nisa was a cupid.

By some cosmic quirk, when Nisa died, her soul didn't move on. Instead, she was drafted. Now she spent her time matchmaking for the preternatural. Who'd have thought the afterlife was a crapshoot for employment recruitment and assignment?

"You had The Dream again last night, didn't you?"

Judging by Nisa's tone, she already knew the answer. Saari sighed. "I used to think I only had The Dream the night before my birthday because that's the actual day I was cursed, or that maybe so much time has passed I'm actually subconsciously *worried* about having The Dream because it's the night before my birthday," she proffered in an unguarded moment of self-analysis. "Now I don't know what to think."

"That is some seriously circular reasoning. You're crazy, girlfriend, you know that?"

"I think maybe I am. Just a little anyway." Saari rubbed her forehead. "At least the shrink I'm seeing hasn't told me I'm nuts."

Nisa snorted. "I don't like you spilling your guts to a human psychologist. This isn't some 'my parents screwed me up' issue. Yours is a life altering 'a witch killed my boyfriend in a ritual that made me immortal' issue. That's not something you chance exposing."

Saari gripped the wheel, her fingers clenching the worn leather cover. "I didn't know what else to do. The dreams are affecting my work. I can't filter right. I'm afraid to sleep. When I do, I'm right back in the meadow, watching Miko die. I *know* Miko's dead. But with all Doctor Lytton's pushing, I'm having the nightmare every night!"

"And this helps you *how*?"

"I don't know. He's supposed to know why I'm having The Dream—that's why I went to him in the first place. Besides, it's the other dreams that really make me crazy."

Because of the other dreams, she remembered everything: the feel of Miko's skin sliding over hers, the warmth of his touch heating her blood. Though more than five centuries had passed, her body remembered like it was yesterday. Sometimes, she almost believed he was still with her. But that was impossible. Those dreams were just wishful thinking.

A sharp pang of loneliness cut through her heart as old memories resurfaced.

"And you think this *doctor* can help? How many lifetimes of experience does he have?"

Saari stared at the beach between passing cars, catching glimpses of white-capped waves breaking against the shoreline. How many more things would she see change with each passing lifetime? Would she ever find the answers she'd spent her life searching for?

"All right then, 'Doctor Cupid,' why do I keep dreaming about him?"

"Because you haven't let go," Nisa told her, the quiet words hushed with patience.

"How can I?" Saari's voice cracked. "Do the words, 'His love will be your curse. Death for him, immortality for you—and your soul forever incomplete' ring a bell? I'll never be able to love anyone else."

Nisa *tskd*. "I think that's a matter of interpretation. If *you* believe you can't love anybody else, you never will. Until you accept that, you'll never be able to have a relationship with anyone."

"I've been married to mortal men twice. I think that counts as a relationship."

They'd had fun. They'd been good for each other. So what if the men she'd married never gave the richness of her and Miko's mind-blowing soul-sharing connection?

"Three centuries ago and 135 years ago. Can we at least move into this century?"

"I did. Remember my engagement to Michael?"

"Of course I remember Michael, but you weren't in love with him. Loving someone is not the same as being in love with them. Everybody knows that. Well, maybe not everybody," Nisa amended. "But you should. Miko's gone, Saari. You need to move on." After a long, silent pause, her sigh poured through the phone. "Sorry about the lecture. Job hazard, you know?"

"No biggie. Nothing you haven't said before."

"At least I haven't tried to set you up on a date." Nisa's amused chuckle echoed with tinny reception.

"Thank God." Saari shuddered at the thought as she exited the highway. Office buildings towered over the city streets. Sunlight reflected off the windows, the glaring flashes disappearing as she turned onto Van Giessen Boulevard.

"But I could," Nisa threatened in jest. "Your profile would read something like, 'S/w/f seeks s/m to spend eternity with. Average height, slender build, pleasantly attractive. Tri-colored eyes and pouty lips are my best physical features. I'm smart, independent…and *psychic*. Eternity means forever, so immortal men only. Sorcerers knowledgeable in curses a plus.'"

Saari burst into genuine laughter. "That was way too canned. How long have you been working on my profile?"

"Not long. I've only toyed with the idea. Don't worry, you're not on my radar—I promise."

She pulled into the medical mall's parking lot and wedged her SUV into a space marked *compact*. Green, flowerless, low-growing hedges marked the perimeter. The sharply demarcated landscaping reminded her of the sterile atmosphere waiting for her in the building.

"I'll hold you to that. I'm at the shrink's office. See you later?"

"Yeah. I'll see you at dinner."

As Saari entered the Corrado Building, heading for the elevators, her friend's unease followed her. She hadn't felt comfortable with this doctor from the get go. And Nisa was right—she couldn't afford to accidentally slip and give away her secret. Which meant she couldn't be entirely honest.

So how much help could the doc really be, and why did she think he could help her?

Because she had nowhere else to turn.

Dreaming of Miko kept her awake most nights. Lack of sleep made her ability to filter auras as unreliable as her spotty cell phone service. For some reason, something told her she needed *this* doctor's help to make the dreams stop.

A slight jolt signaled the elevator had reached the top floor, ending her mental argument. The doors slid open. A shiver wriggled down her spine.

Saari stepped into the hallway, forcing herself to approach Dr. Lytton's office door. Her stomach cramped like she'd eaten bad seafood. *Get a grip. You haven't said anything damaging. There's no reason to be nervous.*

She had to find a solution fast—preferably before she had another anxiety attack. But dealing with the hyper vigilant angst she experienced every time she came to the doctor's office was *so* not worth it. She wiped her moist palm on her jeans and reached for the doorknob.

The human head shrink had one more chance to figure out why she was losing her mind. If he couldn't, this would be the last time he saw her.

Chapter Two

Late Afternoon, May 22, 2032

"Saari," Clayton Lytton coaxed in the smooth voice that always lulled people into trusting him. "How did your fiancé die?"

His patient's facial features tightened, telling him she was seeing the incident again behind her fluttering eyelids. A small whimper escaped her throat, and he thrilled at the sound. Each time Saari went under, he took her deeper into her past. Nobody could hide things from him.

"You are safe and protected. Nothing can hurt you," he reassured her, whispering the words into her ear.

Except me, if you don't start talking.

The lupine in Clayton had smelled the difference between this woman and the rest of his clients the instant she entered his office. Her scent had tantalized his senses: a sweet combination of honest frustration mingled with fear, hidden behind a veil of secrecy—all wrapped in an exotic package of something-more-than-human he'd never encountered before.

He circled her, stopping in front of his desk, and stared at the woman. Time to play follow the leader.

"You have plans to meet the man you love. Where are you going?"

Her forehead creased. "To the meadow."

In previous sessions, Saari had told him she met her fiancé Michael at a restaurant. His lips twitched, fighting a triumphant smile. He'd pushed her into new territory.

"When are you to meet at the meadow?"

"At sunset."

He gripped the edge of the desktop with excitement. More new information. Last week, she'd related a lunch meeting.

"You're at the meadow now. Do you see your fiancé?"

Her eyelids snapped open, fear contorting her features. Her shoulders lifted and her arms dropped tight to her side, held rigid by an unseen force. His gaze devoured her severe body language, the visual clues as valuable as her spoken words.

Her head whipped sideways, her gaze focused on a private memory. "I see him," she whispered.

Clayton couldn't help himself. He leaned closer, sniffing the fear rolling off her body in waves of perfumed terror. A shudder of delight rippled his skin. "What is he doing?"

A tear rolled down her cheek. "Nothing." Her voice cracked. "He's hurt. I see blood on his head."

Clayton already knew all about the man's tragic demise four years ago. The name and facts surrounding the death of her fiancé Michael were accurate. The information was public knowledge, and he'd tracked it easy enough. But she still refused to allow her memories to match those facts. There must be something the police hadn't found during their investigation.

He caught the teardrop on his fingertip as it rolled off Saari's chin, making sure not to break the session by touching her. The bead of moisture lay warm against his skin. *Such intimate contact.* With a tilt of his finger, the droplet landed on his tongue. A salty tang exploded across his taste buds.

She *would* tell him what he wanted to know.

He just needed to redirect her focus.

"Why is he bleeding?"

Her head dipped. "Because someone hurt him."

"Is anyone helping him, the police maybe?"

"There are no police here."

Her answer took him by surprise. In broad daylight, a robbery suspect killed the man she dreamed about. Police were at the scene when the shooting happened. *How could there be no officers present?* Was this part of her secret? Clayton wondered. Did something happen *before* the robbery or did a different man die? The discrepancies between last week's session and today's made no sense.

Unless a different man had been killed.

Clayton rounded his desk. He stood in front of his black, leather chair, analyzing this newest bit of information.

Had Saari killed her fiancé ... an earlier one? Not the one he'd researched?

He dismissed the thought as quickly as it came. Everything she said, even her posture, pointed to her innocence. He'd smelled her fear. Tasted her terror. She wasn't responsible for her fiancé's death. *Had she helplessly watched this other man die?* That would explain why she dreamed of her "fiancé's" death. She knew what happened to this secret lover, and the details were emerging under hypnosis.

"*Who* is bleeding, Saari?" He pushed her, hoping they'd breached the last of the barriers protecting her private memory.

"My betrothed," she answered, her chest heaving with each rapid breath.

Betrothed?

He placed his hands flat on the lacquer-finished desktop, willing his growing frustration to calm.

"*Which* fiancé?"

She shook her head with such force, her ponytail bounced from side to side. "No."

"*Which* fiancé?" he repeated.

"*No*," she growled.

His hands balled into fists. Perfectly formed handprints on the desk, left by his sweaty palms, mocked his lack of progress. Saari's secret lay beyond his reach, and he wouldn't get anything more from her today willingly. For a moment, he wrestled. He *wanted* her secret, wanted to push, cracking the fragile shell of her mind like an egg. He sensed a power in her just calling out for domination.

Her appearance in *his* office, though, didn't feel like random coincidence. More like she had an ulterior motive for seeking him out. Combining that with an unidentified scent that marked *her* as different, it stood to reason she knew or suspected his lupine existence. And that made her a threat. Whether the threat was to Clayton himself or to lupines in general was what he needed to discover.

But if he squeezed too soon and she broke, the answers would scatter to the jagged recesses of her mind. He just had to find the right trigger.

Tomorrow's session would start with the meadow. He still had time to breach her remaining barriers. Then he *would* discover what she was and if there were others like her.

Because nothing and no one was going to interfere with his becoming alpha of the local werepack he'd chosen. Not even rejection from the pack's dominant, Maurika. Of course, Clayton had wanted Maurika to come to him on her own and choose him willingly. Not that her decision ultimately mattered. He'd take her by force—before next month's full-moon cycle.

He stretched his fisted hands open. His training reasserted itself, the doctor in him controlling his lupine side. A glimpse at his watch told him only minutes remained in the session. "My office is your only safe haven, Saari. You *will* have The Dream tonight, and every night thereafter, until you share with me this burden you carry."

Her head twitched.

"Ten. Nine. Eight," he counted. "Your emotions are calm and centered. Seven. Six. Five. When you wake, you'll feel tired but relieved. Four. Three. You're waking up now. Two. One."

He snapped his fingers.

Saari blinked several times. Her fascinating tri-colored eyes opened and focused on him with her usual intensity. Where did she find such unusual contacts?

"So what am I missing? I've been here *every* afternoon because you asked me to come in if I had the dream. *Why* am I having The Dream every night now instead of once a year? And how, exactly, is having the dream every night helpful?"

Her conscious mind continued with the question they'd stopped on earlier. *Oh, but I am good.* Clayton picked up his pen and tapped the end against the edge of his notebook. "We've talked about the underlying traumatic event, but I can't help wonder if there's something else you're struggling with. Another reason behind the dreams."

She didn't blink.

Interesting.

What secret was she hiding in that delectable head of hers?

"I'm a psychologist, Saari." He spoke with his hands open, a gesture calculated to re-enforce an honest impression. "I look for the causal nexus between emotional distress and physical or emotional trauma. One stems from the other. Oftentimes, how the original incident is dealt with relates directly to present emotional disturbances that can exhibit themselves physically."

He watched irritation flash across her face. Her eyes hardened and she lifted an eyebrow. "That's what brought me here in the first place. *I'd* already figured that much out. You're supposed to help me resolve my issues so I quit having The Dream!"

"Knowing there's a reason, and dealing with the issue are two very separate things. The fact that you're having The Dream more often is a good sign. Your subconscious is working on this issue, bringing it closer and closer to your conscious thought process."

The clock chimed, announcing the end of their session.

Saari tensed in her chair, her facial features tightening to sharp angles of distrust. Heat warmed the back of his neck as the burn of uncertainty lodged between his shoulder blades. Maybe he'd pushed her too far, and she suspected he had ulterior motives. Without her trust, their therapeutic relationship was compromised, and he'd never get her secret.

Clayton smothered his moment of doubt, radiating a calm demeanor.

"Okay, then." Her shoulders lifted, ending an internal debate.

When the door closed behind her, he exhaled on a grin of satisfaction.

Saari *would* have The Dream again tonight.

And she'd be back tomorrow.

Chapter Three

Late Evening, May 22, 2032

    Saari followed Nisa past the bouncer into the carpeted hallway separating the street and the bar. Music, something upbeat and funky, thumped in a solid rhythm of resonating bass that traveled through the floor and made the soles of her feet tingle.

    "I can't believe I let you drag me here. My alarm is set for 5:00 a.m. Tomorrow morning is going to come way too early."

    Nisa's carefree laughter brushed her concern away. "Good music and a couple of beers is just what you need to dull that introspective edge of yours. Besides, I still haven't given you your birthday present. Come on."

    Her none too gentle tug pulled Saari forward. At the end of the hallway, the music grew louder. The walls reverberated with the lyrics of the song. Words pinged around the bar, pinballing off any object in their path, the people merely bumpers redirecting the course around the room.

    Almost on cue, individuals turned and stared in their direction. Saari was used to her cupid friend's auric pull. The rest of the world didn't stand a chance. Nisa's looks registered in the bombshell category. The fact that she could have been Marilyn Monroe reincarnated—at least twins in physical appearance—never failed to draw attention. Her stacked figure, naturally blonde curls and honest-to-God mole sold the image hook, line, and sinker.

"They're staring at you, Saari. Smile and work the room, honey."

"Yeah, right—like they even notice me standing next to you." Her lip curled in amusement at their inside joke. Together, the two of them created a striking pair, her dark hair to Nisa's light. When Saari wanted attention, their contrasting looks generated plenty of it. Tonight, she wanted to blend with the masses and ruminate over the vagaries of life.

She caught the eye of a passing, thirtyish cocktail waitress. "Do you have any Negro Modelo?"

"We do. Just one?"

Nisa answered for her. "Bring three to that table, please." She pointed to the far side of the room.

The server nodded and headed for the bar. She maneuvered through the masses with the grace of a professional dancer, lightly brushing against several people along the way.

Saari envied her poise as *she* wobbled on the tips of her toes and lifted her chin to see over the crowd. A man, obviously the intended recipient of the third beer ordered, sat at the table Nisa had pointed to. "Tell me you did *not* set me up for drinks with a blind date?"

"He's not your date, silly. He's your birthday present!"

"I knew you lied about using my profile," she grumbled, trailing in Nisa's wake.

When they got close enough to the table to see the man clearly, recognition curdled the shrimp and asparagus risotto that had pleasantly filled her stomach. *Having seafood for dinner was such a bad idea.*

She gripped Nisa's elbow, pulling her to a stop. "That's Jordan Stevens—the psychic that reads people's memories."

"I know. That's why we're here."

Her heart stuttered in panic. "I'm already seeing a shrink over a memory I can't talk about. Now you want me to let a psychic crawl around in my head? You do realize how dangerous that would be, right?"

Her friend faced her, compassion swimming in her blue eyes. "He's helped hundreds, if not thousands of people retrieve lost memories. I think taking a chance to learn some useful information about your family tree is worth the risk. Do *you*?"

Hope steadied her irregular heartbeat. She'd tried just about everything else she could think of, without exposing her secret of immortality, to discover where she came from. Maybe this would work.

"Besides, I have it on good authority meeting Jordan Stevens is supposed to have a major impact on your life."

She snorted in disbelief. "By who?"

"Not who—by what." Nisa dragged her forward again. "Remember that assignment I had almost a year ago in the Yucatan?"

"The Chupacabra?" Saari clamped her teeth down on her laughter, but a chuckle managed to escape.

Her friend's glare silenced her mirth. "They're first-rate soothsayers, you know. All it takes is fresh blood from a sacrifice to bring on a Chupacabra's second-sight. That hairless mutt killed more rabbits and goats than I care to remember trying to bribe me with self-induced visions."

"I'm not convinced by your client's remark. He spent years avoiding contact with anyone. How accurate could he possibly be?"

"Spot on. He knew I was a cupid, but before I showed up, he had successfully avoided being tied to one territory with a mate and pups. So, he tried to buy me off. Didn't work. I got a half a dozen good readings before he gave up—your connection with Jordan the most important." Her voice dropped to a low whisper. "Too late to change your mind anyway—the psychic spotted us."

Her gaze jerked to the table and settled on the blond-haired man watching her with an amused expression.

He stood and offered his hand when they approached. "Hi, I'm Jordan. Pleasure to meet you."

Her arm shot forward thanks to Nisa's shove. "Uh, hello. I'm Saari."

His hand closed around hers. Cold seeped into her skin. She wasn't sure what she expected—a jolt of energy, hot skin, a painfully hard grip maybe—but a freezing handshake hadn't even occurred to her. "Are your hands always this cold or does that only happen when you give a reading?"

"Huh?" Jordan glanced at his hand. "Oh, I see what you mean. No, I haven't done anything yet. My hand's just cold from holding my beer—sorry."

Well, color me stupid.

Jordan already occupied the chair that put his back to the wall, so she took the chair on his right so *her* back wasn't facing the crowd. Nisa slid into the chair on his left so she could people watch—another one of her occupational hazards.

The cocktail waitress materialized out of the crowd.

"Here you go." She slid three beers and frosted mugs across the table.

"Thanks." Nisa dropped two fifty-dollar bills on the table. "We won't need anything else for the evening."

"Much appreciated," the woman nodded. She scooped up the money and headed back toward the bar.

"People usually have questions about how a reading works." Jordan touched her arm. "Is there anything specific, Saari, you'd like to know before we start?"

She stared at his hand, wondering if he'd already begun wading through the centuries of her life. "Do you think you could explain exactly what it is you do and how you do it?"

He took a drink of his beer before folding his hands together on the tabletop. "I'm a reminiscence psychic. By touching others, I 'see' images from their memories. The process is a bit like herding cats. The trick is finding the first doorway."

How many things has he seen *since he's already touched me twice?*

"Wouldn't touching people all the time create like sensory overload or something for you?" She pulled her hands off the table and gripped them in her lap.

"It can happen if I'm not prepared," he admitted. "I always envision a mental cape covering myself from head to toe. The safety mechanism keeps everybody else's memories from touching me. When I do a reading, I mentally take off the coat, ask the person if they're ready, and *then* purposely touch them."

Oh, thank God. I'll know when he starts.

Her hands flattened over her knees.

"Do you want me to leave the table and give you two some privacy?" Nisa asked.

"We're pretty secluded here in the corner, but you could make sure we're not interrupted—as long as Saari doesn't mind." His gaze cut toward her, eyebrows lifted in question.

"You should stay," Saari agreed.

"Okay, that's settled." He laid his hands on the table, palms up. "When you're comfortable, place your hands palm down on top of mine."

She pulled her hands from under the table and took a deep breath.

"Ready or not, here we go." Her arms lowered until her palms rested atop his.

A dome of silence shrouded them. Everything but Jordan faded. Images appeared in her mind, popping with the special effects of a 3-D movie. A meadow, under a full moon that colored the sky midnight blue, emerged. Firelight danced in the shadows.

Not Miko.

She shoved the memory away, watching it swirl into a passing stream of colored pictures.

Jordan's eyes widened, but he remained silent.

A park bench materialized under a pre-dawn sky. A dark-skinned figure sat alone, his neck resting against the back of the seat as he stared at the moon. His arms rested on his legs, his thumb dug into his wrist. Crimson drops fell into the growing puddle beneath him.

I didn't see the blood. How did miss that when I first saw him?

His head turned at Saari's approach.

The dripping flow of blood ceased.

She sat next to him, waiting.

They spoke, but no sound came with the vision. Her mind filled in the missing conversation.

"I sensed your heartbreak from the other side of the park."

His lips parted and she caught the flash of sharpened teeth. "This is the last sunrise I will ever see."

"What is so terrible about being a vampire that you would choose death?"

Pain and anger swirled in his chocolate brown eyes. "Christ, a wannabe groupie. Don't you understand how dangerous I am? I wasn't even trying to attract prey, and here you are."

Gut-wrenching sadness poured out of him.

"Your emotions drew me, not any vampire ability. I'm psychic. Helping people is what I do."

He gave a bark of humorless laughter and stared at the sky. "Can you give me back my stolen humanity? Restore my soul?"

She lightly cupped his chin and turned his head toward her. "Your soul is intact, your definition of humanity merely changed."

"I don't understand?"

"Evil, soullessness—it's not defined by what you are, only by what you do. How you live your life, choosing not to deliberately harm others, that's what defines a person's soul."

Lines of confusion marred his forehead. "I have my soul—truly?"

"Absolutely." Shades of gray lightened the sky. "So if you want to keep it, I think you'd better come with me. I know someone that can help."

She stood and reached out a hand.

Hope chased the bleak acceptance from his expression. He gripped her fingers.

The cocoa-colored skin changed to a much paler shade, the female in the image now a redhead. Sheets tangled around their legs as they came together in a fevered pitch of ecstasy.

What the hell? This isn't my memory.

Jordan yanked his hands from underneath hers.

The bar around them roared to life as sound shattered the vision.

"Forgive me, Saari." Jordan swiped a napkin across his sweating forehead. "I must be more tired than I thought."

That was Jordan's memory? Wow. I wonder how often fragments of his life have cropped into other readings.

"I think I'll head back to my hotel room. It was nice meeting you both." He nodded his chin toward her and Nisa before leaving their table.

Nisa folded her arms and leaned on the table. "Well he sure left in a hurry. I wonder if he saw something big, bad, and scary."

She shook her head. "Nah. The meadow where Miko was killed popped up, but then a memory about Mag replaced it."

Her friend's shoulders drooped in disappointment. "I'm sorry. I had hoped for a life-altering report about discovering your real name, or what your parents looked like."

She reached across the table and squeezed Nisa's hand. "Remembering the first time Mag and I met, seeing it from a completely different perspective, is a priceless gift. That you orchestrated such a feat—well, I shouldn't be surprised. I bow to your unparalleled skills."

Her friend's delighted laughter dispelled her sulk. "And so you should." She turned her wrist and checked the time. "Okay, this party's a wrap. Time to go."

"What? I figured we'd be here half the night."

Nisa stood. "Did you not catch the 'we won't need anything else for the evening' comment—guaranteed by the huge tip?"

"No. I missed that."

An airy wave dismissed Saari's lack of attention. "You know I'd normally close the place, but I have to catch a red-eye flight to South America."

Saari spoke to the back of Nisa's head as they walked toward the door. "What's in South America?"

"My next assignment—in the Amazon of all places—is a Djinn that refuses to accept a his 'n' her bottle."

"I can't wait to hear this story when you get back."

When they passed the bar, Nisa pointed. "Now I know why he wanted to meet at the bar. Check out psychic boy. He's already got his arm around that auburn-haired gal. If only my job was *that* easy to hook up couples."

The woman listed to the side, her head pressed against Jordan's shoulder. Charming. His date must have gotten hammered while waiting for Jordan to finish her reading. Apparently he had a thing for redheads—and their state of sobriety was optional. *Glad I didn't see more of what he likes.*

She stood next to Nisa at the curb in front of the bar. Her friend didn't even need to whistle for a cab. She turned a hip toward the street and lifted her hand. Before she could wave, a cab pulled up beside her.

"You know how these assignments are, so I'll be incognito for awhile."

She gave Nisa a quick hug. "Be careful, and call me the minute you get back in town."

Saari watched the cab pull away before walking to her Explorer. Light reflected off the windshield. She glanced at the sky and noticed the lustrous full moon. A blue hue covered the surface, dripping color onto passing clouds that shaded the heavens.

A shiver of déjà vu made her twitch.

Tonight's sky looked nearly identical to the one Jordan pulled from her memory.

If that didn't serve as an omen, she didn't know what did.

Chapter Four

Late Evening, May 22, 2032

    Clayton threaded his way through the knot of people crowding the sidewalks.
    Horns honked while cars jockeyed for the next empty space along the curb. Snippets of music blared now and then as doors opened and closed up and down the boulevard.
    His gaze roved the scene, looking for just the right choice. He ignored the loudest women. They drew too much attention. The really quiet ones were too suspicious—and not his type anyway. A confident woman, out to enjoy herself for an evening, that's what appealed to him.
    As he breathed in the night air, a staggering number of perfumed scents assaulted him. The women, as well as the men, reeked with chemical saturation. A cell phone's high-pitched ring tone arced across his eardrums with an acoustic whine. He wanted to mash his hands against his ears, blocking the sound. Cramps gripped his abdomen, nearly doubling him over. A tingle rippled across his skin.
    He dug into his pocket, then withdrew the shaking hand, his palm filled with multi-colored tablets. Without hesitation, he popped them all into his mouth and chewed. The tickling sensation he'd felt moments before receded. With the full moon's arrival, his lupine abilities had sharpened with stunning clarity. Some days, having a lunate's heightened senses made his human existence a pain in the ass.

But after years of experimenting, he'd finally found a way to maintain control.

Being a lunate, unlike his werewolf cousins who answered the call of the moon three days every month, Clayton only heard the call of the second full moon in a month. Fortunately, the phenomenon commonly known as a blue moon didn't happen often. He had to be prepared for a forced change only once every two or three years.

Confident he'd once again mastered his lupine side, he stared in challenge at the full moon. *Every* night belonged to him again.

"Excuse me." A voice carried across the crowd.

Clayton jerked his head in the direction of the speaker.

He knew that voice.

Lifting his nose slightly, he searched for her scent. An exotic aroma of rich soil, blended with a hint of pine and berry leaves reached him. A door opened and light illuminated the auburn curls of the solitary woman entering the Zinful Bar.

Maurika.

He elbowed his way to the entrance and stepped into the hallway. Self-preservation stayed his approach. One deep inhale identified the bar's bouquet: alcohol, leather, stale cigarette smoke, salted peanuts, and popcorn—and Maurika alone. No other wolf or lunate waited in the bar for her.

A feral smile curled his mouth.

His diligent patience was about to pay off.

He followed the hallway into the bar, concentrating on Maurika. Each breath drew more of her unique scent into him, filling his senses until he smelled nothing but her. None of the other people around him registered.

"Thank you." Maurika spoke again.

Her smooth-as-silk tone drew his gaze toward the bar. Light played over her. Each time she moved, deep red highlights shimmered in curls that fell past her shoulders. He rubbed his fingers together, imagining the feathery softness of her hair.

His heartbeat raced with euphoric anticipation. She had started this game of chase when she'd blocked the vote allowing him to join the pack. He'd been furious—until he understood her motives.

She hadn't given Quinn, the lunate she was dating, a child yet. Either she didn't consider him her dominant, or Quinn couldn't father a child—which meant he wasn't capable of becoming her dominant. Either way, she remained the pack's surrogate dominant.

And as the pack's dominant, she held the power.

Clayton's request to join the pack had been viewed as a challenge to her position. She had recognized his strength and was afraid of losing to him.

So their courtship marked a battle for power.

A genuine smile touched his lips.

He sat in an empty chair a few tables behind Maurika and pushed the beer bottles blocking his direct line of sight to the side.

A man's voice interrupted his thoughts. "What the hell do you think you're doing?"

Clayton snarled a quiet warning. "Leave."

The pills staved off his change, but they weren't a hundred percent effective—and the side effects dampened some of his abilities. His hearing wasn't as keen, eyesight not as sharp, and sometimes his lunate aggression bled through.

This idiot trying to hold his gaze didn't sense any danger. His date did. She grabbed the beer bottles with one hand and with the other, tugged the man toward another table.

The fight for dominance was a game as old as time, a contest of wills as much as physical strength. Clayton stared toward the bar and considered his future with Maurika and the werepack.

He had hoped she'd submit to him willingly. The pack would follow without question if she did. But they were beyond that stage. Maurika would never submit to another male by choice—which meant he would take her by force. That would make him the pack's dominant, but challenges of retribution would surely follow. Every male wolf in the pack would probably challenge him to a death match out of loyalty to her.

In order to keep the amount of bloodshed to a minimum, more specifically by shedding none of his own, he planned to keep Maurika on her knees until she grew heavy with his child. Their offspring would cement his position as the pack's dominant.

He reached inside his other pocket for the pills that would guarantee Maurika's submission. She would be his by the end of the night—once he found a way to slip the concoction into her drink unnoticed.

A cocktail waitress delivered drinks at the table next to him. He waved, catching her attention. She nodded and approached him. "What can I get you?"

"Two long beach iced teas."

She slipped between the tables to get to the bar.

His gaze lingered on Maurika. *Had she caught his scent, as he had hers?*

She hadn't moved from her barstool or looked behind her even once. So unless she was ill, she couldn't have missed him. He studied her body language to determine if she was snubbing him or clueless.

"Two long beach iced teas." The cocktail waitress slid the drinks onto the table in front of him.

"How much do I owe you?" He pulled a twenty from his wallet.

Someone bumped the waitress, and she stumbled against the table. "Hey, watch where you're going."

"Sorry. Hey isn't that that psychic guy, Jordan Stevens?" a woman asked.

"Where?" The waitress spun toward the other side of the room.

Clayton opened the capsules and dumped the contents into one of the drinks. He picked up the glass and swirled the liquid, watching the crystals dissolve into the cranberry-colored beverage. After pushing the drugged drink across the table, he set his own on a napkin and used the extra one to sop up the spilled juice on the tabletop.

The waitress turned around, her eyes wide with excitement. "That *is* Jordan Stevens."

He handed her the twenty bucks and smiled, playing on her enthusiasm. "I heard on the radio he's in town for a show. Maybe he'll tip you with a couple of free tickets."

"Yeah, right." She looked across the bar again. "You never know, though. I might get lucky."

Clayton lightly held her wrist, stopping her from leaving the table. "Speaking of getting lucky. See that gal sitting straight across from me at the bar?"

The waitress stared in the direction he'd indicated, then back at him with a knowing smile.

"If you could deliver that drink to her, I'd appreciate it."

"No problem. Want me to tell her it's from you?" She placed the glass of sedative laden iced tea on her tray.

"No." He shook his head. "I'll talk to her myself. It's all about the timing, you know?"

He watched as she placed the glass in front of Maurika. The cocktail waitress smiled and then shook her head. *Good girl. Don't tell her about me. I want that part to be a surprise.*

When the server made a beeline across the room, Clayton followed her progress, curious to see if the psychic Jordan Stevens was really in the bar. He took a sip of his drink, and nearly spewed liquid everywhere.

His patient, Saari, sat across the table from Jordan Stevens, holding his hands. *What the hell is she doing here—with him?* As he watched, Jordan Stevens yanked his hands away from Saari. The psychic rubbed his face and left their table. He watched Saari and another woman chat for several minutes, wondering why the psychic hadn't returned to his chair.

When Saari and the woman with her grabbed their purses and stood, he wanted to curse his rotten luck. They would pass his table on their way to the front door. He couldn't afford for Saari to spot him. She would think he had followed her. If she had come to his office with ulterior motives, seeing him here would only strengthen her suspicions.

The bathrooms were behind him, a convenient refuge until Saari left. Clayton bumped into someone coming out through the men's door. "Move," he mumbled, hurrying past the man. Once inside, he edged away from the door to keep from being seen and leaned against the wall.

Five minutes later, he left the bathroom and scanned the crowd for Saari. He didn't see her or the woman she was with anywhere. He sighed with relief and then checked the bar.

Maurika was gone.

A howl of rage threatened to rip past his throat.

He searched the crowd again, hoping he'd missed her. Instincts told him she'd left. A deep breath confirmed her scent had weakened with her departure. She must have known he was in the bar after all and left the first chance she had.

Her trail led him out of the bar and down the street to the Vagabond Inn. Even with his muted senses, enough lingered for him to track her—as long as he concentrated and blocked out the myriad of other scents. Once inside, he crossed the lobby and stood in front of the row of elevators. She had taken one of them, but which one?

He pushed all of the arrows and waited for the doors to open. First one and then another chimed. She hadn't been in either of them. The last two elevators arrived at the same time. A pine and berry aroma hovered in the elevator to his right. He slipped between the closing doors.

Her scent was strongest in one corner. He pushed all of the buttons, figuring he'd find her scent on one of the floors. After reaching the top floor with no success, he realized Maurika hadn't walked off the elevator. The drugs he'd given her had kicked in, and someone must have carried her.

Damn it. Now I'll have to check this place room by room—all thirty floors. I don't think I gave her a big enough dose to keep her unconscious until I find her.

Stepping off the elevator, he walked along the hallway, inhaling in front of each door. He repeated the process, floor after floor, until he wanted to tear doors off the hinges.

A familiar burn radiated in his muscles. It spread through his body, penetrating the angry haze wrapped around his brain. His medicine was wearing off. Without it, he couldn't maintain control. He popped a couple pills in his mouth and swallowed before continuing his search.

He'd reached the end of one side of the hallway on the seventeenth floor and still hadn't found her. Rolling his wrist to check his watch, he noted an hour had passed in his search for Maurika. She was probably already awake.

The door behind him jerked open. He spun toward the doorway.

"Hey, did you see a redhead out here?"

Clayton growled in fury.

Maurika's scent covered the psychic from the bar. He grabbed the man by the shirt and tossed him back into the room. "Where is she?"

The door slammed, echoing in the small room.

"I don't know. She left."

He lifted his nose and sniffed. The pissant was telling the truth. Maurika had been here, but she'd left the suite. Since he hadn't smelled her in the hallway, she must have taken the stairwell.

She knew I'd come after her.

Jordan Stevens picked himself up off the ground. "I don't know what you want, but you need to leave before I call the police."

Pain lanced Clayton's jaw. He ground his teeth, fighting the agony. A loud pop split the air. The bones in his face shifted, the muscles pulling hard enough to stretch the tendons on either side of his neck. His pills hadn't taken effect yet.

"Hey, are you having a seizure or something?" Jordan Stevens took a step toward him.

The skin on Clayton's arms dimpled. Change wriggled beneath the subcutaneous layers. His back bowed, and an undulating wave rippled across his body in one, long motion. Thick hair followed in its wake, covering his arms and torso. He'd fought for control, managing to stop his change at a partial shift.

"Holy fuck. You're a Yeti." Jordan ran for the door.

He caught him by the neck with a massive claw and lifted him off the ground. Jordan couldn't be allowed to tell anybody what he'd seen. The psychic's fear stoked Clayton's desire to hunt. He wanted to rip the man limb from limb for interfering with Maurika.

His rage tipped him over the edge.

Chapter Five

Pre-Dawn, Friday, May 23, 2032

Dhelis Guidry circled the block twice before he found a place to park. Police cars blocked the end of the alley, their flashing lights casting alternate colors that distorted an already grisly scene. Though it was nearly three a.m., a large crowd of all-night bar hoppers was gathered across the street, craning their necks to catch a glimpse of the carnage hidden behind a wall of officers and crime scene tape.

He and Brogan Vincent shouldered their way through the throng of gawking drunks, thankful no TV crews had arrived. Dhelis hoped there was still a chance to contain the scene. The more "routine" this murder seemed to John Q Public, the better.

Heading for the barricade, he scanned the area, looking for his contact. Officer Donnie Thompson, with the South New Angeles Precinct, had sent Dhelis a coded text message, urgently calling him to the scene of the latest questionable death. Though Dhelis's position as a forensic psychic explained his presence at the murder scene, he wasn't there just on police business.

This situation involved the Tueri Council as well—which was why he'd dragged Brogan along with him. Keeping human injuries or casualties to a minimum protected the Tueri and other preternatural races from being discovered. So standard protocol required a Tueri healer be present when carrying out an execution order—an order that came too late to stop whatever had happened here.

He spotted Stevens standing beside one of the marked police cars. Pulling his I.D. badge from his pocket, Dhelis held it up so the surrounding officers knew he was a cop.

"Thanks for getting here so quickly." Donnie stepped forward and shook Dhelis's hand. "We're going to need your help on this one."

"Well, look who's here. It's Tanto Guidry, and he brought his friend the UWOP—I mean from UFOP along." Detective Hall leaned against the trunk of his department issued car and flicked his cigarette butt into the street.

Dhelis stepped toward the bigoted jerk.

Brogan laid a restraining hand on his shoulder. "Following you into the crime scene will just make things worse. You go ahead. I'll wait here."

Anger at Hall's blatant prejudice raced like fire through his veins. Resentment at Dhelis's psychic status on the forensic team fueled Hall's comments about Dhelis being a Mexican Indian. Filing a complaint with the Department would only make things worse on the squad, but Hall's digs at any other civilian psychic, especially Brogan, were unacceptable.

The WOP, Without-Papers, slur—a play on UFOP, United Forensic Organization of Psychics—had had been aimed at Brogan's Italian heritage, but Dhelis knew part of the reason for the insult was Brogan intimidated the hell out of Hall. At 31 years old, his friend's body-builder physique put Hall's sagging midline and departing hairline to shame. Brogan's good looks, in spite of his bald head, drew more female attention than Hall had had in his entire life.

Of course the other part was Hall was just an asshole.

Donnie turned and ushered Dhelis into the alley. "We should go check out the scene."

Dhelis raised an eyebrow, but deliberately refrained from asking any questions as they walked the length of the alley. He didn't want their conversation overheard. Donnie's code indicated this was already a potentially explosive situation.

People in general, outside of the science versus séance population, accepted Dhelis as a forensic psychic. The preternatural world knew him as a vampire executioner. If humans, in their blissfully ignorant, day-to-day existence, realized vampires and other equally scary things lived in their midst, the hunting phrase "open season" would take on a whole new meaning.

A cat hissed somewhere above his head. He looked up, scanning the edge of the roof. Nothing moved. His gaze dropped to the fire escape. It clung to the side of the chipped plaster wall at awkward angles, as if the metal rails had climbed the building in a desperate effort to escape the fiery flames.

The smell of burning flesh confronted him, overpowering the stench of rotten garbage that filled the trash bins lining the alley. "Ughh," he growled in frustration, putting the back of his hand against his nose.

He stared sideways at Donnie, nodded his head once at him, and then shifted his line of sight toward the human lumps of charcoal, silently asking the question he dare not say aloud: *You burn the bodies?*

"Yeah." The officer whispered in response to the unasked question.

Dhelis moved as close to the dead couple as he could without searing his skin. Heat rolled off the smoldering corpses, adding to the noxious odors, making it doubly uncomfortable at this end of the alley. He cautiously circled the immediate perimeter, not wanting to disturb any retrievable evidence.

There wasn't much left to visually identify either body, but the presence of two skulls, separated from the skeletal remains, made it apparent death had visited in the plural. Donnie had burned the corpses to destroy all evidence of a vampire attack. It also gave Donnie, who wasn't registered on the psychic rolls, an excuse to call Dhelis—the other cops loved dumping the "weird" supernatural cases on him.

He brushed a smudge off his pants, hoping it was only dust. "I'm sorry," he said to the officers watching him intently. "I can't tell you anything without my partner, and she won't be able to tell you anything until these remains are cool enough to touch."

His partner, Thana, was the real psychic.

He was listed on the registry as a medium.

Turning, Dhelis made his way to the front of the alley. He ignored a couple of South Precinct officers' narrow-minded comments about his special kind of help, or lack thereof. Being a psychic, Mexican-Indian police detective made him a bigger target than usual with law enforcement.

His stride lengthened, anxious to be on his way. With the vampire killing this blatantly, his latest Council assignment had just gone from bad to worse.

Donnie followed. "Were you able to pick up anything?"

"No," Dhelis replied, his words laced with frustration. "The fire burned away any genetic traces I might have singled out. There's no essence for me to follow."

"I was afraid of that." Donnie sighed.

"You had to burn them before the other cops showed up," he assured him in a near whisper.

"I know. If the bodies hadn't burned, there would have been other questions about who or rather *what* really killed them."

He understood Donnie's underlying message and clapped the young officer on the shoulder for reassurance. "Nothing you could do about it. Thanks for calling anyway. If you hear anything, let me know immediately."

"Will do," Donnie promised, turning back into the alley.

Brogan fell in step beside him. "Did you find anything?"

"No," he shook his head.

Avoiding the crowd, Dhelis stayed on the blockaded side of the street and headed for his car. After a couple of blocks, the mob of people disappeared. He reached for his phone. The Council handled psychic interaction in the normal and preternatural world alike, but the highly sensitive execution orders came directly from the state's ruling vampire, Alarico Montez.

"Dhelis here. It's your rogue vampire all right, and he left a freaking mess. The bodies had to be burned to destroy the evidence of an attack, so I couldn't find the creature's signature on them. By the way, no picture of him accompanied the execution order faxed to me earlier. Find me a picture of this vampire and email it to my phone. Otherwise, tracking him will be like looking for a vampire at an all-night blood bank."

Of course, if Alarico's man had bothered to show up and help track this nasty piece of vampire vermin, they wouldn't even be in this jam. Dhelis could have read the entire file, detailing every bit of information that might lead to a faster capture.

Closing his phone, he reached for the door handle. The sign for Howard Amon Park glowed under the streetlight. "If you were a hungry, pissed off vampire, where would you go?"

Brogan followed his gaze. "Into the park for a late-night snack."

"That's what I was thinking."

They entered Howard Amon Park, moving swiftly. The park was close to the last killing, and the most logical place the rogue vampire might go. Fairly empty and quiet this time of night, the vampire could slip away undetected.

"At this point, I'd take stumbling across our targeted prey through blind luck. Without knowing what the vampire looks like, the odds for catching this creature before it kills again are slim and heading toward none."

Dhelis clenched his arms, grasping the twin crystal daggers where they rested solid and ready against his forearms. Glancing over his shoulder, he checked the path behind them to make sure they weren't being followed. Though he told himself he was just being careful, he knew the excuse wasn't entirely true. Looking over his shoulder, avoiding Josie Stuart, had become as much a habit as dodging rogue vampires or nosy humans. Of the group, Josie had become the main nuisance.

Friends had fixed him up with Josie on a blind date nearly a year ago. She'd been nice enough, but he hadn't been interested. Aside from the lack of instant attraction, he sensed a hidden edge to her personality that frankly he found unappealing. He never called her for a second date.

A few months later, he'd run into her at a mutual acquaintance's birthday party. She'd tried to rekindle some interest. He'd tried to keep as far away from her as he could. For awhile it seemed like everywhere he went, he ran into her. Initially her presence was explainable—then it became obvious she was stalking him in the literal sense of the word.

He'd had to rethink his position toward Josie at that point. He still had no interest in dating her—at all—but if she went to Council and petitioned for a match, Council would have to grant it under their laws. So he saw her occasionally: often enough to keep her happy, but infrequent enough to keep their relationship in a platonic "getting to know each other" stage.

When the offer for reassignment to New Angeles came, he welcomed the opportunity. The transfer put almost two thousand miles between Josie and him. He'd told her he needed six months of dating space to settle into his new job in a new city. And he had. The position as a detective with the New Angeles Police Department came with a promotion, advancing his law enforcement career. His new tactical execution team with the Council had the highest success rate in the country.

Most importantly, though, the move had brought him to his intended mate.

A seer had told him she lived in New Angeles.

The other half of him, his soul mate, was here somewhere. Now he just had to find her.

He had been in the city almost six months without finding her, and time was running out. In a couple of weeks, Josie would be breathing down his neck. Again. That horrifying thought left him constantly looking over his shoulder, expecting to see her swinging a manacled chain his direction.

I will not marry that head case.

A woman's terrified scream shattered the night. The horrendous shriek raised the hairs on the back of his neck, reminding him why they'd entered the park. He bolted toward the sound, focusing on the trees ahead. With a little luck, no unseen bystanders would observe his faster-than-humanly-possible speed. Brogan's footsteps pounded the ground behind him.

When he rounded a bend in the bike trail, he skidded to a stop. A massive figure stood under a red oak, holding a woman by the neck, high against the tree's trunk. As far as Dhelis could tell, the monster hadn't bitten her yet. The creature merely toyed with her, playing with its food, like a cat would a mouse.

Sliding the crystal dagger from his sleeve, Dhelis smiled grimly. He could only see the back of the creature, but he concentrated, taking in the figure's height and gray, hooded sweatshirt. Before he moved an inch, the vampire whipped its head around and stared straight at him.

The vampire flung the woman at him, as if she weighed nothing. Dhelis saw her arc through the air and leaped to catch her. The screaming female landed in his arms with a jarring thud.

He stared at the spot he last saw the vampire.

The gigantic creature had vanished.

"Ahhh," he yelled. "Damn it." The woman startled at his violent eruption and tried to scramble out of his arms. Frantically pushing at his chest, she nearly toppled to the ground.

Dhelis swallowed a bubble of frustration. He wanted to chase the vampire before he lost the rogue's trail, but he had to make sure the woman hadn't been bitten.

He knelt and carefully set the woman on the grass. Looking at her neck, he confirmed what he already suspected: the woman hadn't been turned. "It's alright. I'm a police officer. You're safe now," he assured her in a soothing voice.

Tears rolled down her cheeks. Her hands alternately pounded her chest and pointed at her throat. Hoarse, choking sounds escaped her lips.

Brogan caught up to them and dropped to his knees beside the woman. "Okay, just relax. Let's see if we can make it easier for you to breathe." He placed one palm behind her neck and gently pressed his other palm across her throat. The ring on his finger flared once before returning to its normal amethyst color.

Dhelis held his breath while he listened for the woman to breathe normally.

Her hands settled on the ground, and her chest lifted with regular rhythm.

"How's your throat?" Brogan pulled his hands away from the woman.

"Better," she croaked. "How did you—"

"Your neck was out. I just popped it back in alignment." Brogan gave her hand a reassuring pat.

Dhelis dialed Donnie's number. "I've got another victim at Howard Amon Park. This one's alive. We're on the bike path about four hundred yards from the Lee Boulevard entrance. I can't leave until another officer is on scene, so make it fast."

Glancing at the woman, he noted finger marks around her throat. The mottled bruising explained the harsh sound of her breathing. The vampire had crushed her windpipe.

Brogan's eyes cut toward him. "Go after him. I'll stay with her until the police get here."

Brogan's tactical training kept him from being a liability.

His psychic ability made him the best Tueri healer in the city.

Watching him save this woman made Dhelis damned thankful he was part of *his* execution team.

The blare of sirens echoed through the trees, announcing the police were close. Soon lights bobbed down the path, heading straight for them. Now he could leave. He ran for the next bend in the trail, moving out of sight. Opening his phone, he hit speed dial for Alarico again. "I found him. He headed toward the hospital. *Now* I can track your vampire. I know what the bastard looks like."

Chapter Six

Pre-Dawn—May 23, 2032

    Saari followed the hospital exit onto Washington Avenue. Turning into the parking lot, she wound her way through the first levels of the building's round parking structure. Cars of different models and colors occupied all the parking spaces she passed. Up and around, up and around the path climbed, like some giant, inverted gumball machine.
    As she rounded the second to last level, she spotted an empty parking place about halfway down the aisle closest to the elevator. Not a bad walk.
    She continued down the row and noticed a woman helping a little girl get out of a blue Ford Taurus. The woman picked the child up, and the pint-sized pixie wrapped her legs around the woman's waist, nestling her head against her mother's shoulder.
    When she drove past the pair, all she could see of the child was a head covered in black curls, big eyes that stared vacantly out of a flushed face, and a pink pair of pajamas that looked soft and fluffy and had those little slippered feet attached. Pulling into the open parking space, she wondered what was wrong with the little girl and made a mental note to look for her in the E.R.
    The dashboard clock read three a.m., which meant her shift at the hospital didn't start for almost four hours. With a sigh, she collapsed against her seat. After her appointment with Doctor Lytton, dinner with Nisa, and the psychic reading by

Jordan Stevens, she'd gone home and fallen into bed. Of course, she'd had another nightmare. And after having The Dream again, she'd known she wouldn't get any more sleep tonight.

On nights like this, she was grateful she had a job at the hospital to go to. As a nurse, she could wander the hallways, using her gift to seek those who needed her.

Her *gift*. She snorted. No one could explain the phenomenon. She had no family to ask. The healer who raised her never allowed Saari to talk about her curative skills. Healers were burned at the stake as witches in the 1500s. Miko was the only person who understood her extraordinary ability. He had taught her how to sense the emotions of others without revealing the source as her extra-sensory skill.

Three hundred years of trial and error had given her some idea how to use the psychic talent to help others. So most days, because she had no choice, she accepted her extrasensory trait without question.

Her birthday, stirring centuries of doubt, *always* made her question where her ability came from.

Dismissing the entire line of thought, she grabbed her backpack off the passenger seat and climbed out of the Explorer. She locked the doors and headed for the elevator. Her mind jumped ahead, focusing on the night's tasks.

As she walked, she mentally reviewed the list of visits she would make on her rounds. Without consciously registering her routine, she dropped her keys and cell phone in the front pouch of her backpack and dug for her hospital I.D. badge. The electronic card was stuck to the back of a pack of sugar-free gum.

Preoccupied with separating the two, coupled with the fact her empathic ability wasn't working properly lately, she nearly walked right into a man the size of a linebacker. The back of his gray sweatshirt filled her vision, and she had to look up in order to measure his full height. The guy was *huge*. When the top of his head came into focus, her head bent so far back she could hardly breathe.

A high-pitched wheezing echoed through the parking structure, like that of a child's, and her heart dropped to her stomach.

Leaning to the right, she looked around the man and saw the woman and little girl she'd seen a few minutes before. The woman stood trapped between the man and the cinderblock wall. She had turned her body away from the man, shielding the child from him and whatever danger he might pose.

This was definitely not good.

"I said give me the kid, you stupid bitch," the huge figure said, shifting back and forth on the balls of his feet.

Shock spider-webbed across her face, and a shiver of horror crawled up her spine at the cold sound of death carried on his words.

She looked down at the man's right hand. He held a large, wicked-looking knife. His fisted knuckles shone white from gripping the hilt so hard. Her heart climbed from her stomach into her throat.

The child plastered herself against her mother, whimpering in fear. She buried her face in her mother's neck and locked her legs in a crushing grip on her mother's waist. Terror made the woman's eyes wide with fright, but she stood fast against the attacker.

Completely focused on each other, neither the attacker nor the woman had noticed her presence yet. Light flashed off the knife blade, drawing Saari's gaze in hypnotic terror.

Jesus, he's gonna kill them both.

"Help us, please!"

Her head shot up, locking on the woman's tearful gaze. Taking cautious steps away from the man, she circled to where the woman and child stood.

The man's eyes blinked once, visibly acknowledging her presence when she came to stand next to the woman. Saari stepped in front of the pair, blocking the giant's view of them. Shielding them with her body forced him to focus on her.

For someone who had been so jumpy just a few moments before, he stood eerily still now. She looked into his eyes and stretched out a hand, palm facing toward him. Her breath leaked between her lips with measured control, the subtle push of energy a calm and peaceful suggestion.

Sometimes, she could imagine an emotion in the form of a blanket, something tangible to wrap around an individual. She could project that blanket of emotion and envelope the recipient. Many a time, she had used this ability in the emergency room with trauma victims in shock. The doctors were better able to treat calm and receptive patients.

"Nice try." The giant laughed at her gesture, a horrible scraping sound that grated Saari's nerves.

Her mouth opened on a stunned 'O.' Her influence had no effect. Nothing about this man defined calm. In fact, he radiated cold energy. Frosty undercurrents exuded from some auras. Not his. This force appeared solid, like a wall of ice, with no continuous flow to his energy.

Dread mingled with shock, making her hand shake.

Normally, she could filter emotions from children, adults, unconscious or wounded individuals, vampires, even from animals in a pinch. The mentally disturbed were difficult. Their tangled and erratic energy folded in on itself in an ever-changing ebb and flow of mixed electrical impulses.

She could not, on the other hand, filter soulless vampires. Their energy solidified, becoming unyielding.

Her energy couldn't touch this man because he wasn't a normal vampire. He'd gone rogue. A total freaking lunatic who derived pleasure from the woman and child's terror. *That's* why he drew out the attack.

She considered her options.

There weren't many.

"You can still walk away. Nobody's gotten hurt." *Yet.* She kept her right hand out, palm toward the man. Since she couldn't filter his energy, maybe she could distract his focus. "Anybody could walk into the garage and see that knife you're holding. All they'd have to do is pull a fire alarm and security will come running."

Her other hand motioned behind her for the woman to ease to her left, toward the stairs. Shadows wavered across the pavement. The woman edged away from her. God help them all if she hadn't picked up on the not-so-subtle command.

She attempted to maintain eye contact with the vampire, but the hood of his dark-colored sweatshirt obscured his face. Shadows blurred his facial features, the shape of his eyes eluding her. A glimpse of the color froze the breath in her chest.

Black. A solid obsidian iris. Staring into a pair of black eyes was frickin' scary. No depth or definition to show emotion or personality. Just a cold, vast emptiness that seemed to absorb every bit of light and warmth.

"So we're gonna play?" rasped the creature, flashing a smile filled with the promise of pain.

A wave of fear threatened to paralyze her.

She didn't stand a chance against the vampire.

But if she didn't do something drastic, there would be a bloodletting. For him, the woman represented a bonus. He really wanted the child. Innocent blood, young and untainted. An intoxicating high so pure a vampire could ride it for days.

The vampire's fangs slid down and out from under his lip. Saari shivered at the ghastly imitation of a smile. A quick yank pulled the sleeve up on her left arm, exposing the skin from wrist to elbow. "I don't think so."

With her arm in front of her, bent at the elbow, each fingertip pointed toward the ceiling. Raising her eyebrows to him in direct challenge, she canted her head toward her raised limb. Her tattoo for safe passage among the vampires circled her wrist. The design's vibrant colors sparkled against the pale backdrop of her skin.

His gaze dropped from her face to her moving arm.

"I know you can see Alarico's mark," she said quietly. "I'm under his protection, and that makes me *intocable*. Untouchable."

"Then get out of my way," he snarled, the tip of the knife pointing straight at her. "Mark or no mark, you're standing between me and that sweet little snack."

His eyes shifted to the woman and the small girl she carried. Saari could see them out of the corner of her eye now. The pair had reached the exit.

"No," the vampire howled.

The woman shouldered her way through the door. He lunged after them. Footsteps pounded up the stairs, drowned out a moment later by an alarm's piercing ring. The siren's tinny noise echoed off the gray, cement walls of the parking garage.

His head swung around, dead eyes paralyzing Saari with the intensity of his anger and hatred. "For that, I'll take you on principle alone."

The vampire moved toward her so swiftly, she didn't have a chance to react. His knife slid between her ribs and into her chest. He buried the blade to the hilt, driving the serrated steel through her heart.

The vampire caught her to him when she collapsed, cradling her against his chest like a deadly lover. He was so tall, her legs dangled uselessly above the ground.

His lips parted, and he smiled, purposely giving her a glimpse of his pearly points. "Don't worry. I'm not going to suck you. I promise, though, you'll feel every last drop of blood as it drips from your dying body."

Instead of biting her, his tongue darted out and licked the pulse at her neck. The smell of congealed blood and death buffeted her senses. Her stomach cramped with a wave of nausea. He tightened his arm, squeezing her body as if she were in a vise. She gasped when he forced air from her lungs.

A warm wetness spread along her skin where blood soaked her shirt. Unsure if her mind had begun to play tricks on itself, she thought she heard the sound of her blood dripping onto the pavement below.

The irony of the situation stung with bitter familiarity.

Dreams about the night she'd been cursed had chased her from her bed, prompting her to leave home and lose herself in work. And here she stood, in the parking garage at her job, on her birthday, stabbed through the heart. Again.

Immortality was a bitch.

Pinpoints of light flashed before her eyes. Centuries of experience told her a death would soon stop her heart. Then, she wouldn't see anything at all—until she woke up again.

Physically dying sucked. The pain that came with death *really* sucked.

And, of course, there was the problem of never knowing who'd be around when she woke up. She hated that part most of all.

The vampire gripped the blade buried in her chest.

A surge of air rolled through the parking garage.

She heard two different male voices filled with shock and rage roar, *"NO."*

Just before her head rolled back, she spotted a shadow behind the vampire. Her vision failed, shrouding her rescuer in a blurred fog. The vampire jerked in surprise. He momentarily tightened his hold on her before exploding in a cloud of dust.

Everything happened within the space of her next heartbeat.

Gravity pulled her toward the ground.

"Saari," a familiar voice whispered fiercely.

Strong arms closed around her.

Her eyes drifted closed and she tumbled into a dark, gaping void.

Chapter Seven

Morning, May 23, 2032

Saari floated, in a sea of blackness, carried by a steady current that pushed wave after wave of nothingness out into forever. A burst of disparate energy streaked through the undertow, suddenly sending her in a different direction. The new force in the ocean rocked her peaceful drift, and her blissful comfort changed. Waves rolled furiously, hurtling her forward.

Her eyes flew open at the exact moment her mind crashed into reality, and she gasped in pain. Though immortal, her body still experienced physical death each time she was fatally injured.

"Oh, God," she moaned. "Consciousness is overrated."

She remembered the 8-inch blade of a psychotically strong, seriously tweaking vampire had caused today's inflicted pain. Having a knife slam through her heart topped her "personally-experienced" list of *Most Painful Ways To Die*. Her chest ached as if it had been wrapped in gasoline-soaked elastic and set on fire.

Blinking away grit, she forced her eyes to focus. Painted stars on the ceiling winked at her through the mosquito netting draped over the rod-iron railing of her pine, four-post bed. A careful sigh of relief escaped. Mag had found her and brought her home.

If she was in her bedroom, her secret of immortality was safe.

The world couldn't know of her eternal existence. A new search for the "elixir of life" would lead to her front door. She'd end up as a pin cushion for some ego maniacal entrepreneur if anyone got a hold of the security tapes at the hospital.

After not showing up or calling, did she still have a job at the hospital?

A very masculine and wonderfully familiar chuckle drifted from her right. "I can see from your frown you've jumped right to worrying. Quit. After I found a broken camera in the parking garage, I called the hospital and let them know you're home sick. They didn't mention anything about the attack, so I doubt they have any viable footage."

Feather-soft linen brushed her cheek as she rotated her head across her pillow with measured caution. She needed to see her adopted sibling, but she didn't want to set off a new battalion of pain marching in a different direction somewhere else in her body.

Her gaze moved up his face until their eyes met. "Mag." Her voice cracked with gratitude. He would keep her safe until she could care for herself.

His lips turned up in a smile, showing perfectly straight teeth. Even his pearly points seemed whiter against his mahogany skin. She wondered for the umpteenth time how he could form a comforting yet cynical smile, all at the same time.

Mag leaned in toward her, the chair creaking in complaint. "Thank God you woke up," he whispered against her ear. He lifted a curl of hair off her shoulder, twining the strands around his shaking fingertip. "I swear you gave me a heart attack, stepping in front of that blood-crazed vampire."

"You'd have done the same."

"I just knew you were gonna die."

"I did," she groaned.

"Not funny."

He pulled back from her enough to lean his forehead atop hers. The solid pressure behind his touch anchored her awareness. Chocolate eyes shot through with amber bored into hers as he rolled his brow across hers.

His deep sigh brushed her cheek.

"You know, Saari, our friendship has a lot of perks, but dying vicariously through you is *not* one of them," he murmured fiercely.

A bark of laughter burst from her mouth, only to be cut short by a moan of pain. Her chest burned in retaliation. "Don't make me laugh," she begged. "It hurts."

His head shot up. "I'm sorry, *Nefer Ka*."

He looked so noble.

Coffee-colored skin and sharp angled features spoke of an Egyptian heritage that lent credibility to his calm and regal demeanor. But hearing him use his pet name for her waved a mental red flag. *Nefer Ka* meant "beautiful soul" in his native language. They'd been friends, each other's family so long, he only slipped into such personal vernacular under highly charged emotions—good or bad.

Today, worry lines marked the grim set of his jaw.

He shifted away from her, careful not to jostle her and accidentally cause more pain. The weight of his left hand settled around her smaller-fisted right hand. She stared intently at their clasped hands before looking up again.

He followed the direction of her glance, looked back up and shrugged. His eyebrows lifted. "Made me feel better, holding your hand."

The memory Jordan had shown her flashed behind her eyes: Mag, unwilling to hurt anyone, intent on killing himself. *I came so close to losing him and didn't even know it.*

She raised their joined hands to her lips and pressed a kiss to the back of his hand before rubbing her cheek gently over his skin. "Now let go of my hand so I can feel better."

His fingers loosened, allowing her to shift in measured increments on the bed. Her lungs filled with a calming breath, preparation against the coming pain. She rested her fist directly over her heart, fingers clutched tight together. The air in the room crackled. A teakettle's hiss burst from her lips, teeth grinding against the pain.

Healing energy burst from her palm, heat scorching the sensitive skin.

The energy output flared past the barriers that defined her personal space, pulling strength from every available outside source, augmenting her minimal reserves. She couldn't sustain this level of flowing power for long. This injury was severe and needed more than the use of her usual ability.

She required time and sleep to heal.

Exhaustion forced her to shift her hand off center on her chest. The crackling in the air subsided to a low hum. Heat radiated in a tolerable wave across her skin. Psychic walls she'd thrown up in an attempt to contain the energy pouring out of her dropped.

Awareness expanded beyond her body, encompassing the familiarity of her bedroom: the quilt she lay under, scented candles on the dresser, and framed pictures on the wall. Each calmed her in a way nothing else could. This was her home. Saari's energy meandered around the room, pulling comfort and strength from the known around her in a metaphysical blanket of security.

Her auric senses circled to the chair—and encountered a man with an unknown source of power. Saari's body bounced on the bed from the psychic contact. Up to this moment, she hadn't sensed anyone other than Mag in her bedroom. Such a lack of perception could be deadly. Her stomach knotted, the chink in her extrasensory armor a testament to how gravely she'd been wounded.

Something had gone drastically wrong.

Why was this stranger in her room?

Her gaze shot sideways. A man sat up straight in his chair, literally on the edge of the seat. Hands, palms down, gripped his knees. His knuckles showed white against the black of his pants, suggesting his own nervousness. The intensity of his emotion pounded her intuitive shields, and his body language struck her as downright disturbing.

~ ☾ ~

From the other side of the bed, Dhelis watched the interaction between the vampire called Mag and the striking woman in the bed. Joy and tenderness radiated from their every touch, making him feel like a voyeur. He presumed they were lovers, his presence an intrusion on a private reunion.

Doctor Conzatti had to have been mistaken about her healing abilities. Dhelis hadn't sensed anything from her.

He considered leaving.

Until the woman rested her fisted hand over her heart.

He *felt* the air in the room shift, every molecule of oxygen sizzling with therapeutic energy. She hissed in pain, the sound escaping through her gritted teeth. When her hand relaxed on her chest, the currents of power flowing toward her changed direction and disbursed throughout the room, passing through him.

His gut churned with certainty that *this* woman was the source of a power shift so intense the hairs still stood up on his arms. Could she be clutching a healing stone? His heart raced with anticipation and excitement. That kind of energy displacement meant she held *something* gripped in her hand. The heel of his boot tapped the floor, his leg bouncing with nervous energy. His hands ached from the tight grip on his knees.

He willed the woman to look at him.

One look at her eyes, and he would *know* if she was Tueri.

Her head turned sharply. For an instant, he wondered if he'd spoken his thoughts aloud. The woman boldly met his gaze. Her eyes rounded with surprise.

Shock rippled through him.

No matter what he had thought he expected, he was in no way prepared when her full attention settled on him. Her tri-colored eyes were striking; the most incredibly beautiful color he'd ever seen. More so, he thought, than even his own. His people all had crystalline-like eyes, amethyst and silver combined with a third shade based on talent and purity of bloodline.

The color of this woman's eyes reflected pure Tueri descent. But she was an Unknown, and for the life of him, he couldn't fathom how this could be. The fact they shared the same eye color went beyond incredible. Only Stone Riders had his color of eyes—and only men were Stone Riders.

Except a Predecessor.

Predecessors were always women.

There had been no female Predecessors for centuries—at least none that he knew of in the last five hundred years of Tueri history.

That *this* woman was a Predecessor defied all logic.

"Who are you?" His whispered words smashed through the moment of hushed silence.

Chapter Eight

Dhelis dropped to one knee and, without asking, took hold of the woman's hand, enveloping it within his own larger hands. The instant they touched, energy arced like a burning flame from a welder's torch. Like coronal waves from an exploding sun, light and heat blasted the room.

The force of the psychic connection slammed into him, punching the breath from his lungs on an outward surge of rolling energy. A returning wave refilled them with supercharged oxygen.

Disbelief shone in the Predecessor's eyes. Her mouth opened and closed several times, trying to speak. "You aren't healing me," she finally gasped. "So why is your energy reacting with mine?"

"I don't know." He shook his head back and forth, perplexed.

Every nerve ending tingled, his entire body aware of the woman in front of him. He knew he'd never met her. He hadn't even laid eyes on her before tonight. So why did his energy connect with *and* respond to this woman?

Realization dawned like a clapping thunderbolt.

Only a true Tueri soul match generated this kind of energy connection.

He'd found his *mate*!

The vampire placed both arms on the bed and levered himself out of his chair. "Enough," he roared.

With surprising strength, the woman jerked her hand from his grasp and turned toward the vampire.

An audible sigh of relief sounded from across the room at their broken connection. The blinding light winked out of existence, their separation triggering the flip of a psychic switch. The searing heat lessened, dissipating in noticeable amounts.

His gaze was drawn to the woman. She stared at him in wide-eyed astonishment, her chest rising and falling with each rapid breath. He yearned to touch her again, to bathe in their joined energy, but he held himself in check. Her injuries were severe, and he didn't want to risk her health.

"What the hell was that?" demanded Mag.

He shrugged. "As I said moments ago, I'm not sure. I've never experienced anything like it before."

"Well, isn't that helpful," Mag groused, sarcasm biting the edge of his words.

The vampire sat back down in his chair. He placed one hand on the woman's arm, the other on her knee. The gesture was both a proprietary statement and a challenge to him. Though the man didn't say a word, his meaning, *I have such a right. You do not,* could not have been clearer.

His eyes narrowed at the vampire's territorial actions, but he kept his mouth shut. Now wasn't the time to claim his status as her mate. Especially since he knew very little personal information about the vampire and absolutely nothing about the woman.

With conscious effort, he reined in his emotions. He sat back down in his chair, affecting a disinterested attitude he had yet to achieve. The chair's arms supported his elbows, while his folded hands rested on his stomach.

Whatever connection the vampire had with the Tueri Predecessor didn't matter. Not in his world, the Tueri world. A psychic connection was for life. And the woman was *his* destined soul mate.

"Saari, love, are you okay?"

Mag's whispered question reached him. *Her name was Saari.*

And the blood-sucking leach called her "love." His jaws clenched. Irritation spiked his triumphant mood. He changed his mind about the undead freak of nature and his mate. Her relationship with the vampire was unacceptable.

He killed vampires for a living. As his mate, Saari would have to understand that and disassociate herself from the nocturnal parasite. The way the vampire gripped her knee, and the fact she let him, all but screamed of a physical relationship between the two.

Grinding his teeth, he held back a possessive claim. As much as he wanted to, he couldn't just knock Mag over the head and drag Saari off to his cave. The utterly ridiculous image nearly made him laugh. This was not how he'd imagined his first contact with his mate.

With fisted knuckles, he brushed his lips, covering a sigh of resignation.

~ ☾ ~

A muffled sigh from the stranger reached Saari.

The level of tension in the room relaxed palpably after she wrenched her hand from the man's grasp, but a low hum of invisible current—that hadn't been there before—circulated between them.

His energy drew her, and the familiar sensation tickled a memory at the back of her mind. Such raw power sang to her on a primal level, reminding her of centuries long gone— reminding her of Miko.

Past memories merged with present, and the importance of the memory hit her. Saari's energy had reacted to Miko's energy in much the same way as this man's. *Had Miko found her?*

"It's not possible," she whispered.

She mentally kicked herself. Miko was dead. She *watched* him die. That this stranger's energy could affect her so intimately was inexplicable. The force of his aura touched her differently than Miko's, but the effect was just as strong.

He couldn't be Miko. *Could he?*

She had to know who he was, assure the exhausted butterflies knocking against her ribs he *wasn't* Miko. Because Saari had no doubt the energy buzzing through the room related directly to this man.

"What's wrong, Saari?" Mag asked, his words clipped and sharp.

She flopped her hand, waving his question aside.

What if the man was Miko? How had he survived? And if he lived, why had he waited over five hundred years to find her? Anxiety churned her stomach. Emotions buried deep in her heart warred with the logical arguments in her head.

Miko. Was. Dead.

Could this man be Miko reincarnated? Had she been given a second chance at love? Was such a thing even possible?

She turned toward the stranger, fastening her gaze on his chest.

From her brief perusal earlier, she'd guess he was in his mid thirties. The dark hair and sharp features could be Spanish or Indian heritage. He didn't look anything like Miko, but that didn't necessarily mean anything.

He had touched her and changed everything. She and this man were connected. To what extent they were connected was the question. Once the thought buried itself in her mind, improbable possibilities took root and blossomed.

Insecure and apprehensive, she avoided the man's intimate stare.

Cautiously, she widened her examination of the stranger. He wore a sweater of muted indigo, a beautiful shade of purple really. The material fit smoothly over a wide chest and broad shoulders, giving her an underscored appreciation for his physique. She took a pained breath and raised her eyes further, taking in the square shape of his jaw. A dark, five o'clock shadow covered his tanned skin.

His nostrils flared, as if in direct response to her inspection. She couldn't tell if his reaction indicated a sign of irritation or anticipation. Either possibility was a bit alarming. His energy wrapped itself around her, vibrating the very air she breathed. Her nerve endings hummed.

Steeling her riotous emotions, she forced her chin up and stared into the stranger's eyes. Time slowed down. Everything except the stranger faded from her awareness. Her vision narrowed further still, and this man—more specifically, his *eyes*—became the pinpoint of her attention.

They were the most amazing color. Not violet. Not amethyst. Not silver. They were some amazing combination of all three, and yet not any of them. The most astounding point about his eyes, they were almost the exact color of eyes that peered back at her every time *she* looked in a mirror.

She had only seen one other living soul in the last 510 years with the same color of eyes as herself, and he died the night she was cursed. In all her searching, Saari had yet to discover who she was and where she came from. The fact she and this man shared the same eye color and some crazy psychic connection was no coincidence.

He had to know *something*.

"Who are you?" She whispered, echoing the stranger's earlier question.

"Dhelis Guidry." The man stared back, his intense expression focused entirely on her.

A small bubble of hope burst. He *wasn't* Miko or Miko reincarnated. He was someone else entirely. But she already knew that. His energy reminded her of Miko, but it was very different.

The irony of her situation, again, glared with appalling absurdity. She was seeing a shrink to get over her one true love, and fate dropped a new man into her life with the ability to physically curl her toes.

"This is unbelievable," she muttered.

"And you're Saari." The stranger with the amazing eyes leaned toward her. "But I didn't catch your last name."

The scent of his Baldessarini cologne—her favorite Hugo Boss of course—tickled her senses. Her skin warmed, her blood pressure rising. Conflicting emotions skittered along the thrumming energy between them, forcing her to concentrate on her fleeting thoughts.

"I didn't give it." She answered, somehow managing to correctly remember the question he'd asked.

The burst of energy that enveloped her when the stranger touched her had been invigorating, making her feel strong and alive. His energy hadn't consumed hers, but instead joined with hers, carrying them to the center of a burning supernova.

His energy's power hummed to her seductively, and she wanted to touch him again. Only the joining, merging of their psychic existence would satisfy her desire to touch him. And like an addict looking for a fix, her need bordered on uncontrollable yearning.

A rope of clarity whiplashed her emotions. Touching the man would be a mistake. Their connection had created a compulsion, stronger than anything she'd ever experienced, to bond with a complete stranger.

So not going to happen.

"Just keep your hands to yourself, Mr. Guidry," she warned.

By keeping *her* hands to herself, controlling her emotions, she noticed her energy level had dropped. She didn't have the strength to handle the emotional turmoil her questions were bound to raise. She needed rest. Her body needed to heal. Only peaceful, uninterrupted sleep would accomplish that, which she wasn't going to get if she tried dealing with him now.

She looked back and forth between the two men flanking her bed. Both were prime specimens, men larger than life. She understood the strength and power of one. The other was a complete mystery.

The answer to that secret, however, would have to remain unsolved a while longer. She glanced first at Mag meaningfully, and then at the stranger, before looking back at the ceiling above her head. From the looks on both of the men's faces, they weren't going anywhere soon.

The thought held frightening, yet comforting appeal.

Her eyelids grew heavy. A deep, dreamless sleep beckoned, and she was hard pressed to resist. She hung onto consciousness to inform the men, in her most imperious tone, what she expected of them.

"I'm tired. I need rest in order to heal quickly." To punctuate her statement, she tightened her fisted hand around her healing crystal and placed her hand against the covered wound.

Energy arced again, and every one of her nerve endings stung from the healing force.

She clenched her teeth, holding back a shout of pain, and looked directly at the stranger. "We have unfinished business. I will know who you *really* are and exactly what just happened between us. You will be here when I wake up."

The man nodded his head affirmatively.

Though leery of the stranger, Saari accepted his nod as agreement. Rolling her head to the right, she met Mag's gaze. Her eyebrows rose in question. "You'll stay until I wake?" she asked quietly.

"I'm not going anywhere, *Nefer Ka*," he promised.

She breathed an inward sigh of relief. "Drop the window covers and draw the drapes. The 'fridge is stocked with fresh blood, so you should be fine," she ordered, forgetting that he was more than familiar with everything in her home.

Mag nodded, and the corner of his mouth quirked up as he fought the beginning of a smile. "Anything else?" he asked, his tone dripping with sarcasm.

Her eyes drifted closed. "Yes," she smiled. "If either of you harms the other while I sleep, I'll kill you both."

Chapter Nine

Late Morning, May 23, 2032

Dhelis sat in his chair, head back, facing Mag over Saari's still-sleeping form. His eyes, however, never left the vampire's face.

Sunrise had come and gone, making the never-sleeping city aware of the new day with its bright sunshine and quickly warming temperature. Engines revved and horns blared, announcing the morning traffic.

Saari slept undisturbed, in a near-comatose state.

"Your tri-colored eyes identify you as Tueri, but I've never seen you before tonight, Mr. Guidry. So why does your name sound familiar?"

Is he serious?

The vampire had seen at the hospital what he could do. How could he not know who and what Dhelis was? Unless he was playing dumb because of Saari. He could be part of the reason Saari was an Unknown among the Tueri.

"Who's asking?" Dhelis's harsh tone landed like a brick wall between them. His hands dropped to his sides, arms loose, shoulders lifted in a defensive stance.

Mag leaned forward, placing his crossed forearms on his knee. "Mag Nicola, Blood Court Prosecutor."

The answer snapped Dhelis between the eyes with the force of a popping rubber band. Council's vampire liaison had finally shown up. He didn't bother to hide his distasteful sneer. "Alarico's man. I should have known."

Maybe Mag wasn't the only vampire keeping secrets.
"What's that supposed to mean?"
His lips curled in a mirthless smile. "Oh nothing. Except I've been in New Angeles for almost six months, and tonight's the first night we've met. Why is that?"
"I've been out of the country," Mag shot back.
"You got back last week, I heard." He pointed a stiff finger in the vampire's direction. "You're supposed to be my link to Alarico."
Mag's chin lifted in recognition. "The new Tueri vampire executioner."
"If you and I had been working together, Saari wouldn't have been injured. I'd have killed your rogue vampire before he managed to escape and terrorize the mortal population."
The accusation, laced with a healthy dose of insult, hit its mark. Mag's hands fisted on his knees, the gesture telegraphing his desire to pound Dhelis for pointing out the vampire's obvious failure.
Bring it.
For a split second, he reveled in the idea of dusting the arrogant creature—but the moment passed. Sanity overruled his jealous reaction. Clearly Saari cared about the vampire. If Dhelis killed him now, he'd no doubt destroy any chance at a relationship with her. And nothing would interfere in bonding with his mate—including his own stupidity.
Experience cleared his head.
All vampires eventually flipped. He just had to bide his time.
Until then, to make sure this played out in his favor, he had to build a working relationship between himself and Mag. All he needed to do was keep his emotions under control so the vampire didn't sense his turbulent thoughts.
"Much as I detest the fact, you're right. My blood court caseload could have waited. As soon as I returned to the United States, I should have met you. If I had, that dead

couple would still be alive. Saari wouldn't have gotten stabbed." He stared at her, carefully rubbing a spot on his arm.

"Maybe. Maybe not. Neither of us could predict what would happen."

"A rogue vampire always kills—especially humans. That's why the creature is executed." He held up his hand, forestalling a response. "There's no benefit in arguing semantics. Neither of us can change the circumstances, so let's just agree to move on from here. Fair enough?"

Dhelis quirked an eyebrow, but didn't utter a word.

He was too busy staring at the patch of darker skin on Mag's forearm.

Is that a burn?

When he and Saari first touched, the room's sudden brightness had been blinding. Heat had ridden the energy that had vibrated and throbbed in the air around the two of them like a living entity. The longer their contact lasted, the more the energy grew. Could the force they had created be as destructive to vampires as the sun's rays?

He made a mental note to ask Council about the situation.

Right after he talked to them about Saari.

A loud vibration startled both men. Their silence was so intense, each of them jumped in response to the noise. Dhelis stretched his right leg out and reached for the cell phone attached to his hip. He looked at the screen on the telephone briefly while debating whether to answer the call.

Obligation won out over his inclination for privacy.

"Yeah."

He knew the vampire could hear the other end of the conversation as clearly as if the caller stood between them.

"*It's me. I need you here right now.*"

"I can't. I won't be mobile for awhile yet," he answered, being purposefully circumspect.

"There's been another one. This one's bad, and he's definitely one of ours."

He closed his eyes and pinched the bridge of his nose with his thumb and index finger.

"Where?"

"The Vagabond Inn. Room 227."

"I'm Riding."

"My car's out front. Use it."

The line went dead.

He snapped his eyes open and looked straight at Mag. "Don't go anywhere. I have to take care of something for the police department, but I'll be back."

Mag lifted an eyebrow but didn't respond.

Dhelis pulled a business card from his pocket and placed it on the dresser next to what he assumed was Saari's cell phone. "My cell number's on the back. Call if there's an emergency."

The air in the room puckered, and Dhelis willed himself to the Vagabond Inn. He knew his disappearances created no shimmer. No slow fade out—merely a snap and *just gone*.

"I *so* hate it when they do that."

Mag's mumbled complaint followed him as he blinked out of the room.

He smiled, knowing he'd gotten under the vampire's skin.

Wait until you see what else I can do.

Chapter Ten

Dhelis ignored the instructions he'd been given and, concentrating on his partner Thana Brunges, rode straight to room 227. Well, to the bathroom in room 227. He checked his appearance in the wall-covered mirror. Bleary eyes and a five o'clock shadow marked his reflection. A wrinkled sports jacket and lack of tie rounded out the impression of a long night.

Watching over Saari had kept him awake through the night.

Touching her had forever changed his world.

A flash of Mag's arrogant face popped into his head. *Why'd she have to be involved with a vampire anyway?* Even that thought didn't spoil his mood. He grinned at his reflection. He'd done it. He'd found his soul mate.

The smile faded. He'd also broken the first promise he'd made to her.

He'd given his word he'd be there when she woke up, and he didn't trust that walking parasite to tell her the truth about his absence. The vampire had heard every word of his conversation on the telephone, but just to be sure, he'd told the bloodsucker he had to leave for work.

Dwelling on the issue would only make him more frustrated. Nothing could be done about the situation with Saari right now. He'd waited his entire life for her. He supposed he could wait a few more hours to talk to her.

His sigh of resignation echoed in the silence. Time to start his day job.

Collar slightly askew, he adjusted his jacket. After running his hands over the sleeves, brushing out the worst of the wrinkles, he stepped out of the bathroom—and nearly smacked into a patrolman.

The young, uniformed officer guarding the entrance took a quick step backward, clearly startled by Dhelis's appearance. "Sorry, sir. I didn't see you come in."

"No problem."

Dhelis turned into the room and stared at the horrific scene. The splattered blood and gore reminded him of the aftermath from last month's vampire rave—and smelled even worse.

"You've got to be more careful." The petite, red-haired woman leaned against the wall with her arms folded over her chest. A stern look crossed her face. "It freaks people out when you just appear."

"I'm always careful." He dropped his voice to a near whisper. "Nobody from the department's ever seen me actually materialize."

She watched him for several moments, her gaze a deliberate perusal of his appearance from head to toe. Partner or not, he had given up trying to hide things from his cousin years ago.

Growing up next door to each other had made it impossible to keep things from her. Once they'd gotten older, became a psychic team and then law enforcement partners, he'd demanded more privacy. Now, if he wasn't in the mood to talk about his personal life, he just told her to butt out. And his situation with Saari qualified as a whole different level of personal.

So." She tilted her head. "Where have you been?"

"Sorry, I didn't have time to call you with a heads up. I had to help track a vampire last night. That damned creature wreaked havoc all over the city. I finally tracked the thing down at the hospital."

That's where he'd first seen Saari, but he kept that piece of information to himself. He needed to find out who Saari was before he mentioned her. Besides, his news wasn't something you just blurted out to your partner, even if she was your cousin—especially at the scene of a murder.

"You're holding out on me, Dhelis. Spill it."

One look at Thana's face told him she'd gnaw on him like a rawhide chew bone until he gave her an answer. "I told you," he said in his clearest 'butt out' tone, "I was working."

Dismissing the whole topic, he cleared his mind and concentrated on the task at hand.

"What happened here?" he asked, as he neared Thana.

With a sigh, she pushed herself off the wall using her shoulder. She turned and faced the center of the room. "He's all over the floor, quite dead as you can see for yourself."

He could certainly see for himself the man was dead. There was too much blood and too many body pieces for the victim to be alive. His nose wrinkled at the coppery smell of blood and other odors that reached him. "What a mess."

She looked over at him. "You have no idea. This is bad. I mean really bad. There are pieces *missing*."

He was going to ask about the missing pieces until he noticed the pallor of Thana's skin, the slight trembling of her slender frame. Her hands were now shoved deep into the pockets of her jeans.

"Quit worrying." She lifted an eyebrow. "I'm just making sure I don't accidentally touch anything before I'm ready."

When they worked scenes like this, he understood her need for control.

His thoughts circled back to the case. "You said he was one of ours. Is he a uniform?"

"No," she shook her head.

His shoulders drooped with fatigue. "I was afraid of that."

"He's a psychic," she lifted her chin toward the room in general, "and he's definitely one of ours." She held up a Ziploc bag containing a shimmering crystal on a gold chain. At his nod, her fingers curled around the bag and her hand disappeared into her pocket again.

Damn. He'd hoped for no double meaning behind her words, but the crystal left no doubt. A headache from lack of sleep pounded behind his eyes. He didn't have time to be tired. His life just got more complicated. The dead man had been a Tueri psychic.

"Are there any Teuri associated with the case?" His question delayed the inevitable audit of the room.

He heard her breathe an audible sigh of relief. "No."

Looking up, he watched Thana wrap her arms in a tight grip across her middle as she looked around. Following her gaze, he noticed for the first time a hot tub in the middle of the room. A steady hum announced the jets were on, circulating the water with pink, frothy bubbles.

He could see through the living-room area into the suite's bedroom. A scarlet path marked the psychic's attempt to crawl away from whatever had attacked him. The now dark-shaded carpet marked his failure to escape the horrifying massacre.

No sleep, combined with the visual and overbearing smell in the air, made his stomach shudder. He focused on the muted colors of wall paint and hanging pastel pictures of cottages and gardens. Neither inspired warm, fuzzy feelings.

And Thana had been in the room longer than he had.

He turned and watched his cousin carefully. No matter what she told him, she wasn't okay. For some reason, this murder scene was affecting her differently than others. He wondered if she had a connection to the psychic, though he couldn't fathom how. They had both been assigned to New Angeles five months ago as consultants on loan from UFOP.

A few years back, New York City had been brought to its knees when the entire subway system was destroyed. Immeasurable devastation reached far and wide. After a complete investigation, the press received a tip many legitimate psychics had tried to warn the government about the impending disaster. Public outcry lead to the formation of a group of registered psychics that worked throughout the country, giving birth to the United Forensic Organization of Psychics.

Dhelis and Thana's initial assignment in New Angeles had been missing persons' files and unsolved cases. Things changed abruptly three months ago when Thana audited some property in a missing person's file that turned out to be related to an unsolved murder case.

As a residue impressionist, she could touch items and gather impressions or signatures from the energy people left behind. Her connection between the missing person and the unsolved murder helped their department bring in a killer on the FBI's Ten-Most-Wanted list. They also managed to close five related cases, all victims of the same man.

The publicity that followed the arrest brought the police department to the Governor's attention. The Governor's office contacted the Attorney General, who then met with the Chief and inquired about the status of the UFOP members on loan to the city, and politely asked when they would be offered a permanent position.

Which all lead to the reason they were here, working a crime scene after the detectives and forensic team had completed their scene work first.

Another tremble wracked Thana's body as she stared at the carnage around the room. There was definitely more to her reaction than just a violent crime scene. But what?

He cleared his throat, drawing her attention to him and not the rest of the room. "You said he was a psychic. That must mean you already know who the victim was."

"Yeah, we do," she nodded. "The hotel manager said this suite was booked for Jordan Stevens. He always uses the same room when he comes to town."

He dropped his chin to his chest. His jaw ached from

gritting his teeth, as he stared at the floor. Jordan Stevens was only about the most publicly famous psychic for the last twenty-five years. Shaking his head in obvious disbelief, he raised his eyes to Thana. "How do we manage to catch every high-profile case that happens in this city?"

She just looked at him with a blank expression.

He raised a hand, halting any response she might give. "I know. I know. That was a stupid question."

She snorted loudly. "I guess that's how things will be from now on. We're permanently assigned to the homicide division. If the case goes well, we'll get paraded around as the new breed of cop. If the case goes down the crapper, we'll get flushed right along with it."

He inhaled sharply, surprised by her last remark. Neither of them had completely settled into their new assignment with the police department, but Thana already sounded like some of the more negative officers in the detectives division. As her psychic partner, his job was to help keep her as balanced and free of negative energy as possible.

Although these last couple of months had been hard on both of them, she had taken on the extra burden of continuing to work the missing persons and unsolved cases on her free time. The task was a huge undertaking, but compulsion drove her to be the voice for the people lost.

Worry for her sparked a new possibility. Had she taken in too much? Maybe that was the difference he noted in her reaction. Dhelis made a mental note to keep a closer eye on her. He would talk to Brogan later and see what he thought about increasing their healing sessions to filter her negative energy.

He checked on Thana. Her demeanor didn't exactly shout, "I'm relaxed," but at least she'd stopped clenching the material of her jacket in a death grip. He heaved an internal sigh of relief. She had her emotions under better control now.

That meant she was ready to work.

Chapter Eleven

Dhelis walked to the suite's entryway, stopping just in front of the open door. He reached into his jacket pocket and retrieved a mini recorder. Looking over his shoulder, he glanced toward Thana. "The other techs are done gathering evidence. You ready?"

"Whenever you are." She joined him at the suite's front door.

He held the electronic device toward her with his right hand and reached for her with his left. "We're recording."

His safety measures, a recording of her detailed audit and his solid, physical connection, he knew eased her mind.

Next came her ritual of focus to prepare her body.

She took a deep breath in through her nose. Inhaling slowly and filling her lungs. He mentally counted to three before she exhaled every bit of air. After the next inhale, she reached out and touched the electronic lock, bare skin to bare metal.

Thana's body jerked, her hand twitching in his. Air hissed through her teeth. Every time he watched her audit something, her initial shock reminded him of a bandage being ripped from a scab.

He knew from experience, the instant immersion kicked her extrasensory perception into overdrive. Hopefully she'd get the information they needed without having to audit the entire room. *That* was something neither of them wanted to do.

"I've got flashes of anger, fear, excitement, and frustration sparking harder than an exposed livewire. Everything's a mixed cluster of feelings."

"You're a psychic deep-sea diver, gal. Plunge your mind into the knotted tangle and find a specific thread for us to follow," he murmured.

Her fingers traced the metal handle. "There's a bunch of different signatures here."

The young patrolman stuck his head into the room. His eyebrows lifted in question, likely wondering if Thana was talking to him. Dhelis shook his head and lifted his chin toward the hallway. The officer got the message and retreated from the room.

Thana talked through her audits, not just for her own benefit, but to keep Dhelis aware of everything she picked up. People assumed Dhelis could see and feel everything she did when he held her hand.

They assumed wrong.

Dhelis was her rock. He kept her anchored to the present whenever she forayed into the metaphysical realm. If she became tired or oversensitized, she drew from his strength, his energy. He served as her *amarrer*, and it was his job to keep her from venturing too deeply into an emotion.

"I hate doorknobs. *Everybody* touches them," she grumbled. Lightly, she ran her fingertips around the edge of the passkey lock again. "I'll recognize the Tueri's signature when I find it, but this will take longer than I expected. There are different strings of emotion within the signatures, and each feeling has to be sensed and rolled separately to separate it from Jordan's."

How would she know Jordan's signature? He remembered the plastic bag containing the crystal. Right, she must have gotten his signature from his stone. Thana always thought ahead.

"I've picked out two separate emotions carrying the same energy signature." Her thumb and middle finger traced circles in opposite directions.

The repeated motion meant she was closing in on Jordan's energy trace, a psychic predator locating the scent of prey.

"I've got it." She smiled at him in triumph. "He entered the room twice. The first signature is filled with excitement and tinged with nervous energy. He came into the room alone then. The second signature is full of anxiety and frustration. And that time, he had company. He had a woman with him."

Hopefully, the other detectives are already canvassing the hotel with Jordan's picture, questioning guests as well as staff. Maybe someone saw him with the mystery woman. Footage from the security cameras would be even better. A description of her at least gave them a place to start looking for his killer.

Confident steps carried Thana into the room, following a trail only she could see. He matched her steps, cognizant of her extra senses that propelled her forward. A psychic beacon, that pulled her straight ahead.

"Stay tight to me, Dhelis. This audit's gonna be messy."

No kidding.

They crossed the darkened carpet that led straight into the bedroom.

"He brought her in here." She approached the right side of the bed and placed her hand on the bedspread. "He put her down on the bed." With a feather-soft touch, she tracked the fabric's pattern toward the headboard. When she reached the indention on the pillow, she pressed her hand into the center of the hollow.

"She fell unconscious. And was very sick. No, wait. That's not right." She chewed her lip in concentration. "He thought the woman was sick." She traced her hand in slow, lazy circles around the center of the pillow. "Her energy signature is here. She had a *very* high fever."

Placing her knee on the mattress, she pulled her hand off the pillow and dragged her fingertips across the bedspread toward the opposite side of the bed. He crawled onto the bed next to her, straining to maintain their connection.

When she reached the other side of the bed, she rocked back on her heels. Her body jerked as if an unknown energy slammed into her solar plexus, constricting her chest. Puffs of air squeezed from her lungs as she panted like a dog in the summer heat.

"Thana?" Had she sunk too far into the other woman's emotions?

She squeezed his hand twice in quick succession, a signal they'd worked out in case she couldn't speak: one for trouble, two for safe.

"Okay. We'll keep going."

"Something's not right," she finally managed. Her gaze locked onto the far wall. "The psychic stood there last night, watching—something. I wish you could see what I do. I'm not sure how to explain what I'm feeling."

"You're explaining things just fine. Tell me what you see."

Her left hand clicked the head of an imaginary pen, the movement keeping time with something he couldn't see or feel. "It's like a jigsaw puzzle, but the pieces don't fit: his signature, her signature, no signature."

He squeezed her hand lightly, hoping to direct her thoughts with his question. "What do you mean no signature?"

"The woman's signature is gone." Her hand fisted in the covers marking a position. "I can't sense her anymore."

Turning toward the foot of the bed with urgent insistence, she pressed forward. He scrambled over the far edge and stood next to her.

She knelt and reached for the psychic's arm. His hand tensed around hers, ready to yank her to him, but he knew he wouldn't. If he pulled her back before she was ready, she would never forgive him.

Once Thana started an audit, she had to finish it.

For her, it ranked as a compulsion. She couldn't *not* finish.

She touched the ravaged stump, and air hissed through her clenched teeth. "God, this hurts." She swayed, but caught herself before she actually bumped into him.

He dropped into a crouch next to her. "Why do you hurt?"

"I found another energy," she indicated. Her forehead creased and her eyebrows scrunched together in frustration. "This signature is crazy, almost frenetic. I get a shadow of something. It's big, but I can't make out what it is. I've never felt anything like this."

"What happened?"

"That *thing* ripped his arm off first." She shook her head a couple of times. Her eyes cleared once she separated herself from the pain that belonged to Jordan Stevens. "The strange signature is full of such primal anger, and the psychic's is bright with fear."

She crept forward. He kept pace in their awkward three-handed crawl across the rug. Together, they followed the path the psychic had taken until she stopped next to his torso.

Dhelis didn't know how she managed to go on. The next wave of pain the psychic endured would be immeasurable. Maybe he should stop her now, before she goes any further.

Thana took a deep breath and placed her hand on Jordan's slashed back. "It clawed through his back. His lungs were damaged, it pierced him so deeply."

Her breath hitched. She stood up fast and approached the Jacuzzi in the middle of the room. Without hesitating, she plunged her hand into the swirling water. "His leg was ripped clear of the socket next."

He tried to tug her away from the Jacuzzi. "That's enough. You have to stop now."

She grabbed the edge of the Jacuzzi and held on. Her eyes widened in surprise, and she jerked back in stunned silence.

The sudden movement caught him by surprise. Though he stumbled and dropped to a knee, he refused to let go of her hand. When she strode toward the sliding glass doors, he scrambled to his feet and followed. The grinding crunch of broken glass accompanied their footsteps through the open doorway and onto the terrace.

Thana stepped to the edge of the balcony and reached for the metal rail. She twitched with the shock of a fork in a light socket. "The same frenetic energy covers this surface. It was here."

She turned her face into the breeze and lifted her nose toward the sky.

Before he could stop her, she climbed onto the railing and turned toward her left.

"Jesus, Thana. Are you trying to kill yourself?" He slammed the recorder down on the rail and wrapped his right arm around her legs to keep her from falling to her death on the street beneath them.

Jordan Steven's suite was on the twelfth floor.

Loud clapping echoed across the balcony from somewhere behind them. The startling noise wrenched Thana from the audit, and she swayed on the ledge with the balance of a drunk performing a sobriety walk.

"*Thana*, be careful." He tightened his grip on her legs.

He turned his head and glared as Detective Hall and Detective Strege approached the terrace.

The two reminded him of the comedic duo Laurell & Hardy. Strege's shorter, lanky build, light eyes, and fake "aweshucks" smile played against Hall's opposite looks. Unfortunately, neither had a sense of humor.

Detective Hall stopped just inside the doorway, crossed his arms over his chest and leaned against the empty doorframe. "Well, look who's—working."

Dhelis ground his teeth. Before he could actually tell Hall to shut his mouth, Thana spoke.

"It threw the psychic's head in a fit of anger."

Hall looked Thana up and down, taking note of her appearance. His gaze cut to Strege and he smiled. "She must be rehearsing for a remake of Carrie."

Strege just shook his head and turned away from Hall.

Thana continued, as if there had been no interruption. "His head's there," she pointed with her left arm, "right in the hollow of the O on the sign for the Vagabond Inn."

Detectives Hall and Strege strode to the railing, careful not to touch Thana. Dhelis knew their distance had nothing to do with the blood on her.

Neither of the men knew exactly what Thana could "see" or "audit" when she touched things. They hadn't worked with her long enough to understand her ability, let alone be comfortable with it. As within UFOP, trust among the New Angeles detectives was paramount. They didn't trust her, so they weren't taking a chance on her finding out anything they didn't want her to know.

Which meant they weren't getting anywhere near her.

Strege looked at the sign. "How can you see anything that far away?" he asked. "That's impossible. I can't make out anything other than a large O."

Without leaving the balcony, he yelled back into the room for a pair of binoculars. One of the uniformed officers in the hallway brought him a pair. Strege nodded his thanks before turning back toward the sign.

Dhelis watched Strege look through the lenses and focus.

Strege slowly shook his head. "I'll be damned. There's a head in that sign."

"Jordan Stevens' head," Thana clarified quietly.

Chapter Twelve

Late Morning, May 23, 2032

Night had descended, and Saari couldn't move.

An ominous fist of foreboding pressed against her. She couldn't breathe around her fear. No amount of struggling loosened the ropes that bound her, standing, to a red cedar tree.

The hint of movement flickered at the corner of her eye. Sap from burning wood hissed and popped, disturbing the night's unnatural quiet. She craned her neck toward the sound. Miko lay unconscious in the middle of a stone circle, next to the fire. Blood oozed from the side of his head and dripped onto the ground.

A shadow fell across the fire, momentarily blocking its light. Her friend, Heika, paced in jerky strides next to the flames. Saari didn't see anybody else with her. She nearly called out to Heika, but instincts checked her impulse.

Something had gone terribly wrong.

Fighting a spike of panic, she closed her eyes and found her center. With some effort, she dropped her mental defenses and opened her senses to the night. She drew out the emotions riding on the wind, separating Miko's pain from the other feelings.

A tremendous hatred rolled off Heika.

The intensity of the emotion stunned her.

Her eyes snapped open and her chin shot up, slamming the back of her head against the tree. Her skull throbbed.

Flashes of light danced in front of her eyes as she fought to stay alert. She pulled her thoughts into focus.

Who did Heika hate? Miko lay unconscious, but she was tied to a tree.

She glanced toward the fire where Heika mumbled to herself. Candles circled the ring of stones. The pungent scent of herbs blended with the smell of smoke. Heika planned to perform a death ritual. The realization slapped Saari with terror.

Miko stirred, bringing both women's attention to his inert form. Heika dropped to her knees, stroked Miko's cheek, and smiled.

Saari's jaw dropped with a shock of understanding. Her breath left her in a great rush. Heika loved Miko! Her stomach clenched, the pain of her friend's betrayal a physical blow. Saari had only just learned how to sense other's emotions, but how had she not seen this before?

Heika gripped Miko's shirt at the neckline and ripped the material off him. Saari cringed at the passionate display. Heika then lifted a small vial filled with a shimmering liquid and poured it onto his chest. She rubbed the oil into his skin with slow, deliberate strokes until it gleamed in the firelight.

Saari wanted to look away, to save herself from the torture of picturing this scene over and over in her mind, but she couldn't. Razor-sharp jealousy compelled her to witness this duplicity. Each time Heika touched Miko, Saari's heart shuddered, flayed by emotions.

Heika looked up at Saari and smiled. "So now you know." She stood and walked to Saari's side.

Saari licked her dry lips. "Why are you doing this? Untie me."

Heika placed a finger over Saari's lips, silencing her words.

Cold, numbing fear spread through Saari's veins, blunting her ability to read Heika.

Silently, she watched Heika pull on the ends of the ribbon that held Saari's blouse closed. The ribbon unraveled and the neckline loosened. Heika drew the material off of each shoulder, pooling the fabric around Saari's waist.

Shimmering oil again spilled from the vial into Heika's palm. With a shaking hand, Heika reached reverently toward Saari's breasts. Then her palm tilted over Saari's collarbone and the warm oil dripped onto her skin. The thick liquid left a shiny trail of iridescent sparkles gleaming in the firelight.

Saari's eyes grew round with revulsion as Heika's fingertip followed the path made by those glinting sparkles. She chased the oil toward its ultimate goal: the dusky rose-colored aureole with its involuntarily erect peak. Heika's eyes closed and her head dropped back on her neck.

Saari sucked in her breath and rounded her shoulders forward, pulling her body away from Heika's moving finger. Heika's breathing hitched, and her head snapped forward. She brazenly stared at Saari's body.

Disbelief flared in the pit of Saari's stomach, leaving her speechless with shock. Heika desired her, not Miko! Oh, God. This was so wrong.

Heika had been her best friend. The closest thing to family she had. She had loved Heika like a sister. But Heika's touch violated her both in body and soul. How could she do this to me?

"Don't touch me." She pulled against the ropes.

Heika didn't respond. Her eyes glazed over as she poured the rest of the oil across both of Saari's breasts. The oil slithered down her skin, and Heika circled her palm over first one breast and then the other. The woman's nostrils flared as she cupped Saari's breast and gently held the full weight.

Saari cringed at the soft caress, the gentle squeeze of her breasts.

"Heika, please. Don't," she begged, willing her to stop.

"Dear God," Heika whispered with awe. "This is what it means to love."

"This is not love!" she shouted in protest, violently shaking her head in denial. Her actions startled Heika. "I don't want this."

The hope in Heika's eyes bled to bitterness at her rejection and her features hardened. "So be it. This is how things could have been between us. Instead, you chose him."

She reached into her gown's pocket and pulled out a dagger. The firelight glinted off the blade.

"What are you doing?"

Heika's smile held madness. "He was to be the sacrifice that bound us together in immortality. Now, his love will be your curse. Death for him, immortality for you—and your soul forever incomplete."

Horror doused her rage. Heika placed the tip of the cold blade over Saari's heart, and her mouth went dry with terror. Blood roared through her head. Her ears buzzed from the sudden pressure.

Heika meant to kill her.

The blade twitched, cutting a perfect crescent-shaped slice on her left breast. She hissed with pain. The cool night air brushed the wound, making it sting. Blood ran down her chest, over her breast, and finally slid down her ribs.

Abruptly Heika turned and approached Miko. Saari's blood glinted on the blade. With the flick of her wrist, Heika created an identical crescent-shaped cut on the left side of his torso. She lifted her head and gave Saari a vicious smile.

The knife arced downward, toward Miko's chest.

Saari strained wildly against her bonds, screaming violently. Helplessly, she watched the dagger plunge toward Miko's heart. At the last moment, Miko opened his eyes. He jerked to the left, and reached toward Heika. His eyes, though, remained locked on Saari.

The blade sank into his chest, and Saari gasped with pain. Her chest burned like fire, her heart ached with emotion. Miko's pain became her pain. In the next instant, a mere blink of an eye, he disappeared.

She stared at the empty stone circle he had moments before occupied, stunned by his death. One moment Miko was her future, and then he was gone. Just—gone.

"His soul's been consumed—as if he never existed." Heika turned to Saari, her eyes empty and dead. She walked forward, stopping only when their bodies were a few inches apart. "It is done."

In a movement so quick Saari had no time to prepare, Heika struck like a rattlesnake. She drove the knife through Saari's heart. She brought her face so close they were nearly touching, each stealing the other's breath. "You, Saari, are cursed to wander a barren existence through the wasteland that is humanity for all eternity."

Heika lifted her chin and gently kissed Saari's lips. Her touch was more than Saari could bear. She closed her eyes, blocking out sight, the only sense she could control.

Heika nuzzled her cheek and whispered in her ear. "A gift, my love. Your first true death. You'll always experience death's pain, but never your soul's release."

~ ☾ ~

Saari's eyes flew open wide, her hoarse cry echoing in her head. She expected Mag to fuss like a mother hen over her waking so soon, but no questions or scolding came. Once her eyes focused, the shadows around her room took shape. Thankfully, she was alone.

"Just a dream. It didn't happen again. It was just a dream." The chanted words became a mantra of safety. She fought to slow the mad thumping of her heart.

Tears dampened her cheeks. "Miko," she whispered, closing her eyes tight against the flood of memories. Loneliness buffeted her soul, a winter storm raging with emotion. Anger pounded her eardrums with the force of thunder. Bitterness crackled through her veins like streaks of lightning.

Her life and everyone she loved had forever changed that horrific day.

And because of that damned shrink, she remembered every detail, every minute.

Night after night she dreamed of Miko's death, unable to change the past or accept his loss and move forward. Nisa said she had to let go, but how was she supposed to love somebody else? Who would ever truly understand her, accept her being psychic *and* immortal?

A new memory skirted the edge of the maelstrom, swirling with the bounding energy of an early spring. Dhelis's face appeared before her mind's eye. She remembered his touch and the warm rays of light that had whispered across her skin.

Maybe there *was* someone who could accept her.

She concentrated on her breathing, forcing her emotions to calm. Dhelis's touch reminded her how exhilarating being alive felt—and how desperately she wanted that again.

Could she have found such a connection?

Hope carried on those remembered rays of light. The possibility became a fragile yearning that wrapped around her heart like a vine, clinging to a new source of life. Working through her issues over Miko became even more important.

I can handle the dreams.

Dealing with the reasons behind the dreams would help her move on.

Saari opened her eyes and stared at the sparkling constellations painted on her ceiling. Her gaze traced the stars, her thoughts following in a connect-the-dot pattern.

She'd gone to the shrink because she had The Dream once every year since Miko's death. Now, she had The Dream every time she slept.

Doctor Lytton said that was normal. Something didn't feel right, but she needed to talk to him. He *had* to figure out why she kept having the dream.

She turned her head and checked the clock. It wasn't quite 9:00 a.m. The doctor's office didn't open for another hour. That didn't matter. He'd given her his cell number in case she needed to call him outside of business hours.

With measured caution, she reached for her cell phone on the dresser. The device lay under her palm. Her fingers bumped the bottle of sleeping pills she kept for emergencies. Considering she'd only had a few hours sleep and her chest still screamed with agony, today qualified as an emergency.

She gripped the bottle and phone, pulling them to her side. Gritting her teeth against the pain, she popped the top and dumped a couple of pills into her mouth. Reaching for a water bottle meant stretching her chest muscles again. No way. She chewed the bitter pills instead, ensuring they hit her system faster, and swallowed.

A quick tap on the cell phone's screen opened the voice command window. "Call Doctor Lytton," she directed. Another tap put the phone in speaker mode. After four rings, his voice mail kicked on.

"This is Doctor Lytton and you've reached my cell phone. Please leave a message, and I'll get back to you at my earliest opportunity."

"Doctor Lytton, this is Saari Mitchell. I had The Dream again, and I really need to speak with you. Unless I hear from you, I'll come by your office at 6:00 this evening. Thanks."

She ended the call and dropped the cell phone. A wave of pain wracked her body from even that small movement. If only she could heal faster. Her eyelids drooped as the sleeping pills hit her system. Maybe if she concentrated on Dhelis, she wouldn't dream about Miko again.

Memories of heat and light swirled in her head, obscuring the line between her past and present. A man with dark hair and a five o'clock shadow gripped her hand. His stare, their connection made her yearn to touch him—and be touched.

Her drugged subconscious whispered encouragement. Here, in the privacy of her mind, it was okay to dream. She could have the love she'd always wanted.

All she had to do was reach for it.

Chapter Thirteen

Bright morning sunlight invaded Clayton's soothing gray fog of slumber. Consciousness came with abrupt lucidity. An unknown disturbance jerked him from his sleep, sending his senses into overdrive.

He lay prone, stretched out fully on his back. In one smooth motion, he rolled to a squatting position, coming to rest on the balls of his feet, the tips of his fingers pressed hard against the earth. Holding his breath, he searched for any vibrations traveling through the ground.

The drugs he'd used to stave off his change had burned off hours ago, allowing his lunate senses to thrive. He cocked his head sideways and listened. There it was: the noise that awakened his keen sense of hearing.

A female wolf growled in the distance.

The familiar smell of pine trees, berry leaves, and soil dampened by the lake assured him he'd spent the night at the reserve.

How did I get here?

He remembered tracking Maurika's scent to Jordan Stevens' room. She had already left, but the psychic had been there. Clayton had wanted to rip his head off for letting Maurika get away. He flexed his fingers, recalling the way the man's neck collapsed in his grip.

Knowing what the psychic had been talking to his patient about would have been nice, but it didn't matter. When Saari came to see him today because she had The Dream again, he'd ask her once he put her under hypnosis.

"Let go, Inyegar. I'm awake." The voice carried on the breeze.

Maurika.

He couldn't be that lucky, could he?

Did I find her here and claim my right as her dominant?

Curiosity propelled him to the top of the path he had slept next to. He picked his way through the wild growing Natal Plum shrubs. He crested a small hill, stopping in the shadow of a black acacia.

Maurika lay stark naked, buried under her pack of wolves...instead of waking up next to him. Well, that answered the question of his position in the pack. He was still an outsider. He lifted his nose and sniffed. No other lunate was near, and being downwind kept Maurika from smelling him.

A triumphant smile curved his lips.

The pack structure was about to change.

"Where's Quinn, girl?" Maurika asked.

A wolf huffed, nudging her hand.

Not here.

An engine's mechanical whine came from somewhere to his left. The gears mashed, changing as the automobile's speed decreased.

One of the wolves issued a low growl, alerting something approached. Maurika sat up, head turned toward the advancing sound. A male wolf took point and stood by Maurika at the front of the pack. Several of the other wolves lifted their haunches and moved in tight around her. Despite his position, Clayton admired the pack, noting their fierce loyalty. They would protect Maurika no matter the threat.

Maurika gave a low bark, drawing the wolves' attention. "There's no danger. It's just Quinn."

Clayton wanted to howl in frustration. To be so close to taking Maurika and claiming her pack as his own, not once but *twice* in less than 24 hours, was a coincidental travesty. Why couldn't he catch God damned break?

Quinn roared into the meadow, the jeep sliding to a pebble-crunching stop next to the pack. He turned off the engine and stepped out of the jeep, a newspaper gripped in his fist.

Sunlight reflected off his dark, white-tipped hair. Clayton knew from watching the pair on the reserve, the color stayed the same in both his lunate and human form. Quinn's eyebrows scrunched over a pair of light brown eyes that glowered at Maurika. He twitched his shoulders and strode toward her, his long legs eating up the ground between them.

As Quinn approached the pack surrounding Maurika, he never slowed his pace. Several of the wolves whined and nudged his legs as he brushed past them, each vying for his attention. He moved into their midst, ignoring the other wolves, finally stopping directly in front of her.

That should be me.

Clayton growled low in his throat, careful to quietly—and from a safe distance—express his intense dislike for the werewolf pack's current alpha male. All lupines had excellent hearing, and Quinn was dangerous enough without Clayton giving away his own presence. He *really* wanted to avoid a direct confrontation with Quinn. As much as the thought galled him to admit, he wasn't sure he could take the other male.

"Are you hurt?" Quinn asked, dropping to his knees and reaching for her.

He ran his hands over her body, testing for broken bones.

"Stop it. I'm fine." Maurika batted his hands away. "You know a change will heal any wound anyway."

Quinn lifted an untamed mass of her tangled hair. "Yeah, well, with all this dried blood I wanted to be sure."

"Huh. I actually got him."

Got who?

Clayton could see the traces of bright fluid that marked her body. Pieces of her prey were woven through her wild curls.

"What's the last thing you remember, Rika?"

Clayton loved the way her nose wrinkled when she concentrated.

Trying to remember wouldn't do her any good, though. Since werewolves—and lunates—could shift at will, they retained their memories after a shift because they were in control. The circumstances weren't the same with a forced change. Once a change was forced, all human control disappeared. Maurika could sit there thinking until the blue moon rose again tonight, and there wouldn't be any memories to access.

"I remember being at the Zinful Bar. *He* was there. I smelled him. I took plenty of Valerian pills to keep from changing, but whatever drug he put in the drink he sent me knocked me for a loop."

Quinn crossed his arms over his chest and dropped his chin.

"He thought he had me. I let him walk me to his hotel room at the Vagabond Inn—I think that was the hotel anyway. There was an elevator ride—and then I woke up here."

She thought that weak, pasty-faced human was me?

Quinn shot to his feet. He opened the newspaper and dropped it on the ground in front of Maurika. "You didn't get *him*. You killed Jordan Stevens."

"What?" Maurika snatched up the paper.

What?

Clayton dropped into a crouch, not wanting to chance Quinn spotting him now that his rival had stood and started pacing.

"No, I couldn't have." Her voice cracked.

That's because I did.

Quinn turned abruptly and stomped back to where she sat on the ground. He reached down, grabbed her by the shoulders and lifted her entire body. Her feet dangled off the ground nearly a foot when he brought Maurika's eyes level with his.

"How could you take such a chance? We have no idea what kind of drug he mixed with the Valerian or how much. You could have done any number of things, Rika. The mixture of drugs could have killed you on the spot or it could have rendered the Valerian ineffective and you would have changed immediately. I told you not to hunt for him alone."

The wolves barked and circled the two dominants in their midst. Maurika roared at the pack, her tone deep and long, calling the wolves to her. Their circle tightened around the pair; lips peeled back showing their deadly sharp fangs.

He gritted his own teeth at Quinn's dominant stance. *How dare he put his hands on her!*

"Rika, stop it." Quinn shook her once.

Maurika growled louder, baring her own teeth.

"I'm sorry. I was just so worried about you." He lowered her to the ground and wrapped his arms around her in a crushing embrace.

One quick bark from Maurika and the wolves quieted, dropping to their haunches.

Clayton's chest swelled with pride at her control. Once he became dominant of the pack, they'd make a fierce pair that nobody would challenge.

"You're right." Tears clogged her voice. "Oh, God. That poor man is dead because of me. I'm so sorry."

Quinn gently pushed her back a few inches and looked down at her. "You didn't kill him on purpose. You were trying to protect the pack."

Her arms lifted in a "so what" gesture.

"We'll sort this out. Come on. There are clothes in the jeep for you. We've got to get you cleaned up before anybody sees you."

He walked her to the jeep. After pulling a robe around her and wrapping her hair in a towel, he got her buckled into her seat.

The jeep started up again and pulled slowly onto the dirt road, careful to avoid any of the wolves watching the moving vehicle. Once the jeep cleared the pack, the SUV's speed increased, leaving a billowing dust cloud following in its wake.

Clayton took his time walking back down the hill, his mind's eye snapping back the mental picture he had of Maurika, naked, laying contentedly among the pack. The need to touch her, to wear her scent, overwhelmed him.

He imagined himself finding her in the meadow. It was *he* who walked through the pack, not Quinn, to get to her. In his vision, her naked body rubbed against his own. Unlike Quinn, he responded.

His hands gripped her waist, crushing her to his hips. Grinding against her, he made her understand exactly how much she was submitting to. Fear and excitement bled from her pores, covering him in her scent. Her small whimpers of surrender fed his arousal.

He stumbled, tripping over a stone in his path. Pain screamed up his leg, and the Maurika in his arms vanished. His rock hard dick throbbed, aching with the need for release.

He roared in frustration.

Rage flooded his system. Each of his fingers curled with the urge to rip something apart. The muscles of his legs elongated, preparing to change. The sight of claws before his eyes plucked at the anger blazing through his senses.

A voice of reason, the shrink buried in him, whispered in his head. *Don't react to the tone of your thoughts. Focus your emotions. Analyze your situation. Determine the risks and set your goal.*

Deep breath in...breathe out.

Pulling his swirling emotions into a directed space in his head helped him relax.

The heavy ache of his erection eased.

Overhearing their conversation had been an unexpected boon.

Maurika took something to keep from changing, but, then again, so did he. Whatever she had ingested was different than the concoction he found worked for him, but he knew how to get around that. He'd been at this longer than she had.

At the Zinful Bar, he had slipped her some of his own special cocktail—mad dog weed—mixed with Rohipnal. The stunning effect from the combined sedatives should have knocked her out long enough for him to get her into his car and back to his cabin.

Then he would have had some *real* fun.

The next morning he'd planned to make a very helpful, but totally anonymous, phone call to the police. Based on the evidence they would have discovered—planted by Clayton himself, of course—Quinn would have been permanently removed from Maurika's life—and Clayton's.

That had been the plan anyway. The fates had decreed otherwise.

Because the pair knew about him—had started hunting *him*, last night had gone far differently than he had hoped.

When he reached the bottom of the hill and approached the area he'd slept the night before, he looked around and really *saw* what he'd missed upon waking. Pieces of bloody fabric littered the ground. The metallic scent of blood floated on the light breeze. Turning, he followed the smell to its source: a piece of bone with torn skin and ligaments protruding from the shrubs to his right.

Without a moment's hesitation, he strode toward the bushes, knowing what he would find. Squatting, he grabbed the end of the mangled bone and pulled roughly on whatever remains were attached to the other end of last night's meal. The upper portion of a female's eviscerated torso slid into view. He briefly recalled the woman.

When Clayton had discovered Maurika's scent on the psychic, he'd been livid. Mount Vesuvius couldn't match his emotional implosion. The pills he'd taken helped him manage a partial shift, before changing back to human in Jordan's hotel room. A few more capsules had kept his beast bottled a while longer. After spending the better part of an hour unsuccessfully tracking her scent in the city streets, he'd given up.

A night's hunting shot. His mood had worsened. On his way out of the city, he'd come across a woman stranded alongside the road. The raised hood on her Honda Civic served as a billboard advertising car trouble. Her drooping shoulders and crooked grin shouted her relief someone had stopped to help her.

Unfortunately for her, his rage at losing Maurika found a new target. He'd simply walked up and with one massive blow knocked her unconscious. After throwing the woman in his car, he'd driven out to the reserve just to feel closer to Maurika. Everything after that was—well, gone.

"Well, damn."

He stared at the bloody mess and heaved a resigned sigh. He wasn't at his playground, and since he ate her, he didn't have a body for last night's full moon to plant as evidence implicating Quinn. That meant he would need two tonight or tomorrow evening to make up for the one he munched on last night.

The forensic team that ultimately investigated would probably be able to determine the last two women he planned on killing died on the same night during the full moon, but there was nothing he could do about the timing issue now.

Perseverance was the key. He would continue to follow the pattern he had established months ago, thus maintaining the credibility of his kills—well, Quinn's kills. That's how the police department and the pack would see things anyway.

That last thought helped to salve his bruised pride.

The wind shifted slightly, and now the coppery tang of blood hung heavy in the air. His nose lifted, tracking the scent, looking for the smell's point of origin. He dropped the woman's remains he held, thinking maybe that's where the odor emanated from. Then he noticed mottled, dry blood covered his skin.

Well, this could definitely be a problem.

He had fresh clothes stashed at his playground, but he would have to trek a few miles to reach it. Naked he could explain to any morning hikers. Naked and covered in blood would just be unacceptable.

He turned and walked toward the lake. When he reached the water's edge, he kept right on going. Cold water slapped his skin, the temperature invigorating instead of freezing. A lunate's core temperature always ran hotter during a blue moon. Changing took a lot of energy, and his body's metabolism had adjusted.

He moved through the gentle ripples until he stood deep enough to submerge his body. Using handfuls of sand he scrubbed himself vigorously, removing all traces of the previous night's kill. He dunked his head, rubbing fingertips through his hair, being as thorough with his short locks as he had been with his skin.

Satisfied he had washed himself clean, he swam back to shore. The cool water and thorough washing left him feeling fresh and renewed. He didn't give the scene before him another thought as he trekked toward his car and fresh clothes. While he jogged along, his mind focused on today's scheduled appointments. His morning was booked, but he'd been keeping his afternoons and evenings open for sessions with Saari.

He'd get more information from her today.

The chance of successfully discovering her secret buoyed his mood.

Absently, he quietly sang the lines to the song he had been humming from the moment he stepped out of the lake. The words echoed with eerie softness through the trees:

*"Through the morning mist I roam,
wearily making my way home;
after a long night on the prowl,
the beast within loosed to howl;*

*The smell of earth floats on the rain,
The thrill of the hunt runs through my veins;
I'll sleep for now and bide my time,
until the sun's gone and night is mine;*

*Another day has taken flight,
and my heart soars in the starlight;
the change to wolf is freedom true,
absolute freedom in the Moonlight Bleu."*

Chapter Fourteen

Early Afternoon, May 23, 2032

 Dhelis stared at the sturdy wood desks, black ergonomic chairs and walls covered in soft beige that made the New Angeles Detectives Division look more like a suite in an office building than the local police department. The painted cement floor destroyed the image, shouting "Utilitarian."
 Thrumming energy buzzed around the room from officers working on cases.
 He usually enjoyed working in the squad room.
 Not today.
 He caught the other male detectives surreptitiously watching Thana walk toward his desk. With her exotic looks, his cousin could easily have been a super-model if she'd wanted to be. Instead, she embraced her psychic ability and joined law enforcement in order to help others.
 Every male in the room was aware of her presence. Their eyes tracked her with the precision of a GPS locater. Their facial expressions betrayed their private emotions. A strange combination of appreciation mixed with wariness, perhaps even a little fear, sharpened their features with distrust.
 He noted her wet hair and change of clothes. "Feel better?"
 "I'm clean." She smiled and gestured at her outfit. "But this was the last set of extra clothes in my locker. I need to do some laundry. You know, no matter how careful I am, some crime scenes will always require a shower afterwards."

He caught the avoidance in her answer. Had she changed the subject because they weren't alone or she wanted to keep something from him?

His instincts told him there was more to this Jordan Stevens thing than she had mentioned. But Thana wasn't talking. She'd closed up tighter than the quahog clams they netted as kids back home on the morning tide. So, he'd just have to be patient and wait for her to open up. Once she worked through whatever she was mulling over in that red head of hers, she would come to him—they were family.

"Does whatever you were handling last night have anything to do with Jordan's murder?" She traced the outline of the psychic's crystal, still buried in her pocket.

He wondered if she even realized what she was doing or if her thoughts were still trapped in her audit of Jordan's hotel room.

"No, I don't see any connection." He rubbed his chin, forcing some of the tension out of his jaw. "I need to speak with the Council and let them know what's going on."

And then get back to Saari. I left her hours ago.

"I'm sure they've heard about his death on the news by now. Besides, I need you to stick around a while."

"What's up?" He dropped his hands on his desk and waited for her to explain.

She picked his cell phone up off the desk and flipped the cover open and closed, listening to the jingle the phone played each time the cover popped up.

"A call came in from the morgue. I'm headed over to see Grimsley," she announced.

"Ah." He grunted in acknowledgement and opened his notebook to read over his notes of the scene without looking up.

She and the coroner had an arrangement for trading information. He flicked through a couple of pages quickly to cover his frustration. The extra readings didn't happen every day, but often enough he worried she might hurt herself by stretching her overused psychic ability with more work.

He bit his tongue, locking a nagging comment behind his teeth. She would just stress over *his* issue about the extra readings, and he didn't want her any more off balance than she already was.

"You're frowning so hard your eyebrows have relocated as an ugly mustache attached to your upper lip." The corner of her mouth curled sardonically.

Dhelis let her think his change of mood related to the notes he read. "Who actually talked to the hotel manager?"

She tapped a finger against the phone. "Hall and Strege did. Why?"

"I just want to check on something." When he got up from his desk to walk toward the other side of the room, Thana flopped into his chair and propped her feet up on his desk. "I'll be right back, you know?"

"Uh-huh, and I'll be right here waiting for you." She rested her head against the back of the chair and closed her eyes.

Dhelis spent a few fruitless minutes going over his notes with Hall and Strege. Neither of them had canvassed the hotel for information about Jordan Stevens or the woman that might have been with him. He should have known talking to the detectives would be a waste of time.

Something he was already running short on.

The quiet ticking of his internal clock grew louder. Saari had been injured, but she wouldn't sleep forever. He wanted to be at her side when she woke. That he still had to go with Thana to see Grimsley grated on his already irritated nerves. At least the ride to the morgue would give him the perfect opportunity to tell Thana about Saari.

He grabbed his keys off his desk and bumped his cousin's leg. "Time to roll."

~ ☾ ~

Dhelis stood next to his car and flipped open his cell phone. He wanted his mate checked out by a doctor for his own peace of mind.

"Why don't you start the car? I need to make quick call." Thana caught his keys midair and slid into the passenger seat. Once the engine turned over, she changed the radio station. A heavy metal song poured out of the car. Her door closed, cutting off the worst of the noise.

He pulled up the recent calls folder and tapped a number. Erik Conzatti answered before the call rolled to voice mail.

"Hey, Dhelis. Sorry you couldn't make it over at lunch today. When *can* you drop by? I really think you need to meet Saari. I'm telling you, she's Tueri."

Erik had been the one to mention Saari's eye color to him. He was supposed to meet with the Tueri physician hours ago. Dealing with Jordan Stevens' death had pretty much taken over his day.

"I've already met her. You were right. She's Tueri—an Unknown Tueri."

"I knew it. Wait a minute. Saari's an Unknown, and you've already met her? When? She went home sick before her shift started today."

He gripped the phone, trying to decide how much to tell Erik. Because he hadn't had a chance to speak with Council, he couldn't confirm Saari's lineage or abilities—hell, he hadn't even told anybody she was his mate.

"She's not at work because the rogue vampire I tracked and killed in the parking garage of your hospital last night injured her."

"Oh, man. Is she okay?"

"I think so. I don't know." He ran a hand through his hair, frustrated that he couldn't be with her. "That's why I'm calling. I need you to check on her for me. Make sure she doesn't need to be in a hospital—a Tueri hospital. Call Brogan if you have to. Also, if you could check with security and make sure nothing showed up on tape, I'd appreciate it."

"Sure. Unless it's an emergency though, it'll probably be another hour before I see her. I can't get away from the hospital until after my rounds."

"An hour's fine." He rattled off Saari's address.

"She's Unknown *and* tangled with a rogue vampire." A snort crackled over the phone. "If she's conscious, can you imagine the questions she's going to have?"

Jealousy flared in the pit of his stomach. "Plenty, but since she's *my* mate, I don't want you answering any of them."

"Whoa. No problem. And congratulations on finding your mate. Just remember, I'm the one who hooked you two up—sort of."

Shame at so easily losing control of his emotions doused his heated reaction. "Sorry, man. There's a lot going on right now or I wouldn't have left her side."

"Apology accepted. So what *can* I say?"

"Just tell her I'll be there as soon as I can."

He shoved the phone in his pocket and plopped into the driver's seat.

Several blocks later Thana turned the music off. "What's on your mind?"

His gaze slid her way before returning to the intersection. The light turned green.

At this time of day, cars crept through the business district at a snail's pace. Though he moved with the flow of traffic, his thoughts sped at lightning pace. The Tueri in him rejoiced at finding his mate. His detective instincts warned him to be cautious until he learned more about her.

"I found my Tueri mate last night."

"What?" Thana's screech pierced his eardrum. She turned in her seat and faced him. "That's amazing news. Tell me her name. What's her ability? And why didn't you say anything this morning?"

"We've been a little busy today, in case you hadn't noticed." She punched him on the arm. "Don't use our jobs as an excuse to keep things from me. That's what destroys relationships, you know."

He couldn't help smiling at her enthusiasm. "Her name is Saari Mitchell. As for her ability—I'm not sure yet."

Her head tilted. "What do you mean you're not sure?"

"I haven't talked to Council, and I *really* need to. I think Saari's a Predecessor."

Thana's jaw dropped.

"I know how crazy it sounds, but Saari has a Stone Rider's eye color. And to really throw a fly in the ointment, she's an Unknown."

Her low whistle filled the car.

"You weren't kidding. You *have* to talk to Council—the sooner the better."

"I figured I'd call after we leave the morgue and set up a meeting for later tonight. That should be enough time to get a few members together."

"Speaking of the morgue." She flopped back in the seat and stared morosely out the window.

He turned into the parking lot and pulled into the space reserved for law enforcement. A Laurel Bay shaded the car, the green lance-shaped leaves creating pointed shadows across the windshield. Thana popped her seatbelt and traced the patterns with her finger. He gave her a few quiet moments to steel her nerve.

Grimsley's help came with a price.

He gave them information, always before the other detectives, and occasionally they received facts nobody else got. In return, Thana audited an object of his choice.

"You don't have to keep doing these audits."

Her shoulder lifted. "The readings aren't that bad. It's never knowing what he wants me to audit that bothers me. There's no way to prepare myself. My ability fascinates him, so he tests me to see what I'm capable of. Each new little 'experiment' pushes the boundaries."

"Not bad?" He shook his head. "Grimsley made you audit a blade he'd found broken off inside a victim."

"That was an especially gruesome one." She dragged her fingers through her hair, pulling it into a loose knot, but he saw her fingers dig into her scalp like she'd like to rip the scene out of her memory.

"Now he only has me audit something a victim wore if the autopsy is complicated. You know my information sometimes gives him more insight into what happened." She shrugged before getting out of the car.

Dhelis locked the car and caught up to his cousin. "Just because these readings are helpful, it doesn't mean I have to like you doing them."

"It's my choice, remember?" Thana nodded as she passed the secretary.

They headed straight for the morgue where Grimsley waited.

Chapter Fifteen

When Dhelis walked through the door, the pungent odors of death assaulted his senses: rotted flesh, congealed blood, and formaldehyde. He immediately breathed through his mouth. It helped. A little.

"You're late," Grimsley growled from his desk in the corner. "I told the detectives I'd be ready for them at 4:00. That meant you two were supposed to be here at 3:00." He pointedly looked down at his watch. "It's 3:30."

He and Thana stopped next to the desk. Without preamble, he reached out and took her left hand in his own.

Thana took a deep breath and flopped her right hand out, palm up. Grimsley dropped a tube of lipstick onto her palm. She curled her fingers around the hard casing. "The metal's freezing."

"It's been in cold storage," Grimsley explained.

"There are only two signatures. One of them is yours, Grimsley. For once, this will be easier than I expected."

Dhelis grunted. "That'd be a nice piece of luck."

"Here we go. Simple as liquid chocolate sinking into milk." Her arm twitched, signaling her connection. "That's weird. The second energy is male."

"Meaning?" Grimsley prompted, waiting for an explanation.

"The lipstick belonged to a man," she clarified.

He heard Grimsley scribbling notes for himself on a piece of paper at his desk. Grimsley never looked at Thana during an audit, but it wouldn't have mattered if he did. His cousin had moved into that other space, that place between here and there, where only she could go.

"He's excited by the color red. That's his favorite color. The shade is sexy and vibrant, full of strength and power. He's anxious to use the lipstick. It's so pretty."

She popped the lid off the tube of lipstick, keeping both ends in her hand. Without hesitation, she pushed her index finger into the tube and wiggled it. When she pulled her finger out, a red mixture of smeared lipstick covered her fingertip.

"I picked up another signature. The energy is faint, almost cold even. What remains is filled with confusion and pain." Her eyes closed. "This lipstick was used on a woman. She was nearly dead. The man knew she would die, and the thought of her death thrilled him."

Another Full-Moon Killer victim.

"The woman's signature is negligible compared to the man's signature. Like a spice left on the shelf too long, the powder is present but the flavor is faded. The man's signature though—"

Her eyes snapped open and her breath hitched.

"Thana?" He waited for her to squeeze his hand, giving him a signal.

A spasm rocked her body, drawing a moan he'd never heard from her before. "What the hell?" He gripped her shoulder with his other hand, trying to pull her out of the audit.

The hand holding the lipstick tube shook.

Her eyes glazed over.

"Damn it. She's too far in. She'll lose herself in the man's signature."

The lipstick tube dropped to the floor.

Useless adrenaline poured into his bloodstream. He hadn't pulled her back in time. His heart slammed against his ribs. He had nothing to run from and he couldn't fight Thana's vision for her.

Thana wrenched out of Dhelis's grip—and screamed.

"Shit. Thana, you're okay. I'm here." He snagged her wrist, trying to pull her to him.

Her eyelids fluttered and her breath hitched. "Don't touch. Makes it...worse."

He let her go.

She wrapped her arms across her middle and crashed to her knees, her eyes closed. Each time her body visibly shuddered, a small whimper escaped.

"Oh, God. Not mine. Not mine. Not mine." She rocked back and forth, moaning in shame. "I'm gonna be sick."

Grimsley slid the trash can in front of her.

Dhelis watched as she purged every bit of emotion until only dry heaves were left. Finally, the spasms subsided. He touched her arm. When she didn't pull away, he rubbed her back, moving his hand in a slow, circular pattern. Grimsley handed him a cool cloth for her forehead.

After a few minutes, Thana took a shuddering breath and opened her eyes.

Grimsley helped her into his chair and placed his hand on her shoulder. "I'm sorry," he said quietly.

She shrugged off his words with a weak flop of her hand. "Just be thankful neither of you *felt* that. Killing her was sexual for him—an erotic fantasy."

Her nonchalant attitude didn't fool Dhelis. A red hue of embarrassment tinted her cheeks, and she wouldn't look Grimsley or himself in the eye. Auditing was always personal for her, but this reading passed intimate on the way to obscene. It was hard enough for her to have him see her reaction—but Grimsley? How would the coroner going to treat her after today?

"Besides, you couldn't have known," she whispered.

"I suspected as much."

Thana's head shot up, eyes searching Grimsley's face. "You knew? You knew, and you asked me to feel that anyway?"

Grimsley knelt down next to her. Anguish colored his usually jovial brown eyes. "I never knew the audit would be like that. I swear, I didn't know. I just knew the bastard had a fascination with this brand and color of lipstick, and that he put it on his victims. I didn't know the rest—that you'd get sucked in so completely." He gathered both of her hands between his own. "Thana, I'm truly sorry."

She sighed before pulling a hand free and patting his larger hands gripped around her own. "It's okay. I know you wouldn't do something like that to me on purpose."

"I did ask you to audit that tube for a very specific reason though," he said with determination. "I needed you to know the difference."

Her attention cut to Dhelis, then back to Grimsley. "Difference? What difference?"

With a brisk nod, like he'd been waiting for her question, he released her hand and stood up.

He walked away from the desk and retrieved the little silver lipstick tube from the floor where it had rolled to a stop. He looked up at them and purposefully wiped the outside clean of any fingerprints.

That wasn't normal. "Why did you just do that?" Dhelis asked.

"Because," he said, as he dropped the tube into a plastic bag, "this is a piece of evidence. There were no prints on the casing, and I've already typed the DNA from the lipstick itself."

"So now you're tampering with evidence?"

Thana shushed him and stared at Grimsley. "And?"

The corner of his lips lifted in a smile. "That's why I like you. You look beyond the surface. You want to know what's lurking underneath."

She leaned back in the chair and crossed her arms over her chest. "Interesting metaphor. Now, how about you tell me why you really had me audit that thing?"

Grimsley approached the far wall and opened one of the many doors sealing the refrigerated compartments. After sliding a tray all the way out, he turned and motioned for them to join him.

Jordan Stevens' remains. The pieces didn't look any better joined together on the tray than they had spread out over the entire hotel suite where Dhelis had seen them earlier that morning.

Thana swallowed loud enough he wondered if she might get sick again. He heard her breathe through her mouth, albeit through gritted teeth.

"First time the Full-Moon Killer's gone after a male." Dhelis pointed at the tray.

"The other detectives are going to try to lump Stevens' murder in with the full-moon killings as well. Even though my findings won't support that theory, they're gonna to do it anyway. That announcement will look better for them in the press. There's still only one killer to look for, not two." Grimsley lifted two fingers for emphasis.

Dhelis tilted his head to the side, his thoughts narrowing in on that last statement. "What do you mean two killers?" He checked his watch. "I don't have time for riddles. The Pony Express will be riding through here for information any minute, and I have to be somewhere. Get on with the lesson."

"Okay, here's what I mean." He pointed to the shoulder joint. "Thana, what do you see?"

"I see a mess," she ground out.

Grimsley stood stone-faced, ignoring her comment. He wasn't going to let this go.

She looked closer. "I see bone separated from the joint. I see muscle and tendons torn. Well, actually they look like they were ripped apart."

"Very good. You've been paying attention. Now, either of you, tell me how that's different from the full-moon killings?"

Dhelis thought about his answer for a moment before he responded, comparing the other victims to Jordan Stevens. "In the other killings, there were bite marks. Even though skin and muscle had been ripped and torn, the injury was due to a bite that caused the ripping and tearing."

Carefully, he looked at every piece of the body on the tray. "There are *no* bite marks here at all."

"Exactly," the pathologist agreed. "Now just because there are no bite marks, you do understand this doesn't rule out the possibility it's the same killer?" He continued to watch them, waiting for them to make the connection.

"True." He nodded in agreement, but saw where this was leading.

"Thana, I needed you to *know* the difference. I cannot conclude that the Full-Moon Killer did not kill Jordan Stevens. I can only hypothesize based on my findings."

"But I felt the difference on the lipstick tube. That was the Full-Moon Killer, and the Full-Moon Killer did not murder Jordan Stevens. Besides, the Full-Moon Killer is a man. Something I've never felt before killed Jordan Stevens. *That* much I'm sure of."

Grimsley crossed his arms over his chest.

"That's why you didn't tell me where the lipstick came from."

His chin dipped once in acknowledgment. "I needed you to make the connection yourself. I can't influence your audits. You see what you see or feel what you feel. However it is you do what you do, it's a damn handy tool."

A quick push sent the tray back into the compartment. The door closed with a *snick*. He crossed to his desk and searched through paperwork until he found a manila envelope. After he returned to Thana's side, he handed it to her. "Your copy of the autopsy report. I have another one for the detectives."

Voices carried down the hallway.

"Speak of the devils." Thana shoved the envelope into the front of her jeans under her jacket just before Detective Strege and Detective Hall walked through the door.

The clock read 4:10. They were obviously running behind.

Grimsley turned and boomed, "You're late. I said four o'clock. I have things to do, you know. I can't spend all day waiting for you two to show up whenever you feel like it."

The detectives ignored him. Everybody knew Grimsley was always at the morgue. He was always doing something, but he was always doing that something at the morgue.

Detective Hall glared at them. If Dhelis had to bet, he'd go double or nothing Hall was trying to figure out how long they'd been there and what they'd learned.

"You know we're lead on this case. What are you two doing here?" Detective Hall growled.

"Our jobs." Thana took a step toward the detective. "What's your excuse?"

Hall immediately stepped back.

"Let's go." Dhelis lifted his chin toward the doorway and headed out of the building. Once outside, he turned to his cousin. "Do not antagonize them. Their closed-minded holier-than-thou attitude makes them dangerous."

"I'm not afraid of jerks like them." A sudden shiver twitched her shoulders. "The Full-Moon Killer, he scares the shit out of me."

Chapter Sixteen

Early Evening, May 23, 2032

    Saari stared at the ceiling, celebrating the fact she hadn't had The Dream again. Willing herself *not* to dream about Miko had worked—or maybe it was the sleeping pills that had done the trick. Either way, at least she had some progress to report to Doctor Lytton.
    She checked her cell phone for messages. Nothing showed in her inbox. Good. Her appointment for six o'clock was still on. The next question: had she healed enough to venture out of bed, let alone out of the house?
    The comforting weight of her stone rested in the shirt pocket directly over her heart. She pushed herself up in measured stages, careful to slide her legs over the edge of the bed without causing more pain.
    Sitting still, she took stock of her injuries. Every muscle in her body ached. Sitting up had made her chest burn like fire. She hunched her shoulders forward, trying to relieve the sting caused by her chest muscles stretching and pulling on the wound.
    A wave of light-headedness rocked her balance. She gripped the edge of the nightstand to keep from falling off the bed. When her eyes focused, the glowing numbers on the clock caught her attention. She calculated the amount of time since she'd last eaten: nearly eighteen hours. Her stomach growled loudly, offering an opinion on the matter.

A soft knock at the bedroom door brought her head up swiftly.

Mag had no reason to knock before entering her bedroom, so that eliminated him as the unexpected visitor. She knew nothing of Dhelis other than their mutual eye color. Besides, Mag would have come into the room before allowing him near her again.

Don't forget the fact his touch set your heart racing, just like Miko did, an inner voice whispered. She hushed the voice. *But you want to be near him again. Touch him. Bathe in that incredible energy rush he gave you.* Her stomach fluttered at the thought—rather than making her want to run screaming in the opposite direction.

No, her visitor wasn't Dhelis.

The knock sounded again, louder this time.

Saari's closed her eyes and concentrated. Her senses sharpened. She let that other source of feeling flow over her, and opened herself to the space around her. Her bedroom, a private sanctuary, always gave her a sense of peace. The quiet stillness wrapped itself around her, soothed her tense body.

Letting her senses reach beyond the door, she moved through the individual on the other side. Concern, mixed with a stronger impression of anxiety filled the person. Oddly enough, a hint of familiarity emanated from the individual knocking at her door. Though she couldn't place her finger on the person's actual identity, the recognizable energy piqued her curiosity.

"Come in." She called out to her visitor.

The door opened slowly. She recognized the dark-haired head that poked around the edge of the entryway. "Doctor Conzatti."

Caution marked his steps into the room. He still wore his green, hospital scrubs. With a tentative smile, he moved closer to the bed, but remained out of reach. "You're awake. That's good. Actually," he stammered, "that's very good."

She made note of the doctor's obvious discomfort. His nervous energy filled the room. He tapped the black medical bag he held against his thigh. Most people can't endure silent pauses in a conversation. If she waited long enough, he would fill the pregnant pause.

The doctor remained where he stood. "How are you feeling?"

She had no idea why Erik Conzatti, a doctor she worked with at the hospital, stood in her bedroom. She had a hunch his presence had something to do with Dhelis Guidry. That meant Erik knew the man who had touched her earlier.

She wanted answers.

Her eyes narrowed with suspicion. She threw her blunt answer out for shock value, seeing if he would take the bait. "As if I was stabbed through the heart with a very sharp knife, by a really big, seriously pissed-off vampire."

The man smiled with infuriating patience. "Okay, I guess I probably deserved that." His head canted to the side. "In case you were wondering, nobody at the hospital really knows what happened. The security cameras in the parking garage stopped working at some point—some electrical interference or something—and you're marked out on the board as sick. I was asked to come by your place and make sure you were okay."

Relief she hadn't even known she waited for flooded her system. Her job still waited for at the hospital, and her secret really was safe. But Doctor Conzatti hadn't blinked at her comment about being stabbed through the heart by a vampire.

He knew *exactly* what was going on.

There were so many things she wanted to ask. Each thought jockeyed in her head to be the first on the tip of her tongue. Surprisingly, the most inane subject won. "Who was the vampire?"

Though he appeared amused by her remark, he just continued to look her in the eye without saying anything else. The nervous tapping had stopped. Erik Conzatti wouldn't give any information away willingly.

She watched the doctor's face, as he weighed his options. Convincing him to answer wouldn't be easy, so she played the only card she had. "You've worked with me in the emergency room several times."

"I have. I've seen you help people." Erik's lips pursed. "Your reputation is...fierce."

"Then you know I'll be relentless in my search for information." She tipped her head slightly. "It would be in your best interest to answer the question."

"I don't know."

"Fair enough. Who sent you here?"

"Dhelis Guidry."

That answer she expected, but before she could ask who the hell Dhelis Guidry *really* was, Erik put out a hand, stopping her from asking more questions. "I'll make you a bargain. I need to examine you, Saari. I promise, after I've checked your injuries and assessed the actual damage, I'll try to answer any questions you have."

Erik Conzatti had an exceptional reputation as a doctor, but she didn't know much beyond that. He seemed to be a genuinely nice man, but she'd been fooled before.

As if sensing her uncertainty, Mag stepped into the room. "Let the doctor look at you, Saari. I did what I could for you, but I may not have done the right thing."

She laughed, the sound echoing flat and humorless. "As if anything you did would make a difference one way or another."

Frustrated, Mag's shoulders twitched. "He has some special...expertise. He may even be able to help you heal faster. That would be something new."

Reassured by Mag's presence, she relented. "Knock yourself out, Doc. But I promise you, I'll live."

Mag shot her a warning glance.

She lifted an eyebrow in a "what did I say?" signal.

The doctor's face showed confusion, but he moved purposefully forward. He set his black bag on the edge of the bed next to her. "I, uh, need to see your chest…I mean where the knife punctured your chest."

The need to see how far she could push him, punish him for not answering her questions overrode her good sense.

She nibbled her lower lip in a coy gesture before unbuttoning the front of her shirt. A slight shrug sent her sleeves down each arm, allowing the fabric to pool at her wrists. With the shake of her head, her long hair flipped over her shoulders.

A rosy flush stained his cheeks.

She batted her lashes at him and added a southern twang to her voice. "Why, Doctor, I do believe yo're blushin'."

"We're co-workers, Saari. We're not at the hospital. We're in your bedroom. Even you have to admit this qualifies as an extremely unusual circumstance."

"Depends on one's perspective," she countered with a sweet smile.

"You have a mean sense of humor, woman." He turned to Mag. "Is she always like this?"

Mag snorted. "Depends on one's perspective, I guess."

She shot him a heated look.

Mag just smiled. "Play nice, Saari. This is going to be a very long night."

She dropped her chin forward and rolled her neck left to right. An audible pop sounded. Her muscles loosened as some pent-up tension sloughed from her body. She sighed in relief.

With a quick look at the doctor, she shrugged as if to say "sorry."

Erik nodded his head in response, accepting her gesture as a truce. She watched him reach toward her chest and carefully pull the edge of the taped gauze back. A hiss of pain leaked through her teeth when the gummy strip took skin with it.

"Sorry," he murmured, concentrating on his task. When he finally freed her skin of the entire bandage, his eyebrows shot to his hairline. She stared at her chest. The flesh separated around the exposed opening, reminding her of the way her prime rib steaks looked as the butcher sliced the meat.

"You have a one and a half inch gaping hole directly over your heart," he measured. "Jesus. It's a miracle you survived."

She stared at the top of his head. "If you say so."

Doctor Conzatti got out his penlight and concentrated the bright beam over the wound. "I can't believe what I'm seeing." His breath puffed in amazement. "The wound is already knitting together. From the angle, I'd say the blade stopped when it hit a rib bone."

Mag came forward to stand next to the bed. He looked directly at her when he spoke. "When I got Saari back here and pulled out the knife, the blade tip stuck out of her back. Once the bleeding stopped, I could see her damaged heart through the hole in her chest."

Erik turned to Mag, his face slack with shock. "That's not medically possible," he sputtered. "She would have bled out. Her wound would have to have healed muscle as well as cartilage. The human body doesn't heal that fast. You have to be mistaken."

She picked up the gauze bandage—then dropped it. Instead, she buttoned up her shirt while the two men discussed her injury. She needed some air, and this conversation needed to end. When she got to the doorway, she stopped and looked back.

"Mag is telling you the truth, Doctor Conzatti. If he says the blade went all the way through my heart and out my back, then it did." Her voice filled with compassion. "Don't feel too badly though. Generally speaking, you're right about the human body. It doesn't heal that fast. I guess I'm lucky, though, because I do."

On that cryptic note, she turned without saying another word and walked through the doorway. Her chest pain subsided into a slow burn, steady, but not sharp. Behind her, Mag encouraged the confused man.

"Come on, Doc. She'll be fine. A little grumpy, but fine."

Doctor Conzatti muttered to himself in disbelief. A metal "clank" echoed through the hallway each time he dropped a piece of equipment into his black bag. She knew he'd finally given up on understanding anything he'd seen when two sets of footsteps followed her down the stairs.

She smelled the food long before she reached the kitchen. Her stomach growled, hunger pains twisting her stomach. She salivated at the thought of a huge cheeseburger with everything on it. When she stepped into the dining room, she saw a plate with a large burger sitting next to a huge bowl overflowing with homemade fries.

Mag reached the dining room just as she squealed in delight. Holding her chest, she twisted sideways and planted a loud, smacking kiss on his cheek. "I'm so hungry I think I could eat a whole cow."

He pulled her chair out for her. "There's more in the kitchen when you feel up to having seconds."

She placed her hand over his, resting on the arm of the chair. "Thank you," she whispered.

He dropped his chin on top of her head. "You're welcome. Now eat, before your food gets cold."

"You don't have to tell me twice."

He chuckled and went back into the kitchen.

She picked up the burger and took a bite, savoring the onion flavor. A brand new ketchup bottle sat near her plate. There was no way she could twist the top off without making her chest hurt.

"Doctor, could you open the bottle for me, please?"

He dropped into the chair next to her and broke the seal. "Tell me when." Ketchup squirted onto her plate, forming a growing puddle.

"That's enough. Thanks." She dipped a couple fries and popped them into her mouth. The tang of tomatoes and salt coated her tongue. "Mmmm, this is good. Have you eaten?"

The doctor perched his chin on his hand. "I did earlier. Thank you, though."

Twenty minutes later half the burger and fries still lay on her plate. She couldn't take another bite. With a sigh of contentment, she pushed away from the table.

"I'm impressed." He stared at her in rapt fascination. "With your wound, I'm amazed you're conscious, let alone eating solid food after that much trauma."

Mag leaned against the counter that separated the kitchen from the dining room table. "If you're still here in an hour," he chuckled, "there will be a repeat performance."

She smiled. "Healing takes a lot of energy. The faster I heal, the more energy I need. Normally, I don't eat red meat, but I lost a lot of blood. I need to build my strength up as quickly as possible. If I don't get enough outside energy, the healing is very painful."

"I don't understand."

She looked at the doctor, gathering her thoughts. "I know you don't. There's a lot I don't understand either. I was too tired to ask any questions earlier when Dhelis Guidry was here. Since he's the one who sent you to check on me, maybe you can clear up a few things."

The man's gaze bounced between her and Mag.

"Look, I don't know how much Mr. Guidry wants you to tell me, but you aren't leaving without telling me everything *I* want to know." She pointed at herself for emphasis.

She pushed her chair back from the table and headed with her plate for the sink. When she reached the middle of the kitchen, the man in question suddenly appeared in front of her.

"Ah!" The plate slipped from her fingers and shattered against the tile floor. The explosion of sound blasted the room like a gunshot.

Mag spun around and stepped between her and Dhelis. The message was clear. He would have to go through Mag to get to her.

Erik Conzatti sprung out of his chair, skirting quickly around her and toward Dhelis. He reached forward and shook hands with him. "I'm glad you could make it back before we started, Dhelis. I wasn't sure I would be able to fully answer all of Saari's questions."

Before Dhelis could respond, she stepped from behind Mag and pinned Dhelis with an inquisitive glare. "How did you appear from nowhere in the middle of my kitchen?"

Chapter Seventeen

Saari waited for an answer Dhelis didn't seem ready to give.

Mag took her elbow and walked her back to the table. "You'd better sit down. This will take a while for Dhelis and me to explain."

She looked up at him. "What do you mean, 'take a while?' How do you know…"

Her words trailed off. Emotions swept through her like a sudden storm at sea, waves swelling from calm to turbulent in the space of a heartbeat, as confusion bled to furious clarity.

"You already know what he's going to tell me."

"I do." Sadness filled Mag's eyes. "The secret I've harbored for forty years popped into your life with the appearance of Dhelis Guidry. Now that the decision to tell you anything about the Tueri has been made for me, I promise I'll give you every answer I have. I only pray my explanation will be enough for you to forgive me."

What did he mean? Forgive him for merely keeping a secret from me or forgive him for the secret he kept?

Until she knew, at this point she was along for the ride.

They could weather the tempest.

She just hoped their friendship would survive.

"Somebody better start talking," she warned, her words clipped with anger.

With the sweep of his arm, Mag gestured toward the table, indicating the other men should take a seat. Dr. Conzatti's face reflected wariness, his unease clearly evident by his hesitation to leave the kitchen. Dhelis, on the other hand, showed no such compunction. He stepped up to the table and pulled out the chair on her left.

Mag's jaw tightened. Dhelis's interest, displayed so blatantly, had grated on his nerves. Good. Maybe he should have considered an accidental meeting like hers and Dhelis's might occur before he decided to keep information from her.

Doctor Conzatti took the chair next to Dhelis, a couple seats away from her. The doctor sat on the very edge of his seat, body wound tight as a spring. She worried he'd bounce like a jack in the box at the slightest hint of trouble.

Though both men came to the table for different reasons, she didn't sense any real threat emanating from either of them. Mag took a seat at the opposite end of the table, directly across from her. His position was tactically a poor choice if she needed his help, but she didn't think the conversation would come to violence.

Besides, Mag knew how her mind worked. If anything, he should be concerned about *her* reaction. She had the amazing ability to shut down her emotions—compartmentalize. If he had truly betrayed her, she would throw up a wall so thick he would never be able to reach her again.

They both knew that possibility terrified him. She was his *Nefer Ka*—his beautiful soul. She'd become the bridge between that treasured part of him, his humanity, and hell. Without her, without their friendship, he would be lost— which meant he'd better have the mother of all explanations.

"Well?" She prompted.

Mag turned to Dhelis and broke the silence. "She already knows who the doc is," Mag nodded at Doctor Conzatti. He shifted his gaze back to Dhelis. "So who is going to start, you or me?"

Dhelis looked directly at him, giving him the small courtesy of attention while he spoke, before returning his gaze to her. "Like I told you earlier, my name's Dhelis Guidry. My partner and I transferred to New Angeles several months ago. We recently received a permanent assignment to the Detectives Division in homicide."

Mag raised an eyebrow at this. "And I'd hoped you were just filling in, on a temporary basis. A permanent position here in New Angeles means you plan to stay. Fan-fucking-tabulous."

Dhelis grinned. "Isn't it though?"

She placed an elbow on the edge of the table and rested her chin on her palm. Staring at the men helped keep her from grinding her teeth together. The hum of energy she'd felt earlier had disappeared when she woke alone in her room. Now it was back. Did she want it to be there? Especially since she had no doubt whatsoever it was tied to this stranger sitting beside her.

The idea her energy resonated so strongly with him was a little exhilarating but a lot scarier than she wanted to admit. A connection meant possibilities. So she *really* wanted to know why there was an energy connection between them, but other questions had to be answered first.

Her gaze landed squarely on Dhelis. "You're one of the psychics that caught that serial killer a couple months ago, aren't you?"

Dhelis's spine straightened, his eyebrows lifting in twin points of surprise.

Mag's hands dropped off the table. "How do you already know who Guidry is?"

"You should see the astonished looks on your faces right now." She flopped back in her chair and snorted with disgust. "I'm not Darla Dimwit. I got stabbed through the heart, not the head."

Doctor Conzatti's lips twitched and he coughed, the noise suspiciously resembling a choked laugh.

"I heard your name mentioned in a news report on the radio," she answered, pointing a finger in the psychic's direction.

Dhelis commented with a vague "Harrumph."

Mag folded his hands on the tabletop. Wrinkles pulled at the corners of his lips. If he even cracked a smile she'd let him have it.

Her eyebrow lifted, her exaggerated stare sweeping the table. "Just so everyone's clear," she added slowly, taking care to enunciate her words as if speaking to a group of children, "they only *talk* on the radio. They show you *pictures* on a television."

She didn't watch much television. And she never watched the news. After 500 years of living, *what* people did to each other rarely changed. Something was always stolen or missing. Somebody always got hurt. Someone always died. The only thing that altered the equation was the "how" and occasionally the "why." She also never read the newspaper, for pretty much the same reasons—except the newspaper also had a lot of misspellings and inaccurate quotes.

The men's amusement irritated her, hardening her attitude. "What I want to know, Mr. Guidry, is who you *really* are, and how you just happened to appear in the middle of my kitchen."

Dhelis took a deep breath. "I guess this won't be completely startling to you since you already know he's," at this he nodded his head toward Mag, "a vampire."

"*He* has a name," she broke in. "It's Mag, and I expect you to give him the same respect you're giving me. You're the stranger here. This is *my* home you popped into. I'd suggest you remember that."

The detective's lips tightened with the barest hint of displeasure. "You're right. My apologies."

She suspected Dhelis Guidry harbored a racist attitude toward vampires. Her defending Mag must have galled the man. Impressively, he kept himself in check. Good. Detective Guidry didn't know any of the facts surrounding her and Mag's relationship, nor should he since her life was none of his damned business. At least he was smart enough to see she and Mag shared a bond.

"We're Tueri," Doctor Conzatti interrupted. His measured tone reminded her of the calm voice he employed with patients at the hospital. His peacemaking effort succeeded. Everyone at the table shifted their attention to him.

"Tueri," she repeated. Interest piqued, she leaned forward slightly. "What does that mean?"

The two men answered at the same time.

"It means several things," Dhelis answered.

"The word *Tueri* is Latin for defend," the doctor explained.

Sharp pains pulled at her chest from sitting up straight. Dropping her forearms on the table to relieve the ache, she considered the two men before her. One of them was trying to answer her without actually giving her an answer. The other seemed to be giving only half-truths.

In her view, both amounted to lying.

Her eyes tapered to unhappy slits. "I've had enough posturing. I want some *real* information."

Dhelis's lips parted on an answer. Before he could get any words out, she cut him off with a chopping motion of her hand. "You had your chance."

Her eyes cut to Mag.

He cracked a smile, obviously pleased with the conflicted exchange.

As angry as she was at him for keeping information from *her*, things had definitely shifted in his favor—at least for a chance to explain why he'd violated her trust. But he only had *one* shot for redemption.

"What the hell are Tueri?" she asked, her eyes settling on Mag in an unwavering gaze.

"They're called Tueri." Mag's hands lifted off the table, palms up in an "I don't know" gesture. "In truth, there is no exact definition. This race came into being after a meteor crashed into the earth thousands of years ago. The same cataclysmic event caused our change. You already know about werepeople and vampires."

He paused, making sure she followed.

She stared back. "I'm with you so far. Go on."

"There are those who feel it was a result of the radiation and/or fallout from the meteor, but, whatever the reason, another cluster of humans also changed: the Tueri. They're a race of people that are only in human form. However, they have evolved in very unique and incredible ways. They are as dangerous and powerful as any vampire."

Her eyebrows lifted at his comment. She had been exposed to numerous species of creatures, each fantastic in its own right. For Mag, a vampire, to give such high praise, the Tueri must be something special indeed.

Mag nodded his head in response to her unvoiced thoughts. "Oh, yes, they are truly special. There are many different abilities among their people. The common attribute they share is their psychic abilities. They range from incredible Healers to Readers to Seers, but the most astounding ability is that of the Stone Riders."

Doctor Conzatti nodded his head in agreement with Mag's description.

"Our *friend* here," Mag tilted his head toward Dhelis, "is very definitely a Stone Rider."

Saari looked at Dhelis for confirmation.

He didn't as much as blink. "I am."

"What's a Stone Rider?" Curiosity made her ask.

Before Dhelis could pick up the thread of Mag's explanation and try to take control of the conversation, she looked back to Mag and rolled her hand, signaling him to answer her question. Sharp, stabbing pain radiated across her chest, reminding her to move as little as possible.

He tilted his head toward her as if to say "as you wish."

"The Tueri use what they call 'stones' in order to focus or access their abilities. These 'stones' were generated from the meteor that crashed upon the earth. I believe the Council has control of several mines that produce nothing but the stone they require."

Everyone again looked to Dhelis for verification.

"You are correct," Dhelis answered.

"But what do they do with these stones?"

"The Stone Riders have the ability to move through, or manipulate space, if you will. I don't mean space, as in outer space. I mean space, as in distance and location. From here to there. From your house to Chez Chaz," Mag explained, using her favorite restaurant in the analogy.

"From somewhere to the middle of my kitchen."

"Yes, exactly," he beamed, like a teacher proud of his favorite student.

She turned to Dhelis. Light reflected off the silver flecks coloring his eyes. Her concentration jumped track, and a distant memory flashed in her mind. Another set of tri-colored eyes stared at her, gently teasing her for being so easily startled. Miko's cat-like appearances made sense now. Miko had been a Stone Rider, too.

Why hadn't he told her right away?

Would you have trusted him, believed him? The voice in her head countered.

No, she wouldn't have.

But he'd told her he had something very important to show her. Could he have meant his Stone Riding ability?

"Saari, are you feeling all right?" Doctor Conzatti stood and reached for his black bag.

"I'm fine. Sorry, Erik. Just thinking." Her eyes snapped to Dhelis, pinning him with her direct gaze. "I heard two different voices in the parking garage at the hospital. Mag's voice was one. Yours was the other," she realized, her mind putting together the missing pieces of the puzzle.

"I was there also," Dhelis nodded.

Her focus shifted to Mag. "You were there after the other vampire."

Mag nodded his head in silent agreement.

Her eyes cut back to Dhelis. "You were there for me?"

"The rogue vampire—and you," he corrected.

"Why?"

"Oh, I can answer that," Doctor Conzatti jumped in. "I mentioned to Dhelis about what I'd seen of you on the ward, including your amazing eye color, and I just knew you were a Tueri. I didn't know how or who you were, but there didn't seem to be any other explanation. I figured if anybody could figure out what was going on, it would be Dhelis. But he wasn't supposed to be at the hospital until around noon."

Saari watched Dhelis, her eyes never leaving his face. "Why were you after the other vampire and how did you kill it? I didn't see a stake come through his heart."

Mag smiled. "She's quick, Dhelis. Not many details escape her attention. You might want to remember that for future reference."

"I'll keep that in mind," he said to Mag. "As to the why-I-was-there part of your question, Saari, I'm part of a tactical team that hunts rogue vampires. I've been assigned by Council to work with Mag, as he's the Blood Court prosecutor. Last night was our first 'assignment' together."

"That's true," Mag spoke, offering his own affirmation.

"How I killed the vampire—that's a longer explanation. Our stone has the same effect on a vampire as a wooden stake, with one exception: it only has to break the skin to kill the vampire. It need not be stabbed through the heart. Humans discovered that destroying the vampire's heart would stop the blood flow and kill the vampire, as it does in a human. Vampires are just harder to catch.

"The church actually propagated the use of wood as the way to kill what they deemed unholy creatures because Christ was nailed on a wooden cross. The religious tone was significant for people, giving them courage and the church's blessing to face and kill evil...of course it only worked if the stake was put through the heart."

She accepted Dhelis's reasoning in silence. His explanation made logical sense. She'd seen everything from priests to presidents manipulate beliefs to suit their purposes—and pursue their power.

She reached into her shirt pocket and pulled out the tri-colored stone she'd been told her mother gave her as a child, the only thing she had of her parents. She laid her arm on the table, turning her hand palm up so the gem could clearly be seen.

"That's a Tueri stone." Doctor Conzatti pointed at her hand.

Her fingers closed around the stone. "So, I'm a Tueri. Okay then."

The movement pulled with an aching hitch, making her grimace. Her wound throbbed without her stone close to her skin. Or maybe her heart ached from a deeper wound. She rarely went a day without thinking about the parents she couldn't remember. And all that time there was an entire people she hadn't known she missed.

For five centuries she'd wanted to belong somewhere. Fit in.

Now she had a place to start.

She lifted her arm, dropping the stone back into her pocket.

The hum of energy connecting her to Dhelis Guidry had dropped to a low level of distraction, rubbing against her nerves in an unsettling sweep of psychic contact. Enough with the mystery. "Why is there some kind of—" her hand fluttered with her lack of words "—between us?"

"Our psychic energies recognized one another as Tueri, establishing a link between us," Dhelis answered.

She'd been alive for over five hundred years. Odds are she'd met another Tueri without knowing. Why hadn't she felt this connection with anyone else—other than Miko?

"You're Tueri, right?" Saari asked the doctor.

"Yes." He answered.

"So how come I don't feel a connection with Doctor Conzatti? Shouldn't I feel this hum of energy with him, too?"

"No, you shouldn't," Dhelis all but growled. "Among the Tueri, our energy seeks the best balance or counterpart—a partner, if you will—to share strength and grow in skill. Our energies have chosen each other."

"Oh."

She digested this last bit of information. So she actually was connected to this man—even if she didn't want to be. *Did she want to be linked with him, in any way?* She really wanted to talk to him about all of this, but she couldn't. Not until she knew the truth behind Mag's withholding information from her.

A stabbing headache was forming right between her eyes.

She looked directly at Mag, holding his stare. "You knew I'm Tueri?"

"I knew."

Pain lanced her heart from his piercing admission of betrayal. Not knowing who she was and where she came from had haunted her, her entire life. And Mag—the brother of her heart—had known. *He* could have ended her search.

"Why?" she whispered.

Her best friend looked directly into her eyes, his gaze never faltering. "I was sworn by blood oath with my maker. Only upon his direction could I share my knowledge."

"Have you been released from your oath?"

"Not by words."

"Then why now?" she demanded. "Why are you free to tell me?"

"The Tueri have come to you. Their approach relieves me of my obligation," he explained.

Her eyes closed in relief. *A blood oath.* Breaking one meant death. That was the only thing that had kept him from giving her the answers she had desperately sought for so long. Answers she would not have pressed him for at the expense of his life. The fist of anger and betrayal crushing her heart loosened, allowing blessed relief to move through her.

A smile pulled at her lips. Liberation percolated in her veins, a delicious warmth spreading in a healing energy. Something shifted in her body, like an out of place vertebra sliding into place, and her senses balanced in harmony. She finally had an idea of who and what she truly was.

Mag's words echoed in her head. *The Tueri have come to you.* Her hidden identity, necessary to disguise her immortality, explained her present exile. But she didn't become immortal for many years after her parents' deaths. Why hadn't they come for her as a child? Why did they wait so long to find her?

Anger at being abandoned simmered low in the pit of her stomach. The peace she'd finally found in discovering her roots waned. Nothing good *ever* came without a sour pill to swallow. Life had taught her that with vicious precision.

Her emotions roiled. This was all too much to handle.

She collapsed against the chair, suddenly aware of how tired she still was. With great care, she massaged the skin around her wound. Her muscles burned like fire, and the thought of pain reminded her of Mag's comment earlier about Doctor Conzatti being able to help her heal faster.

"Doctor," her chin shot up. "Can you heal me faster than I can heal on my own?"

Erik smiled ruefully. "No. I'm sorry. My abilities are most useful in the emergency room. I'm able to find what's wrong and almost always fix the problem, usually without any x-rays or CAT scans or MRIs. They're helpful confirmation, but I don't really need them. I use them, of course, or people would figure out something was different, but sometimes, in the emergency room, there's not time and I just have to help people. I'm compelled to," he finished apologetically.

Compassion prompted her smile. She understood the feeling of compulsion.

"Mr. Guidry," she glanced to her left, "there are others, healers, who could help me?"

"It's Dhelis, and the answer to your question is 'yes'," he replied. "Brogan Vincent's the best healer we have. He owns his own massage clinic here in town. The clinic caters to the general public, but Brogan works only on Tueri and is available any time he's needed."

She slowly stood and started toward her bedroom. "I need to cancel an appointment that frees up my evening. While you're waiting, I'd suggest you give Brogan a call and let him know he has a new patient." She stopped and looked back at him. "Can someone else move with you while you pop all over the place?"

He didn't even try to hide his grin. They both knew the ball was back in his court. "Yes, as a matter of fact, someone else can Ride with me."

"Good. You're driving. You can show me how this Stone-Riding thing works."

Chapter Eighteen

Clayton checked the caller I.D. and recognized Saari's number. He smiled with satisfaction. Her message earlier had said she'd come to the office at 6:00. She must be running late.

He picked up on the next ring. "Dr. Lytton."

"Hi. This is Saari Mitchell. I'm sorry to call at the last minute, but I need to cancel my appointment. I'm not feeling well. There's no way I can make it to your office this evening."

Disbelief left him mute.

She's canceling?

His brain scrambled for a different approach. "I'm sorry you're ill. Are you getting enough rest?"

"If that's your subtle way of asking if I had The Dream again last night, the answer's yes."

Of course she had The Dream. That's why she called me earlier. What else had she said?

"There was something else I wanted to talk to you about. This morning, I was miserable and I just wanted to go back to sleep. So I told myself I would not have The Dream again and took a couple of sleeping pills to knock myself out."

Like that worked.

"It worked."

If he hadn't been gripping the phone, he'd have dropped it.

"That's gotta mean I'm making progress, right?"

"Uh, that's a very real possibility. Why don't I come to you? We can determine just how much of a breakthrough you've had." He drummed his fingertips on the desk, fighting to keep his tone even.

"That's very generous, but I'm not up to having a session today. I'll try the same method tonight and see if it works again."

"I'd suggest not using the sleeping pills if you can," he suggested. "Sedatives can become addictive, and that would only hinder your ability to discover the real reason you're having The Dream."

"Okay. Hopefully, I won't need them."

"Please call me tomorrow, whether you have The Dream or not. If you're feeling well enough, I'd like to have a session whenever you're available."

"Thank you. I'll let you know."

He dropped the phone back in the cradle.

Fury warred with shock.

How had she overcome the post-hypnotic suggestion he'd planted in her subconscious? That shouldn't be possible. The sleeping pills had to be the reason. Nothing else made sense. Still...

Too agitated to sit, he strode to the office window and stared into the night. Saari's memory under hypnosis was real, but it didn't match the story she'd given him when she described The Dream. He'd suspected her motivation from the beginning. Her response—canceling the appointment—made sense if she'd been playing him from the start.

So who had sent her to him and why?

Could Maurika be behind Saari's visits?

He'd learned from overhearing Maurika's conversation with Quinn she'd known he was in the bar last night. Her mistake was thinking the psychic had been Clayton. That meant his drugs had knocked her for a loop. Otherwise, she'd have smelled the difference. Helpful information for use on other lunates, but it didn't answer the pertinent question.

Why had Saari come to see him?

Anxiety crawled up his spine, lodging at the base of his skull. He rubbed the back of his neck in an effort to relieve the nagging sensation. Saari had been sent to expose him. That bitch, Maurika, had gotten away from him not once, but twice. Last night he never made it to his playground, interfering with his precise timeline for the Full-Moon Killer.

Things were unraveling.

He forced his hands to his side.

No. Everything was under control. Maurika didn't know anything—or else she wouldn't have accepted the drugged drink.

I'm almost done. After tonight, only two more women to go.

He needed to stay focused and follow the plan he set in motion so many months ago. Deviations created problems. Problems altered a plan faster than a spreading virus adapted to its environment. Killing that woman last night hadn't forced him to change his strategy. He would need to kill two women in the same night, but that was the only the setback to deal with.

No more deviations—no more problems.

Outside his office crowds of people cluttered the street. Dinner rush hour had started. The need to shift ate at his insides, interfering with his thoughts. His pills weren't going to be enough tonight. He needed to snatch his next victim early and get out of the city.

A list of potential victims he'd put together weeks ago scrolled through his head: overconfident women that took unnecessary risks. That flaunted their bold defiance toward the world and anyone in it who might tell them how to live their life.

From this select group he would choose the next.

He pictured Elizabeth Foster. Warmth spread through his body, his heart pumping euphoria through his veins at his decision. The shade of her gleaming hair matched Maurika's auburn-curls. Such an exact balance in nature signaled a portent of good fortune.

A ruthless smile lifted his lips. He would truly enjoy this night's work; so much so, he grew hard with anticipation.

Turning toward his desk, he checked the clock on his computer screen. He had just enough time to get in place and intercept her as she walked to work.

He bolted for his car.

Once inside, he merged seamlessly into traffic, staying exactly at the posted speed limit. A special on TV had revealed a large number of lesser-talented predators were discovered by, of all things, stops for traffic infractions.

I am much smarter than that.

He knew Elizabeth's route by memory.

A few hundred yards down, Lewis Street branched off the main boulevard and headed toward the highway. The serpentine road wound its way through several blocks of aging businesses and old apartment buildings.

He would snatch her here.

Only a few light poles stood watch against the dark night. Even fewer actually worked at chasing away the shadows. And no windows faced the last two blocks of the street. He parked his car on the easterly side of the road. A considerable column supported the outside corner of the Hartford Building. Completely hidden from view, the nook gave him the perfect place to wait for her.

The moon's brilliant rays lit up the sky, overshadowing the streetlights that lined the avenue. Clayton checked his watch again, staring at the glowing numbers. He didn't have long before the medicine that kept him from changing wore off under the full moon.

He heard her approaching. The sound of a quiet but solid rhythm along the pavement, disturbed only by the swishing sound of her workout pants, announced her presence. She came abreast of him, strode past him, and then collapsed neatly into his arms after he struck her on the back of the head.

A perfectly timed grab. His position was exceptional. He merely had to reach out and open the passenger door. She dropped gently into the front passenger seat. He closed the door. To anyone watching, she looked like she tripped. He caught her and helped her into the car. Not that the scene mattered. No one would be able to identify him from such a distance.

He walked around to the driver's side of the car and got in. Leaning across the console, he buckled Elizabeth in. Her slumping inconveniently in the front seat might catch the attention of a patrolling officer. That would give a policeman reasonable suspicion to stop his vehicle, and *that* would be problematic.

The busy highway held no surprises. Some of the cars that passed him contained families—mom and the kids reading or watching those infernal DVD screens, dad driving. Others held couples. Clayton allowed himself a small smile. From all appearances, he was just like everybody else.

Of course that's where the similarities ended. He chuckled at his own cunning. People believed what their eyes told them, never stopping to question if their other senses conveyed a warning.

Killing someone was so easy.

He glanced to his right, taking in Elizabeth's profile. She lay unconscious, her breathing slow and relaxed. His eyes roamed over her still form, expertly judging her height and weight. The woman's petite stature and slight build gave her an almost fragile appearance.

Her features lent her a childlike quality he figured appealed to most men in an impish sort of way. Lean muscles spoke to her marvelous physical shape, which lead to an absolute certainty her oversized breasts were not created by nature.

Disappointment made him grit his teeth. He detested breast implants. They made women look great in clothes, but out of them—he sighed. Even the best surgeons left minute scars, leaving imperfections that marred their natural beauty. He knew his wasn't a popular opinion, but for him cosmetic "improvements" lessened, not enhanced, a woman's value.

Oh, well. *C'est la vie.* He shouldn't expect her to be flawless. She was just a means to an end. A purpose that for him, indeed, held perfection. He'd kept his eye on the ultimate prize, and success was just a matter of time now—he was that sure of himself.

Though he continued to watch the road, his other senses functioned like independent arms of an octopus, focusing on Elizabeth to detect the slightest change in her consciousness. He'd hit her pretty hard, purposely meaning to keep her subdued on the ride to the reserve.

He saw his exit up ahead and moved into the right-hand lane. After leaving the highway and traveling several miles toward the reserve, he reached a dirt path to his left. He'd been here many times before, creating a stage for his leading ladies. He hoped the effort would not be wasted on the police who eventually visited his exhibition.

Driving deeper into the wooded area of the reserve, he finally brought the car to a stop. She'd wake soon, and he wanted to be ready. Opening the trunk, he felt under the carpet where the spare tire was stored. He popped the hubcap and reached inside to retrieve his tool bag.

From the bag, he grabbed the roll of duct tape and moved to the passenger side of the vehicle. Oiled hinges ensured the door opened without a sound. He dropped to one knee. With a few deft movements, he wrapped the tape around first one ankle and then the other, effectively binding her legs.

Her hands rested limply in her lap. He put her palms together. With practiced ease, he wound the tape around not only the outside of her wrists but also over the back of each hand.

From past mistakes, he had learned not to leave their hands free. That allowed the prey a chance at self-defense, however slight the attempt may be. One woman had thrown dirt in his face after trying to painfully wrench a handful of hair from the top of his head. That had been the first and last time any one of them ever tried escaping from him.

His task completed, he walked back to the trunk and replaced the tape in his tool bag. After dropping the sack into the opening, he rescued the hubcap. He stepped back and checked the contents of the trunk, noting everything sat in its proper place. Nothing out of the ordinary here to attract attention.

Grinning, he closed the trunk and approached the passenger side of the car again. Despite the fact Elizabeth's eyes were closed, the woman was conscious. Her breath came in short puffs now, not the deep, even breathing from someone out cold. The scent of fear rolled off her.

He inhaled deeply, breathing in the night air, savoring her fear as if it were an aroma wafting from his favorite dish—terrified woman. And just last night he'd eaten one! He laughed at the ironic comparison. The sharp sound, in contrast to the night's quiet, caused her eyes to open suddenly, wide and staring.

Ah, such drama.

He stuck his hand deep within the front pocket of his jeans, caressing the tube of red lipstick he would use. Dramatic Red—his favorite shade. When he withdrew his hand, he kept the tube of lipstick at first concealed in his fist, but then stood the small cylinder upright on the dashboard in front of her.

Her eyes rounded like saucers, air whistling through her teeth on a sharp intake of breath. Then came the mewling sounds as she pressed back into her seat, shaking her head in denial.

He never grew tired of hearing their will break.

Kicking off his shoes, he set them on the towel covering the floor behind the passenger seat. Then he undressed. When he unzipped his jeans, he marveled at the echo created by the small metal teeth. Stepping out of his pants, he laid all of his clothes, neatly folded, atop the shoes on the floorboard.

His preparations were complete.

He *would* change under the full moon, which of course meant he'd need his clothes in one piece when he left in the morning. This ritual of dressing and undressing was such a part of his routine, he never gave it much thought.

Stepping away from the car, he stretched his body's muscles in a yoga warrior position, arching his back while lifting his arms high above his head. The asana helped release some of the tension from the moon's growing pull.

He sensed Elizabeth's eyes on him, tracking his movements. Her ample chest rose and fell with each rapid, shallow breath. Her racing heartbeat echoed in his eardrums, her fear causing the organ to gallop wildly in her chest. Adrenaline pumped through her body, an autonomic function of her fight or flight response. Since neither fight nor flight was an option for her, she would reach the point of resigned acceptance before the night ended.

He squatted in front of her and reached for the tube of lipstick. Each time he moved, her body jerked in response. Savoring every moment of power and control, he twisted the lid off the makeup container.

"Please...no." She shook her head sharply, her denial obvious.

He took a deep breath, reached out, and grasped her by the back of the neck.

Her head became instantly immobilized, giving him access to her mouth.

Gently pressing the stick of color against the corner of her mouth, he watched his favorite shade of red appear, as if by magic. The cylinder of makeup glided over the smooth surface of her lips. When he finished, he closed the tube of lipstick and used the edge of her shirt to wipe off any prints from the outer surface.

Satisfied with his results, he pushed the tube into the right front pocket of her pants. He stood up, reached for her bound hands, and pulled her from the car. Her body stiffened. She stumbled slightly, but not really fighting him, numbed by fright. He lifted her with one arm and flopped her over his shoulder. A hip bump closed the car door before he turned toward the trees.

Moonlight danced across his skin. It rippled in answer to the moon's pull. He did not have long. His feet grew, legs slightly elongating as he moved silently toward the meadow. Elizabeth wriggled, trying to throw him off balance. He tightened his arm around her waist, squeezing hard enough something popped.

She inhaled sharply, but got the message. Her struggling ceased, but her body shuddered occasionally as she sobbed without making a sound.

He moved past a stand of trees and stepped into his meadow. Once he approached a particular group of large boulders in the clearing, he scanned the area for intruders. None were present, but he smelled a strong scent, not his own, carried on the wind.

Dropping his burden on top of the makeshift chair of rock, he lifted his nose to the air and sniffed to identify what he'd noticed. A deep growl ripped from his throat when he recognized the scent as male, but nothing more.

The other predator hadn't ventured close enough yet.

Elizabeth whimpered, drawing his attention. She huddled against the rocks, trying to make herself as small as she possibly could. Her dark hair stood out against the pallor of her face, her eyes large with fright. When he reached for her, his hands began to change. The tips of his fingers sharpened to claws, hair sprouted from his skin. He was shifting too quickly. He needed to kill her—now—before it was too late.

He grasped her face between his large hands and jerked her head hard to the right and up. An audible snap ricocheted through the meadow, and she fell limp. He sat her body up tall on the rock chair and turned her head forward. No matter how he positioned her torso, her head hung loosely on her neck. He lifted her chin and leaned her head back on the top boulder.

Elizabeth rested there nicely, as if she were relaxing, maybe taking a quiet nap. He saw her eyes from his position above her, though, and they told a different story. The lids stood wide open, orbs staring sightlessly at the last image she carried with her into the next life.

That thought pleased him. Her last vision was of him, a strange mix of man and beast. He wondered if he appeared more man or more beast, but truly, his appearance didn't matter. It was this blending of the two that would give him his greatest triumph.

After tomorrow night, he had only to take Maurika. That would establish his dominance, and she would belong to him. Quinn would be taken into custody for the murdered women they found on the reserve. Quinn's arrest would solidify Clayton's position as the new alpha male, and that meant the pack would be his.

He loped toward the trees at the edge of the clearing and worked his way around the outer boundary, spraying the tree trunks and shrubs. He marked them with his scent, leaving a clear warning to any males in the area. This was his territory. He would kill any who challenged him for it.

After marking the entire perimeter, he gave himself over to the moon, submitting to the change he'd fought for several minutes. The pressure in his head disappeared with the final phase of shifting, replaced by the predatory instinct to hunt.

Clayton, the man, was gone, and the beast roared with exultant freedom.

Chapter Nineteen

Saari walked back into the kitchen to find Mag standing next to the table beside her empty chair. Dhelis leaned against the breakfast bar's granite countertop. Doctor Conzatti was nowhere in sight. "Where's Doctor Conzatti?"

"Erik left for the hospital," Dhelis told her. "They needed him in the emergency room. I've already called Brogan. He's expecting us."

"Good." She clapped her hands together once in approval. That meant this little excursion would include just the two of them. Obviously, Dhelis would have to touch her in order for her to "Ride" with him. Nervous butterflies fluttered in her stomach. Her skin tingled in anticipation.

Earlier at the table, sheer willpower and her overriding desire to know how she was connected to this man had kept her from rubbing herself against him like a cat against a catnip-covered scratching post. This "Stone Riding" gave her the perfect excuse to touch him again without letting him know she couldn't wait to get her hands on him.

"So," she asked with feigned nonchalance, "how's this work?"

"Saari," Mag touched her elbow, a warning tone in his voice. "We haven't checked into anything about Mr. Guidry, and for all we know, this process could kill you."

She crossed her arms in front of her and rolled her eyes. "Oh, please."

"Fine," Mag conceded, "but you're already hurt, and this Stone Riding *could* aggravate your wound."

Her eyes slid to Dhelis. "Could Stone Riding make my injury worse?"

Dhelis rubbed his chin. "I've never heard of Riding having adverse affects on anyone."

She looked back at Mag, giving him an "I told you" look. "See. Stop worrying. I'll be perfectly safe."

Mag stepped close and looked down at her. He fidgeted nervously. His lips parted, and words spilled from his mouth in a rush.

"And have we, *Nefer Ka*, been adversely affected?"

She leveled a hard stare at him. "You know, I'm tempted to leave without answering you; give you a taste of what it's like to need to know something so badly you ache from the wanting."

"I hurt you. I understand your need to retaliate," he answered with quiet dignity.

Her shoulders dropped with a sigh of resignation. "That's not our way. We've always been honest and respected one another. Nothing has changed that."

His eyes rounded with hope and expectation.

With a smile of reassurance, she placed a hand on his chest, the other against his cheek. "No, my friend, we have not been adversely affected."

His eyes closed on an exhalation of relief and he leaned into her palm. The downy softness of his skin brushed her palm where his cheek lay cradled against her hand. Ironically, the linen shirt he wore lay stiff under her other hand. The fabric rubbed against her skin with each solid beat of his heart.

Funny how the movies had gotten that fact about vampires wrong, too.

If a vampire didn't have a heartbeat, you could bet they were dead.

Mag was very much alive.

He turned his head, brushing his lips against her palm, pressing a soft kiss to her skin. "Go. Mr. Guidry is impatient to be on his way."

With all of their secrets out in the open, her heart lightened. Mag was still her dark knight. She gave him a playful wink and then turned to Dhelis.

"So, are we going to do this or what?" she asked brazenly.

Dhelis reached for her. He gripped her arm over the fabric, avoiding skin-to-skin contact. No burning light filled the room. "Just testing," he assured her. "Good information to have. I don't want to make you feel worse before Brogan has a chance to heal you."

"Good idea." She wasn't sure her body could withstand another energy reaction with Dhelis just yet. The idea of touching him again had overridden her sense of self-preservation. That was definitely something she needed to think about. Later.

He gave her a wolfish smile. "Hang on. The first Ride's always a rush."

"You're the one stalling," she pushed, the rational side of her brain fighting a moment's fear of the unknown.

"Here we go," he warned.

Before she could blink, her world tilted on its axis.

She wasn't sure what she expected, but she wasn't prepared for the force that pulled her body forward at the speed of light—or maybe faster. Her insides squeezed from the pressure. Like some internal force was trying to move outside of her body while the rest of her, attached by an invisible umbilical cord, followed in its wake.

White spots crackled at the edge of her vision, in startling sparks of lightning. She couldn't be certain if they were real or random blasts of her brain's synapses. Rising nausea kept time with her increasing dizziness. Her body had to stop moving, but somehow she suspected stopping would be just as unpleasant.

Her head snapped forward with an audible crack when her body came to an abrupt stop. She heard voices and saw people close by, but they whirled around her so quickly she couldn't be sure what they looked like. Then her stomach flip-flopped, and she reached blindly for something solid to make the spinning stop.

~ ☾ ~

Brogan stood next to the massage table. The air shifted. A fraction of a second later Dhelis and a woman he'd never seen before appeared in the room.

He sucked in a startled breath. She had crystalline eyes that rivaled Dhelis's in color and beauty. Long, dark curls framed her pale face, and the woman did *not* look well. She swayed like children do after spinning around in circles until they were so dizzy they stumbled. Her eyes bounced back and forth, unable to focus on any one object.

She definitely looked like she was going to be sick.

He reached out a hand to help steady her. She promptly bent over double—and vomited all over his pant legs and shoes. Her shoulders heaved, the violent retches jerking her body forward in an invisible game of tug of war. The brutal force of the spasms stunned him.

Dhelis quickly stepped forward, hands extended toward the woman. She lurched to her right and slumped against the massage table. "Don't touch me," she groaned. "Not yet. I might be sick again."

Brogan stepped out of his shoes as the woman climbed up on the table. She lay, trembling spastically, facing the opposite wall. An uncomfortable wetness had soaked through his pants, the fabric clinging in spots to his skin. Without hesitation he unzipped his jeans and stepped out of the soiled clothing.

Grabbing a large towel off the counter, he wrapped it around his waist. He used another towel to scoop his things off the floor. After a couple quick twists of terrycloth, his clothes were wrapped in a tight ball. Thankfully, nothing dripped onto the floor.

Dhelis chuckled.

"Not one word," he warned, juggling the soggy mess.

Dhelis lifted his hands in mock surrender and took a step back.

"If you laugh, I swear you're setting yourself up for some serious payback."

He could see Dhelis fighting a smile. Despite *his* best effort, Brogan laughed first. "You do know how to make an entrance." After glancing once more at the woman, he turned around and walked out of the room.

~ ☾ ~

Dhelis heard Brogan asking his staff to please clean the floor while he took a quick shower. "And use lots of soap," he yelled after Brogan.

He approached Saari slowly, careful to keep some distance in case she threw up again. There couldn't possibly be anything left in her stomach—but he wasn't taking any chances.

Compassion flared in him. With her injury, he should have anticipated this kind of reaction. He had made her feel worse, and he hadn't even touched her to do it. At least she lay perfectly still on the table now. If it weren't for her occasional moans, he'd have believed she was asleep. He squatted, his eyes level with hers.

Her eyes snapped open abruptly, startling him. "You lied to me."

Lied to her? He'd only just met her. "I've never lied to you."

"You told me no one had been affected by Riding."

"Ah." Now he understood what she was talking about. "I said I'd never heard of anyone being adversely affected by Riding."

"That sounds like a distinction without a difference to me."

He covered a laugh with a cough. "I'm not entirely convinced the Riding caused you to be sick. It could have been your injury. Personally, I think it might have something to do with your injury *and* the fact you ate about a half an hour ago."

Saari eyes closed. "I don't know what to believe. Maybe this Riding thing is a little like swimming and the same rules apply."

"What are you talking about?"

"If you plan to swim, don't get in the water for half an hour after eating because you could get a cramp and drown."

"Isn't that a myth?" He kept his tone neutral, careful not to make her mad and upset her further. An argument would only make things worse between them.

"You're the one that's supposed to be the expert," she mumbled.

"Well," he tried, "I wouldn't place Riding in the same category as swimming, but, considering we did break the laws of physics, yes, there are specific rules related to Stone Riding."

She opened her eyes and focused on him. "Do you think you could find me a toothbrush and mouthwash or something? Please?"

He stood. "Will you be all right if I leave you in here alone?"

She paused, obviously thinking about her answer.

"My stomach seems to have settled. Nightmares and Stone Riding—two things I seriously don't want to have or do again." She lifted a hand and touched the top buttons on her shirt. "On top of that, my chest burns like fire again."

He wasn't sure how to respond.

"I'm fine," she insisted in a scratchy voice. "I just really need to brush my teeth."

He stepped into the hallway, then poked his head back through the doorway. "I'll be right back."

He'd been gone less than a minute when he came back into the room carrying a brand new toothbrush, toothpaste and mouthwash. This time he walked right up to the table, fairly certain she wasn't going to be sick all over him.

"There's a bathroom behind that screen. You can even shower if you want to."

She heaved a sigh of relief. "Thank you."

He gripped her covered arm and helped her slide off the table. She plucked the items from his other outstretched hand, making sure to avoid any skin-to-skin contact.

"You said the bathroom's over there?" She pointed the toothbrush toward the other side of the room.

"Yeah, just behind that screen."

He watched her walk behind the privacy divider and let out the breath he'd been holding. Part of him was disappointed at her avoiding his direct touch. The rational part knew she already felt lousy and agreed with her actions of self-preservation. She definitely didn't need a repeat of this morning's surprise.

Besides, he'd been trying to think of a way to help her without actually touching her again. There were too many Tueri in this building who might witness their connected energies. He wasn't ready to give *that* explanation to everyone else just yet.

At least not before he talked to Brogan first—and then the Council.

Chapter Twenty

Freshly showered and dressed in new clothes, Brogan entered the room ready to question Dhelis about the strange woman. But the woman had disappeared. He turned to the Stone Rider and lifted an eyebrow in question.

"She's still in the bathroom," Dhelis explained.

"Too bad you didn't pop in there instead. Flushing the toilet would have been a lot easier than disinfecting the floor and showering." He checked the marble-colored anti-fatigue cushioned vinyl. Nothing showed. Thank goodness it was stain resistant. Somebody had even lit some vanilla-scented incense to cover the smell of cleaning solutions.

Leaning against the massage table, he crossed his arms over his chest. "Her first time Riding, huh?"

"How'd you guess?"

"Are you ready to tell me who she is now?"

Dhelis looked toward the bathroom, making sure the woman was still inside before he answered. "You saw her eyes, right?"

"They're the same color as yours—which isn't possible. Unless...I mean, there hasn't been a..."

"Her name is Saari," Dhelis interrupted, "and she's a Predecessor."

"Wow. Have you guys talked about what her natural ability is—aside from being a Stone Rider? I mean, there's only ever one living Predecessor. They inherit the ability to borrow the skill of previous Predecessors."

"The borrowing ability thing only works when the Predecessor is connected to another Tueri with the same ability—and that it's not permanent."

"So when you Rode her here, tapping into your ability gave her a double whammy of 'go' fuel. I'm not surprised she got sick."

"I don't know, maybe—and no, we haven't talked about her extra abilities." Dhelis's eyebrows V'd in frustration. "Doesn't matter anyway. Her eyes tell me she's a Predecessor."

Brogan lifted his hands in a "backing off" gesture. "Hey, I just wondered if you were sure."

"Sorry."

Dhelis rubbed a finger back and forth under his chin. "She's of the purest descent I've ever seen. I don't know how, Brogan, but she's an Unknown. I've never heard of her, and, until yesterday, Council didn't know of her existence either."

Brogan crossed his arms again, searching his new friend's expression. They'd only known each other for a few months, but Dhelis was too tense for somebody who had just discovered what among their people would be as significant as finding the Holy Grail. Something didn't add up.

"What aren't you telling me?"

Dhelis took a breath. "Saari and I, we're mated."

Brogan's arms dropped to his sides. "Serious?"

"Yeah."

"What does it feel like?" Brogan asked quietly.

"I knew instinctively there was some kind of connection between us. I couldn't have predicted how strong our link would be, though."

Jealousy over wanting a connection of his own slithered through him, striking at his carefully erected walls of solitude. "What happened?"

"When we touched, our energies arced. It was like standing in the middle of the sun while its heat burned everything around us. Rolling my psychic energy into hers was amazing—

unbelievably amazing. I swear, that must be what it feels like to get high. I was seriously juiced from the power surge between us."

He wrestled his jealousy back into its cage. Dhelis deserved to be happy. The choice Brogan made long ago to never search for his own mate had nothing to do with his friend. "Very cool. I'm thrilled for you, man."

"Thanks."

"If she's unknown to Council, does she know she's a Predecessor? Or that she can Ride stones, too?"

Dhelis's gaze shot to the bathroom door. "No. I Rode into her kitchen, and startled her so badly she dropped the plate she was holding. She had no idea who or what I was. She didn't even know she was Tueri until tonight."

At this, Dhelis turned and looked directly at him. "She has a general idea what it means to be mated, but now is not the time to explain everything. I want to tell her myself, and I'd rather do it privately, just the two of us."

The bathroom door opened, effectively ending their conversation. Brogan and Dhelis both turned toward the other side of the room. Saari stepped from behind the screen, wrapped in a towel. Her arms were folded across her chest, holding her clothes. She looked up to see both men staring at her.

"I assumed you would want me undressed for this. Was I wrong?"

Brogan tried not to stare at her. A hot shower had warmed her skin to a healthy pink glow. Her black hair cascaded in looping curls that fell across her shoulders. *Get a grip*, his inner voice chided. *This is Dhelis's mate.*

He ignored the fact a beautiful woman just correctly assumed he wanted her naked—needed to touch her skin. *Enough.* With some effort, he ground his wayward thoughts to a halt and buried his attraction for Saari.

Brogan offered her a professional smile, hoping to put her at ease. "You were right. I need you to be undressed for the healing to be most effective." *There. That sounded appropriately detached.* He motioned toward the table. "I'm Brogan, by the way."

She placed her clothes on a chair and climbed onto the table. "Saari." She looked directly at him. "I'm so sorry about before..."

"No harm done," he interrupted, waving his hand dismissively. "Dhelis said you were hurt, and this *was* your first time Riding. Unexpected things happen."

Dhelis stepped next to the table and gathered Saari's hair without touching her skin. "I thought you might hurt yourself if you lifted your arm to hold it out of the way."

"Thanks." She gave Dhelis a small smile.

Without being asked, she scooted backward on the table, stretching out full length on her back. Her gaze found Brogan, tracking his movements. He turned and gathered several things off a shelf before approaching her side. With only a moment's hesitation, she flipped open her towel. Her arms relaxed at her sides, hands resting against her thighs.

Dhelis stared openly at his mate, devouring the sight of her naked body. Brogan didn't blame him. The woman's tiny waist and rounded hips tapered into a pair of long legs he couldn't help but imagine wrapped around his waist.

"Heal her." Dhelis scowled at him and pointed at Saari's chest.

"Of course."

He glanced in the indicated direction and inhaled sharply. Leaning over her body, he looked closely at the wound over her heart. He reached out to touch her, but stopped just short of actual contact, uncertain how much pain he might cause her.

His chin lifted, meeting her gaze. "Does it hurt as much as it looks like it should?"

"It hurts. A lot."

He rotated his head toward Dhelis. "Over the phone, you said there was a hole *in* her heart. I can see her heart through her ribs, but any hole in her heart has already closed. If she can heal this fast, what do you think I can do for her?"

Dhelis shrugged. "I guess we'll see if you *can* help her."

Turning back to Saari, he extended his left hand out, palm up. His stone lay where she could see it. Her eyes blinked once, an acknowledgement she recognized the stone. She raised her left arm. Her stone balanced in the center of her palm.

He couldn't help smiling. She had followed his lead instinctively. That was a very good sign. Maybe he could help her heal after all.

Dhelis stepped closer to the table to watch their progress. Brogan understood he needed to see any difference in Saari's wound. First and foremost was Dhelis's concern for his mate. Secondly, he'd have to report his observations to Council, and they would want every detail possible.

Brogan plucked her stone from her hand and placed it immediately above her wound. He positioned his own stone right below her wound. There was now a direct line between her energy stone and his, capturing her injury between the two. He looked quickly at her and raised his eyebrows. "Ready?"

She dipped her head in response.

Leaning his thighs against the side of the table for support, he closed his eyes and allowed his other senses to focus. Moving his hands outward in slow, uniformed circles, they hovered over her body. His energy dropped into her space with the *plunk* of a pebble landing in a pond. Energy built in ripples. His palms tingled, and he lowered his hands. The closer he got to Saari, the more heat the stones generated.

Carefully, he placed both hands directly on her flesh over her heart. The instant his skin contacted hers, an explosion of energy as loud and forceful as a sonic boom pounded through the room. His eyes shot open in surprise. Unsure of what was happening, he held fast to the connection.

Dhelis's jaw dropped in shock.

"Can you feel the energy heavy in the air?" He managed to ask Dhelis around the pounding echo in his head.

Dhelis's nostrils flared as he ground his teeth. "Not only can I feel it, I can hear the pulsating tone. I can't believe this."

Heat poured from his hands into her body. He watched in disbelief as her muscle and tissue knit together, responding to his healing energy in a way he'd never seen before.

Dhelis had explained an incredible energy connection between himself and Saari, indicating *they* were mated. Now there was some kind of extreme energy transfer between Saari and himself.

How could she possibly be mated to both of us?

Brogan's hands began to shake.

Saari began to scream.

Dhelis reached forward to separate Brogan and Saari. "Jesus, can't you see you're hurting her? Whatever you're doing is killing her." The massage room door burst open, crashing against the wall. Dhelis whirled toward the sound.

Brogan recognized the group of people that poured through the doorway: other Tueri who worked at his massage clinic. They'd been drawn to the room by the energy they obviously sensed in the air. And he couldn't just order them out. They were witnesses to his energy connection with Saari, a requirement by Council for any Tueri match.

Dhelis turned and strode back to the massage table. Before he got between them, Saari broke their connection. She rolled off the table, away from Brogan, pulling the towel around her before her feet hit the ground. Eyes wild, she stared at the crowd of people gathered behind Dhelis.

"What the hell is going on?" she demanded of nobody in particular.

Brogan heard the insistent whispering behind him. They had no way out of this situation now. Dhelis looked at him, features tight with tension. He knew what Dhelis was thinking. There had to be an explanation for what just happened, for why Saari was connected to both he and Dhelis, but he didn't have a clue what it was.

He was also afraid to move for fear of spooking her. She looked like a deer caught by a hunter in the forest, ready to bolt at the slightest noise. "Dhelis?" he prompted softly.

Dhelis inched toward her, speaking in a quiet, reassuring tone. "Saari, Brogan needs to touch you again."

She pushed her back against the wall, vigorously shaking her head "no."

"Yes, he will. We need to know if there truly is an extra energy between you two. This is very important or I wouldn't ask," Dhelis insisted.

After a moment, she nodded stiffly. "Okay."

Once Brogan reached her side, he raised his hands and gently cupped her shoulders. Energy rolled through the room again. He immediately dropped his hands, breaking the connection, and stepped back.

The other people in the room talked in excited whispers. There were more than enough witnesses to support his match. He knew Dhelis would need a similar demonstration. He lifted his chin, and Dhelis stepped forward before Saari could guess his intent. He quickly enveloped her fisted hand tightly within his own.

The room filled with bright energy, almost blinding in its effect. Saari jerked away, breaking the connection. Dhelis stepped to her side but didn't attempt to touch her again. The muscle in his jaw twitched.

Brogan read his emotions clearly: Dhelis didn't know whether to be amazed or outraged. The poor guy. He'd discovered his mate just this morning, and now circumstances indicated she was mated to a second man—someone he barely knew well enough to call friend.

"Oh my God, did you feel that?" One of the females whispered.

"Both times!" Another voice answered.

"So which one of 'em's gonna be sanctioned as the real deal?" The first woman asked.

He stared at his staff in frustration. Everybody in the room gawked at Saari like she was the newest addition to the sideshow at the circus.

Their interest in her struck a proprietary chord.

Brogan pondered his own situation. Saari was also *his* mate. He hadn't even been searching for his perfect match. A seer had told him when he found his mate, she'd belong to someone else, so he'd decided, why bother looking? But now that he had stumbled upon her, and experienced their own energy connection, he understood Dhelis's protective instincts.

Then, another thought occurred to him. What if she resonates with all Tueri men? Could it be possible?

The observers openly discussed the trio with animated gestures. More of them voiced confusion over how this woman could be mated to both he and Dhelis at the same time, echoing his earlier train of thought.

Dave, one of the physical therapists, cleared his throat. "You know, something like this has occurred before—but the connection was with a set of identical twins. Both men had been mated to one woman, but *they* were identical twins. Matching DNA. Brogan and Dhelis aren't even related, so that can't be a possible explanation."

He considered the possibility Saari was a Resonator. The story about Resonators persisted only as a myth, though. No historical support existed for that particular kind of Tueri. After what he'd just witnessed, he didn't know what to think. Anything could be possible.

"Dave, come here." He motioned him forward with a wave of his hand.

The man jerked in surprise, but moved away from the doorway as Brogan directed.

Saari caught the motion and backed toward Dhelis. "Oh, no way. Not again."

Brogan met her horrified stare. "We need a baseline. We have to know if you resonate with all Tueri men or just Dhelis and me. Please, let him touch you."

Her mouth dropped open. "Like hell I'll let another one of you people touch me. I don't know what's going on, but you're nuts if you think anybody else is getting near me."

He turned, blocking the rest of the room's view of her with his body. He lowered his voice so only she could hear. "I know I don't have the right to ask anything of you, but I am. This is incredibly important, and if there were another way, we'd do it. But, truthfully, this is the only way, Saari. We need an answer, and we need it now."

She hesitated. He considered her position: frustrated at being ignorant of the Tueri and their customs—people she just discovered she came from; indignant at being the object of curiosity to a bunch of strangers; frightened by whatever happened every time she touched Dhelis or him. They were *all* unknown to her, yet somehow she belonged with them.

That probably scared her more than she would admit.

He watched her take a shuddering breath. Her features settled into firm resignation. If he were in her place, he'd want answers. And if this was the only way to get them, then so be it.

"When this is finished," she murmured to him, "somebody better start explaining."

Brogan smiled. He'd guessed right. "Fair enough."

He turned toward Dave. "All right, you're up."

Dave approached Saari quickly, almost as if he wanted this over as much as she did. His hand hovered over her arm, hesitating at the last second. Then he moved his hand swiftly and tapped her, using the same caution one would use when testing an electric fence.

Nothing happened.

Brogan and Dhelis simultaneously breathed a sigh of relief.

"Well, what are the rest of you waiting for?" She asked of the remaining men, shocking everyone in the room. "You might as well give it a go, too."

Brogan almost choked on a chuckle. "You heard her."

She whispered, "I feel ludicrous standing naked, wrapped in a towel, with a line of men waiting to take turns touching me."

Before he could comment, one of the men approached her as if she were a snake, and he was clearly afraid she might strike him. Another seemed way too eager with anticipation. He thought the enthusiastic guy would be rather pleased if there was some sort of reaction between Saari and him.

The man walked away disappointed.

The last male advanced and looked at her as if she was something repugnant, stuck to the bottom of his shoe. "Even *I'm* required to touch her?" he asked of Brogan.

"Especially you," he answered.

"Just my luck to be mated with a woman," the man grumbled under his breath. He reached out and slapped her on the arm. It didn't hurt, but the meaning was clear enough.

Again, nothing happened.

"Thank God," the man exclaimed dramatically, making no attempt to hide his relief. "Can you just imagine how I would explain *that* to Jacob?" He turned back to Saari. "No offense, honey, but you're not my type. You're too—female."

Her eyebrows shot up at that. "O-kay." She cracked a small smile. "At least I'm not the only one less than thrilled at participating in this experiment."

Brogan walked toward the door, ushering people out as he went. "Back to work, everybody. Show's over."

The room emptied, and he finally closed the door. He turned to face Dhelis and Saari. Leaning his back against the door, he crossed his arms over his chest.

Dhelis paced the floor. "I have to brief the Council immediately. They're going to need to know what happened here today. I'd prefer to take Saari with me, but I don't know for sure why she got sick earlier. She'll have to meet them. Since she's about to make a lasting first impression on them, I would rather the experience not consist of her throwing up all over a member of Council."

The mental picture he had of Saari puking on a particular member of Council was amusing, but he agreed with Dhelis. "I don't even know that you could get them all assembled tonight, Dhelis. Her meeting with Council may have to wait until tomorrow."

Dhelis stopped pacing. "I don't know what this means, Saari, but we're going to find out, I promise you. Brogan's right, though. I may not get any answers tonight."

"Brogan, can you take me home?" Saari glanced at Dhelis. "No offense, but I'm none too keen on Riding with you—even if you're only dropping me off at my place."

Dhelis chuckled. "No offense taken. You've had a rough day. I certainly don't want to make it worse—again. Well then, I'll let you know as soon as I know something."

The air in the room shifted, and Dhelis blinked out.

"I've seen Dhelis do that once already, but it's just as amazing a second time." She turned to him. "Do you ever get used to him just popping in and out like that?"

He pushed away from the door, grinning with genuine amusement. "I thought I had."

She grabbed her clothes off the chair and headed toward the bathroom. Her steps halted as she neared him, her gaze penetrating. "You told me you would answer my questions."

"I did, and I will."

"I know you will, but that's not what I meant," she replied, her eyebrows scrunching together in thought. "You asked something of me earlier. Now I need to ask something of you."

He looked at her curiously, but didn't back away.

"I have a feeling things are going to get even weirder than they already are, and I have to be able to trust somebody. I'd like that person to be you, but for that to happen I need you to be completely honest with me. The truth itself is not as important as knowing I can count on *you* to always be truthful with me."

He stared at her, chewing his lip thoughtfully. "Even when it's something you don't want to hear?"

"Especially if it's something I don't want to hear," she verified.

He placed his hand over his heart. "I give you my word," he quietly pledged his agreement.

She watched him, her gaze never faltering. He knew she sensed the truth behind his promise when her features relaxed into a smile. "Okay." She walked into the bathroom without saying another word.

Brogan stared at the bathroom door in silent contemplation. He wondered why she'd chosen to trust him—though he was glad she did.

It would appear they were truly mated after all.

Chapter Twenty-One

Late Evening, May 23, 2032

Saari abruptly realized Brogan had asked her a question. From his tone and curious expression, he'd asked it more than once. She jerked her thoughts from the three-way psychic connection she'd somehow stumbled into and focused on the man driving the car. "I'm sorry, what did you ask me?"

His eyes looked in her direction briefly before moving back to the roadway. "Do you always eat so much food in one sitting?"

She felt a moment's embarrassment over the question, but then noticed his smile. He was trying to lighten the moment, a quality she found endearing since she appreciated a good sense of humor. After answering him with a shake of her head, she realized he still watched the road.

"No, I do *not* always eat that much food. Healing takes a lot of energy, and, as you saw for yourself, I needed some serious healing."

His next question caught her off guard.

"You had your stone, so I assume you can heal yourself, right?"

She had never been seriously injured before she became immortal, so she had no real experience that supported his statement. She always healed. Healing was never the issue. How quickly she healed, now *that* was the important question.

That seemed the safest way to answer.

She turned in her seat to face him, careful not to stretch the still puckered skin on her chest. "I've always been able to heal, but this time—with you, I mean—I healed faster than I ever have before."

That said a lot, since she'd been alive for several centuries, but she didn't think now was the time to share that particular bit of information. Very few people knew of her immortality, and for now, she wanted to keep it that way. She knew nothing about Brogan or Dhelis, but she had a feeling some serious bonding time would be required before that kind of news could be shared.

Which meant she'd also have to spend time with Brogan. *Be honest*, the pragmatic voice in her head whispered. *You're looking forward to spending time with him.*

And she was. His energy was just as intense as Dhelis's, but it affected her differently. Instead of the consuming passion she felt with Dhelis, an underlying calmness drew her to Brogan. Their shared link shielded her from the chaos blowing around her, giving her room to focus her emotions and center.

And she needed to feel centered.

Good Lord, how was she supposed to handle this connection with *two* men?

One thing at a time.

They rode for a while in silence. Since she wasn't driving, she had the perfect chance to covertly observe him. She already knew he was tall, about 6'2", with broad shoulders. She hadn't seen him with his shirt off, but she suspected he had those washboard abs commercials for workout machines were always promising. His form-fitting shirt showed off every ripple of muscle as he moved.

Her gaze shifted next to his profile, noting the squared jaw, the sharp cheekbones. Except for the amazing color of his eyes, she was pretty sure he was Italian. To round out the whole masculine effect, his head was completely shaved. His eyebrows were a dark brown, but that didn't necessarily mean the hair on his head would match. She found herself wondering what color his hair really was, and why he kept his head shaved.

He was a massage therapist, but he had the look of a bouncer. She'd sensed the palpable edge to his energy that radiated an animal-like strength, his easy-going nature covering a dynamic force. Her head tilted to the side as she considered this last observation. The power of his energy stood at odds with his skill of healing, of soothing the body.

Abruptly, he pulled the car over. Leaving one hand on the wheel, he turned from the waist toward her. His eyes found hers, holding her gaze captive with their piercing intensity. "Have you decided yet if you like what you see?"

She sucked in a breath, surprised not at his perceptive nature, but by his bold approach. His stare never wavered from hers. Though his question smacked of conceit, his eyes shone with sincerity. He truly wanted to know what she thought of him. He had been aware the entire time she was looking at him she was forming an opinion based on his appearance.

While part of her cringed at the shallowness, her stomach fluttered at the vulnerability and heat reflected in his gaze. This man was a contradiction in appearance and emotion. She couldn't help but acknowledge being physically drawn to him. The difficulty came in accepting that the attraction was not solely because of the energy connection. She wanted to understand him.

Both were emotions she thought buried long ago.

Squelching her own vulnerability, she remembered their earlier agreement: nothing but complete honesty would ever be offered between them.

"Yes," she smiled, "as a matter of fact, I do. You're a great-looking guy with a body carved by a Greek god. More to the point, you know it."

He smiled broadly at her, pleased with her answer. "I know the way I look to other people, but the way I look to you matters most."

His tone sent shivers across her skin, the strings of her heart jangling in nervous reply. Miko had had the same affect on her. She'd fallen for him, fast and hard. And then he'd died. She couldn't put herself out there like that again—could she?

She shoved her serious thoughts aside, hiding her emotions in humor.

An eyebrow lifted. "We've only just met. Besides, you have an advantage. You've already seen me naked."

He laughed outright at her baiting him. "You already know you're beautiful, but I said I'd always be straight with you, so here goes. I noticed you have one hell of a figure, but that's only part of it. When we touched, the energy connection we shared was incredible. It transcended beyond an auric link. We bonded on a primal level I didn't even know existed. Of course, I'm hoping our link only hurt like hell the first time because you were injured."

She gasped. "Are you saying you could feel my pain?"

His eyebrows drew together. "There was more than just pain, but, yeah, I could. Whenever I've healed someone, it's never been that...well, that intense before, and I've *never* experienced what my patients were feeling."

"Crazy. That's exactly what I thought when I was staring at you. Your aura radiates an intensity that flows below the surface of your emotions."

He reached for a curl of hair lying on her shoulder and twined it around his finger. A gentle tug pulled her toward him. His lips brushed hers in a whisper-soft kiss, drawing away after one booming heartbeat. He turned around and pulled the car back onto the road. "In this instance, only for you. I promise."

Her stomach flopped at his declaration.

Another thought struck her. *What if that's the way this is supposed to work?* Dhelis told her their energy searched for the best match to learn and grow in skill. *Was all of this a physiological reaction? Were her hormones dictating her reactions?*

Too much, too soon.

She decided to let that personal comment pass, searching for a safer topic. Right now, she really wanted—*needed* some answers. "Do you mind if we make a quick stop on the way to my place? I have to talk to someone."

"No problem. If you plug the address into my GPS, I won't have to keep asking you for directions."

"Thanks." She leaned toward the screen below the dash and typed in the club's address. Alarico *would* explain her Tueri history and why he'd kept Mag from telling her the truth. He owed her.

She remembered the first time she'd saved Alarico's life.

He'd planned to marry a friend of Saari's from the village—a very human girl. Before the wedding ceremony, he'd confessed he was a vampire. She'd told her family, and her brother had tried to stake Alarico through the heart. Instinctively, Saari had stepped in front of Alarico—and ended up stabbed through her heart. For the second time.

She woke up to discover Alarico had taken her with him and left the village. When she asked him why, he told her he'd watched her die and then come back to life. Neither of them would ever be welcome in her village with their secrets. After she'd healed, he'd given her his mark. The tattoo had guaranteed her safe passage among the vampires for centuries.

Oh, yeah. Alarico owed her.

In the meantime, maybe Brogan would answer a few questions about the Tueri for her. "Tell me about this Council I keep hearing about. Why do we have to go before them? Who are they, and what exactly do they do?"

He didn't answer right away. "I don't know if I can answer without completely confusing you."

"Maybe a simple explanation would be best," she encouraged. "Because I really need some details to help put all this in perspective."

He took a deep breath and started. "Dhelis already told you all Tueri have some form of psychic ability, but the different kinds of ability and level of skill vary. Ultimately, the level of skill is what sets us apart. Each new skill a Tueri acquires opens new doors to advanced knowledge otherwise unattainable. The combination of knowledge and skill gained over the years is what defines the framework for the Council."

That was only slightly clearer than mud.

"Okay, but who are the Council?"

His eyes cut to her. "The Council is made up of Tueri who have reached the height of their skill level in an individual category of ability. Each member of Council possesses a different ability and specialized knowledge. Their collective guidance is what allows our people to continue to learn, train, and protect humanity."

Now he was making sense.

"That explanation sounds simple enough in theory, but I suspect there's a lot more you're not telling me."

"Like I said before, I don't want to confuse you." He glanced at her before he looked over his shoulder and changed lanes.

They exited the bypass, the off ramp dumping them onto a main thoroughfare. Heavy traffic and flashing lights announced their arrival in the posh party district. Several Hollywood "A" listers regularly visited the restaurants and nightclubs on Columbia Center Boulevard.

The computerized navigator announced, "You have reached your destination."

He pulled into the valet section of the parking lot and threw the car in park. His shoulders twisted sideways. He turned and stared at Saari, his eyes wide with disbelief. "The Chrysalis is the biggest vampire hot spot in town. Are you sure this is where you want to go?"

Chapter Twenty-Two

A valet driver opened the passenger door. "I'm sure. Come on," Saari said.

The line of hopeful clubbers stretched the length of the building. Brogan recognized the restless anticipation on their faces. He'd only gotten into the Chrysalis once a couple of years ago, and that was because his date knew someone who knew someone.

He handed his keys to the valet driver and hurried to catch up to Saari.

Her stare fell squarely on the bouncer blocking the entrance to the nightclub. She walked straight to the front door, like she expected to be let in without question.

The crowd surged forward on a wave of complaint.

She didn't pay any attention. She approached the bouncer standing at the front of the line. "Where's Waldo?"

The man, who looked about as tall and as big around as a side-by-side refrigerator, crossed his beefy arms over his chest and stared at the two of them. "Who wants to know?"

She held up her arms, palms facing the sky. "*Moi.*"

He watched the hulking giant's demeanor change on a dime. Either there was some super secret hand signal going on or the bouncer knew her. He unhooked the heavy chain blocking the entranceway and stepped aside.

She stepped over the imaginary line separating the wannabes from those in the know. The bouncer started to replace the chain, intending to exclude Brogan. She reached out, her fingertips stalling his massive arm with a feather-light brush. "He's with me."

Refrigerator Extraordinaire nodded his head and withdrew the chain long enough for him to pass through behind her.

The crowd yelled obscenities at being kept outside while someone they didn't recognize as a VIP waltzed right in.

The bouncer shouted at the waiting onlookers, but his words were lost in the noise after the club's doors opened. Loud dance music pounded onto the street. The live band's distinctive sound carried on the cool, night air.

The doors closed, cutting off the crowd's reaction.

His eyes adjusted to the dim lighting inside, and he hurried after Saari. She walked between tables, headed for the bar on the far side of the club. Another large bouncer, the Refrigerator's twin, stood at the end of the bar. His massive shoulders rested against the wall, thumbs curled casually around the belt loops on the front of his pants.

She approached the bouncer. He stood up straight, placed his left paw on the wall and pushed. Brogan stared, speechless. The wall moved. A hidden door materialized in the striped décor. A mirrored panel inside the opening reflected the club's neon lights, the replicated colors disguising the barely noticeable space.

This guy may be a bouncer, but Brogan knew he was security, guarding *this* door. And unless you already knew there was a hidden entrance, you would never see it.

So how did Saari know about the entrance?

And why did she have unquestionable access?

He followed her into the corridor without any trouble. Apparently he'd been afforded the special hall pass as her guest. Word traveled fast in this place.

She went straight to a set of stairs that lead to an upper level. A sign on the wall read, "Not accessible to the public." He had no doubt she knew exactly where she was going. He stayed a couple steps behind her as she led the way.

At the top of the stairs, she moved past what could only be described as a viewing section. A glass wall ran the length of the club from floor to ceiling. Lounging chairs and couches filled the room at deliberate angles, so a person sitting in any of them had an unobstructed view of the entire club.

He politely nodded his head in greeting to several people they passed. Seated in groups, the voyeurs watched the human crowd below. His teeth clenched. Vampires filled the viewing room. He moved as close to Saari as he could without actually touching her. He wanted his hands free in case he had to fight his way out of here. His heartbeat raced. Adrenaline sped through his body, leaving him ready to jump at any threatening movement.

Two vampires, even larger than the Refrigerator twins, stood before a pair of thick-paneled doors decorated with an intricately carved design. Each of the vampires sported a duck tattoo, one labeled Huey and the other Dewey. Brogan wondered if these guys were UFC wrestlers moonlighting as bodyguards.

He stopped, expecting Saari to knock or ring a doorbell or something.

"Move," she commanded.

The space before the doors cleared.

His eyes bulged in disbelief when they obeyed.

Without breaking stride, she placed her hand flat against a portion of the door. It swung inward with ease, as soundlessly as the hidden door downstairs.

Looking back over his shoulder, he saw the two vampire bodyguards follow them into the room. This couldn't be good. He turned and looked for Saari, scanning the area for any possible danger. His gaze stopped abruptly when he recognized the man sitting on the edge of a large marble desk.

Brogan made a grab for Saari, but her long strides had taken her beyond his reach. She was moving straight for Nevada's ruling vampire. A cold sweat dampened his palms. If something went wrong, he knew he would never get close enough to her in time.

The vampire smiled in greeting. "Cara Mia, what a pleasant surprise."

She stopped in front of the vampire, pulled her arm back, and slapped him across the cheek. A resounding crack split the air. To Brogan's astonishment, she reared back and slapped him again, hard enough to rock his head back on his neck. A red imprint of her hand appeared on Alarico's cheek.

Alarico's hands shot out, gripping her wrists. "You dare much."

His heart stopped, his chest seized with panic. Alarico would kill her for such disrespect. No way would he stand by and let that happen. He slipped his crystal dagger from his sleeve and raced toward the pair.

"Get your hands off her," he bellowed.

He focused on the vampire holding Saari. There was nothing he could do about the vampires at his back, but he *would* stop Alarico from killing her.

She turned in Brogan's direction, jerking her hands out of Alarico's grasp. Her eyes widened with fear. "Brogan, get down," she screamed.

Without a second's hesitation, he dropped to his knees. A hunting knife flew over his shoulder and clattered against the floor. She flung herself at him. The impact knocked him to the floor. She'd wrapped her arms around him, without touching a patch of bare skin, and had plastered herself against him like a full-length coat. Somehow she'd even managed to keep him from smashing his head open on the floor.

"You Tueri bitch. Did you actually think you could assassinate Alarico?" Dewey grabbed Saari by her hair and yanked her off him.

"Stop," Alarico commanded.

Dewey launched her toward the doors they'd just come through. She slammed into the wall hard enough to crack the plaster. Her leg broke with a bone-crunching snap against the door's casing.

Huey flew at Brogan. Instinctively, he rolled to his side. Cold air kissed his cheek as the enraged man's fist shattered the tiled floor with the force of a sledgehammer next to his head. He shifted the crystal dagger in his hand, gripping the hilt. He thrust his arm backward, trying to pierce the vampire's skin.

Resistance met the blade before the sound of tearing cloth gave way. The blade bit deep into Huey's flesh. A loud *"pfft"* displaced the air—the vampire exploding—and every bit of resistance disappeared. His hand arced downward, the tip of his crystal knife slamming against the floor. The bracing contact reverberated up his arm.

Ignoring the pain ripping through his shoulder, he leapt to his feet. He rounded on Dewey, the vampire that had hurt Saari.

"She'll die first for bringing a Tueri here," Dewey growled.

"Leave her be. She is *intocable*," Alarico roared. Rage contorted his features. Alarico appeared next to Dewey so quickly Brogan barely registered his movement.

The vampire bodyguard ignored Alarico and turned toward Saari. Alarico's hand shot forward, punching through the other vampire's back. He yanked his arm backward, ripping the bodyguard's heart from his body. He squeezed, and the heart turned to dust. The vampire stumbled and then crashed to the floor like a felled tree, exploding on contact.

He stared in shock. "You killed your own man."

Alarico spun toward him, fists clenched with anger. "He broke the treaty. Even if he believed you would hurt me, he attacked Saari after she took you to the ground. That was proof enough she did not intend for anyone to get hurt. The fact that he defied me by hurting her guaranteed his death."

"Brogan isn't here to assassinate you, Alarico."

Saari had managed to sit up, her back against the wall. Her right leg below the knee lay at an odd angle. When she tried to straighten the leg, her lips tightened on a hiss of pain.

He stepped toward the door to help her.

Alarico blocked his path.

"I can heal Saari, but I have to touch her to do it." He lifted his hands in supplication.

The vampire's nostrils flared. He nodded his head once, granting him permission to touch her.

A moment's irritation burned the pit of Brogan's stomach. Saari was *his* mate. She was injured. He shouldn't need anybody's permission to touch her. And he really wanted to know what Alarico's connection was to Saari—especially since he'd just killed one of his vampires for harming her.

He knelt beside her, setting the crystal dagger on the ground next to her thigh. "I need to straighten your leg."

"I know." She whispered.

Alarico sat cross legged on her other side and held out his hand. "I can't take your pain away, but I can help you endure it. Give me your hand, Cara Mia."

She hesitated.

"Squeeze Alarico's hand, Saari. This is going to really hurt," he warned.

"Of course it will." She gripped Alarico's outstretched hand with a groan of resignation.

Brogan placed one hand on her knee, the other under her ankle, careful not to touch her skin. "Ready? On the count of three. One. Two. Three." He gripped her knee, immobilizing the joint. With his other hand, he rotated the ankle, aligning the broken bone.

She screamed as he manipulated her leg. He flinched, wishing he didn't have to cause her more pain. "I'm sorry." Gripping the material of her jeans above her injured knee, he pulled the fabric up and exposed the bloody fracture at her shin.

He picked up the dagger and laid the crystal knife lengthwise over the wound. Brogan opened his healing sense and lowered his outstretched hands. His energy slid into hers like a well-fitting glove. He placed a palm at each end of the blade, wrapping his fingers around her bare leg. A thunderous *boom* filled the air, hammering his eardrums.

Saari's leg shuddered in his grip. Her calf muscles contracted as the bones knitted together with an eerie teeth-grinding crunch. New skin grew, filling the open gash where the bone had protruded through moments before. The hole disappeared, covered by a quarter-sized patch of creased, pink tissue.

"How is such healing possible?" Alarico's gaze landed on him, his eyes wide with surprise.

Brogan released Saari. Her harsh breathing replaced the thumping sound that had filled the room.

"I've never seen a Tueri healer do that before." Surprise colored Alarico's eyes. "I see we have much to tell each other, Cara Mia."

"Yes, we do." Saari let go of Alarico's hand and crossed her arms over her chest. "Starting with why you never told me I was Tueri, and why you blood oathed Mag to keep him from telling me."

Alarico's head tilted to the side.

She shook her head once, her expression tight.

Brogan caught the interplay, noting their silent communication. What the hell was going on? Just what kind of relationship did Alarico and Saari have?

"I believe this conversation would be better had if we all sat down together and included your newest bodyguard." Alarico nodded his head toward him.

Brogan reached for Saari's elbow. "Do you think you can stand?"

"I don't know. Maybe." She stood, sliding her back up the wall to keep the weight off her right leg.

"Lean on me, if you need to," he offered.

Gingerly, she took a careful step. "It's really sore, but I can walk."

There was a slight limp with each step, but he didn't see her wince or hear her make a sound that meant she was in severe pain.

Alarico raised his arm, indicating they should take a seat on the soft leather furniture. He stood before a chair facing the couch, waiting for Saari to sit down. Brogan stayed next to Saari. No way was he letting her out of arms' reach.

The vampire extended his hand toward him. "I am Alarico Montez."

He shook the vampire's hand. "Brogan Vincent."

"*The* Tueri healer. I've heard of you." Alarico released his hand.

Saari perched on the edge of the cushion, and the two men followed her lead. Alarico turned to her. "Mag informed me of last night's debacle. I'm sorry you were injured in the hunt—and again here today."

"Thankfully, Brogan has healed most of the damage. You saw for yourself what he's capable of."

"So I did." Alarico responded.

~ ☾ ~

Saari leaned forward. "So why didn't you tell me I belonged among these people?"

"For centuries," Alarico began, "the vampires and the Tueri hunted the other, almost to the point of extinction. The Tueri's abilities made them as powerful a race as our own. Though they were not as strong physically, their enhanced capabilities, combined with a weapon we were unable to defend against, caused them to be feared among my people.

"Because of that fear, the vampires hunted the Tueri mercilessly. The Tueri retaliated by killing every vampire they could find. This never-ending terror ignited a global war that lasted for thousands of years. A couple of centuries ago things began to change swiftly. The industrial revolution had begun. Larger, better and faster forms of transportation made other areas of the world suddenly accessible. There were also great discoveries being made in the medical field. It was not as easy to hide the battle that raged between our species from the rest of the world."

She listened intently. So far, everything he said tracked with what Mag had told her.

"Our races entered a truce, administered by a joint Council. As mankind continued to progress, both the vampires and the Tueri were in danger of exposure. In a world ruled by mankind's power and greed, both species would be hunted and exploited alike."

"You said Dewey broke the treaty." She interrupted. "Did you mean this 'truce' between the Tueri and the vampires?"

"Not quite." Alarico answered. "The truce became a mutual bond of survival. Representatives from each species worked together to ensure our continued existence. When the Internet came to life, a new revolution began. This time information became the commodity, and it was available from every corner of the world with the touch of a button. Advancements in forensic science also increased the chance of exposure with every new technological discovery.

"We were forced yet again to look at how our existence could continue undetected within the world of man. It was a daunting prospect. Several ideas were proposed before the Council made a decision and implemented it. Suffice it to say, a balance of sorts has been reached, and the two groups now work together to maintain that sense of stability."

Her glance shot to her injured leg before focusing on Alarico again. "I'd say you don't *all* work together. Seems there's some old resentment between our races." A moment's surprise rippled through her at how easily she'd claimed the Tueri as her own race.

"I had not realized until today my bodyguards harbored such bitterness toward the Tueri." Alarico rolled his shoulders, lifting his hands as if to say "how could I have known?"

"Psychotic duck brothers aside, where do I fit into all this?" she asked.

"The vampires and the Tueri work closely together, and you were not known to your people nor did you know of them."

She turned to Brogan. "Is that true?"

"It does happen," he shrugged.

Alarico leaned forward and took her hands within his own. "I knew you would eventually be discovered and brought among the Tueri—or not—for specific reasons. But the ability to give you any information was not my right or Mag's. We could only wait and see if your existence came to light."

The door in her mind opened, the fingers of her gift searching Alarico's emotions. There was more to this explanation than he was telling her, but she sensed no deception on his part. He'd been very careful in Brogan's presence to respect her silence with regard to her curse of immortality, and she could not fault him for staying within the boundaries she set.

But his silence about her being a Tueri—that was a different issue.

"Thank you for helping me understand why you've been silent for so long." She leaned forward and kissed him on the cheek. Then, her voice so low even Alarico would be hard pressed to hear it, she whispered, "But if you ever keep information from me again, truce be damned. I will kill you."

She pulled back from him. His eyes widened slightly in surprise. A weary sadness shuttered them. She had known Alarico for the better part of four centuries, and she had never threatened him harm. His betrayal hurt more than she wanted to admit.

He pulled back and shook his head. She never saw his lips move, but she heard him answer. "*That would be a very foolish thing to do, Cara Mia. We are linked, you and I, for several centuries now; and because it has been so long and our bond has grown deep, you would harm not only me, but also yourself in the process.*"

Before she could ask Alarico what he meant, the air puckered and Dhelis appeared in front of her. "What are you doing here?"

"What am I doing here?" Dhelis's eyes widened in surprise. "What are *you* doing here?" He waved the question away. "Never mind. Alarico, could you please have Brogan's car brought to the Roullier Estate?"

"Of course." Alarico dipped his head toward Dhelis.

Brogan stood. "What's happened?"

Dhelis scrubbed his hands down his face. "I'm sorry to do this to you, Saari, but I'll explain everything later. We have to go—right now." He reached out and grasped her and Brogan each by a wrist.

"Oh, no way. I'm not Riding again."

She stood up and tried to step away from Dhelis.

Her foot never touched the ground.

Chapter Twenty-Three

Light bounced behind Saari's eyelids every time she blinked. Shapes sped past her eyes in a blur of celestial Morse code. When her stomach threatened to relocate somewhere outside her body, she thought she might actually die—for the second time in the last twenty-four hours.

The crazy movement stopped just as abruptly as it had the first time. Her senses whirled like a spinning top. She fell sideways against a rod-iron handrail, barely managing to stay on her feet. Her stomach flopped, threatening regurgitation. Her head remembered she hadn't eaten anything after getting sick at the clinic.

Thankfully, her equilibrium mastered the crazy twirling of her senses. Everything stopped moving.

Dhelis squeezed her arm. "Are you okay?"

"Of course she's not okay. What's wrong with you, Dhelis?" Brogan pushed him away to reach her. "How's your leg—your chest? Anything reopen?"

"Her leg? What happened to her leg?" Dhelis demanded.

"Both of you, stop arguing. I'm fine." She glared at Dhelis. "Other than the lovely nausea that accompanies your cosmic metro railing."

Dhelis's face scrunched in apology. "Sorry about that. I didn't have a choice." He rolled his wrist, checking his watch. "We're due before Council in less than five minutes."

"How did you manage to get them all gathered on such short notice?" Brogan asked.

"I didn't." Dhelis shook his head. "Josie filed a marriage petition this morning. She, of course, neglected to inform me. I only found out when I came to discuss Saari with the Councilor. I had to produce you and Saari immediately to dispute her petition."

"Talk on the way, Dhelis, or you're going to miss the deadline anyway." A petite red-haired woman nudged Dhelis in the ribs.

"Right. Oh. Saari, I'd like you to meet my partner—and cousin—Thana Brunges." Dhelis made the rushed introduction. "Thana's the psychic I transferred to New Angeles with. The one I was telling you about."

Thana stepped forward and shook her outstretched hand. "Nice to meet you."

"A pleasure," she replied, burying her surprise at Thana's familial connection to Dhelis.

"Come on, they're waiting for us inside." Dhelis rushed the group through the ornate front doors. They moved through a large foyer. Natural stone, laid out in intricate, geometric patterns, covered the floor. Her gaze followed the design, finally recognizing the pattern as the Roullier's family crest.

Dhelis canted his head. "This way."

Following his lead, they turned left into a long hallway. He walked through two oversized doors at the end of the stately hall.

"Hey, what did you mean by a marriage petition? And who's Josie?" she called after him. When she stepped through the doorway, her eyes bugged.

She stood in a magnificent ballroom. Crystal chandeliers designed by world-renowned artist Francois Borgeali adorned the ceiling. Gold filigree added elaborate detail at the top of the room. Elegant Italian marble graced the dance floor. Moonlight sparkled through large windows, casting streamers of pale radiance across the room.

She felt like Alice falling down the rabbit hole into the world of beyond the rich and famous. Nothing she'd ever seen before matched the grand scale of opulence surrounding her.

Dhelis and Thana climbed the stairs leading to the upper levels. Brogan walked by her. He casually put his fingers under his chin, and closed his mouth, demonstrating her jaw had physically—not metaphorically—dropped.

She clamped her lips shut. She'd just shown a disgusting worldly naiveté for someone who'd lived over five hundred years. But those years had been spent hiding her existence from the world, avoiding detection. Knowing such affluence abounded was different than *seeing* it firsthand.

Her rational side gave a mental slap to her forehead. The unknown woman named Josie and her petition for marriage screamed for an answer. She rushed after the others. At the top of the stairs they exited the ballroom. The new level presented with yet another hallway. This corridor stood much wider than the first, with several sets of doors along its length. Dhelis and Thana waited halfway down the passageway.

Once they were all together again, Dhelis turned to her and Brogan before opening the door. "I've already talked to Council about what's occurred. They'll want verification, Saari, so you'll be required to touch Brogan as well as me."

"I can do that. That's not a problem." She glanced directly at Thana and then back at Dhelis. "Not knowing what's going on, *that's* a problem."

"I understand, and I'm really sorry about you going into this blind, but we have to stand before Council and present our connection. Now." Dhelis reached for her arms, making sure he didn't touch her skin, and squeezed lightly. "I'll explain everything after the meeting. I swear I will."

She squelched her disappointment at the sensible contact. Now wasn't the time to indulge in a private high-energy connection. They were here to handle this Council business.

Frustration flashed through Dhelis's narrowed eyes. Tension lines pinched the corners of his mouth. She opened her senses, catching a gust of worry swirling around Dhelis. Something big was going on, and he was asking for her help. He didn't need her piling attitude onto his already burdened shoulders.

"Okay." She smiled and squeezed his arms once in reassurance. "Let's go."

Besides, she was curious about this Council that Brogan and Dhelis kept talking about. She had to admit, though, standing before a group of strangers and allowing them to pass judgment on whatever this energy connection was between Dhelis, Brogan and herself was a little intimidating. And irritating.

As she stepped around Dhelis and entered the room, she overheard him speak quietly to Brogan. "Josie's seated in the viewing section."

She really wanted to know who this Josie person was, but she didn't hear Brogan's response. Brogan caught up to her, staying close to her side. They followed the carpeted walkway until he stopped and turned into an aisle on her left.

A thin, blonde-haired woman sat at the other end of the row. Her elbow rested on a crossed knee, leg bouncing with barely-contained energy. She looked at Brogan, dropped her chin on her hand, and grinned like a kid who'd snuck the last cookie from the cookie jar.

Saari disliked her on sight.

Before she could ask Brogan about the woman, he sat down. He grabbed the back of the seat in front of him, his arm blocking any movement past him. When Thana dropped into the seat on Saari's right, she realized they had sandwiched her between them, with Brogan effectively blocking her view of the other woman.

Dhelis didn't acknowledge the woman either.

He continued down the walkway to a podium centered between the ends of a horseshoe-shaped table. Men and women sat at this table, ranging in age from forty-something to possibly ninety-something.

A man seated directly in front of Dhelis spoke first. His elegant robe shimmered in the light every time he moved. "A petition has been submitted to Council requesting mating consideration between Josie Stuart and Dhelis Guidry. What say you in response, Dhelis Guidry?"

Saari's head jerked toward Brogan, her eyebrows lifting in question. Instinctively, she knew the woman on the other side of Brogan was Josie. She leaned over and whispered. "He said mated. Do *they* have some kind of connection like the one I have with you and Dhelis? Because he said he'd never felt anything like it before. Did he lie to me?"

Brogan didn't answer. Instead, he dipped his head toward Dhelis and the people Dhelis was about to respond to, indicating Saari needed to pay attention. An intense wave of jealousy broke over her, swamping her senses with a shocking deluge of emotion. She didn't know anything about Josie's interaction with Dhelis, but she wanted to slap the smug expression off the woman's face.

Her thoughts percolated in the back of her brain like a computer with a program running in the background. She considered the visceral reaction to another woman's interest in Dhelis. The ferocity of her response forced her to admit she was more than just physically attracted to Brogan *and* Dhelis.

That realization held a frightening appeal.

Her thoughts leapfrogged in logic.

This other woman's interest in Dhelis threatened Saari's link with him. Since she knew nothing about the Tueri, her ignorance could only be a disadvantage. She didn't want to consider the possibility of Dhelis's energy bonding with someone else, the link forging an unbreakable connection with somebody else. She had to learn everything she could about the Tueri—fast—if she wanted *any* kind of relationship with Dhelis.

She sat back in her seat and focused intently on the proceedings in front of her.

Dhelis cleared his throat and spoke. "I was unaware of the request made by Josie Stuart, Councilor. I had no knowledge of her arrival in New Angeles or her intention to file such a petition at this time."

Several members seated at the table raised their eyebrows at this, but none made any comment. The man with the shimmering black robe spoke again. His control over the meeting, as well as the white hairs left on his head displaying his old age, suggested to her he served as head of the Tueri Council.

"Ms. Stuart, please step forward."

The woman stood up and sashayed to the front of the room next to Dhelis.

To Saari's complete surprise, the Councilor looked directly at her. "Ms. Mitchell, would you step forward please?"

She stood, wondering what *she* had to do with this petition thing, and moved to the end of the aisle. When she reached the walkway, she hesitated. *What is my role in all this? Do they expect something from me?* She looked first at Brogan and then Dhelis. They both nodded their heads in silent consent, prompting her to walk to the front of the room and stand on Dhelis's right.

Several of the Council members murmured quietly among themselves, and a few commented openly about her sudden appearance and tri-colored eyes. Finding another Tueri couldn't be this important, could it?

"I have been informed there has been a new pair mated?" the same Councilor asked.

"There has," Dhelis answered.

Josie tapped her foot impatiently.

Saari waited for Dhelis to announce what had happened when he touched her.

"There must be an open declaration made by the pair," stated one of the two women seated at the table.

"Ms. Stuart first," the old man ordered.

What? She unconsciously held her breath. If Dhelis touched the other woman, and energy filled the room, what would that mean for her and Dhelis? She hadn't decided what her connection to Dhelis meant, but she didn't want this group of strangers deciding for her.

Her insides churned faster than the wheel on a paddleboat.

Dhelis turned to the woman named Josie and took her hand in his. Nothing happened. He stood perfectly still until the ancient Councilor nodded his head. Dhelis immediately let go of Josie's hand.

Saari's lips parted on a relieved breath.

The Councilor's eyes narrowed. "Now take Ms. Mitchell's hand, please."

Her stomach did a flip-flop.

Her heartbeat filled her ears.

Josie turned toward her, surprised, eyes wide with shock. Her gaze moved back and forth between Dhelis and Saari. "What's going on? You haven't filed a petition, so what's she doing here?" Josie reached toward Dhelis, but he turned his back to Josie and faced her.

"Ready?" he asked. Tension and joy sparkled together in his quiet tone.

The intense look in his eyes set her nerves jangling like musical chimes clanking in the wind. Being near him filled her with a disconcerting excitement.

Dhelis cleared his throat and spoke in a loud, clear voice. "Dhelis Guidry." He raised his right arm straight out, palm facing the ceiling.

Realizing what was expected of her, her voice matched his tone. "Saari Mitchell." She lifted her left arm straight out and placed her hand atop his outstretched palm. Their fingers reflexively curled around each other, tightening their hold and thereby sealing their connection.

The instant they touched, a blast of brilliant light exploded in the room. Ripples of warmth rolled on the energy flowing from their joined hands. Shock and surprise rode bursts of exclamation.

A surge of heat, like a steam-filled blast from a sauna, brushed her skin. Her entire body warmed under the pressure. Instead of pain, desire roared through her in a pulse of energy. She gripped Dhelis's arm, anchoring herself to him. Her gaze sought his.

Silver swirled with amethyst and violet as his eyes darkened with need.

A single, commanding voice rose above all others. "Separate," it thundered.

She and Dhelis relaxed their grip, their hands falling to their sides. They stood close to each other, careful not to accidentally touch.

The Councilor rose and smiled. "Council is satisfied. Dhelis Guidry and Saari Mitchell are declared a mated pair."

Josie gave a stunned hiccup. Her mouth flopped like a guppy on a riverbank, trying to breathe. It didn't last. She quickly gained control of herself. "I'm entitled to a second match of my choice."

"As you are a chimera, a breeder of lineage, our customs so allow," the Councilor agreed.

What was that supposed to mean? Saari's ignorance of the Tueri reared its frustrating head yet again.

Josie turned toward Brogan. "I choose Brogan Vincent as my mate."

Brogan gaped pop-eyed. Despite the seriousness of the situation, Saari was hard pressed not to laugh at such a comical sight. Then her humor fled. She didn't want to lose her connection with Brogan either. This Josie was really starting to piss her off.

Brogan shook his head no in denial.

"Step forward, Brogan Vincent." The Councilor commanded.

Brogan didn't hesitate. He approached and stood on Saari's right.

The Councilor spoke again. Not only his age, but also his aura of presence demanded respect. All eyes turned to him.

"A balance check is always required. Saari is now mated to Dhelis, so she will be the touchstone for Josie and Brogan's petitioned match."

Josie smiled triumphantly, but Saari knew *she* had no way of knowing Dhelis had already spoken to Council. At least she prayed he'd spoken to Council. He'd left the massage clinic to inform them of what occurred earlier between the three of them.

She recalled his earlier comment to Brogan about Josie's petition. She guessed Dhelis hadn't known Josie would be present. And from the look on Josie's face over Dhelis and Saari's match, odds were pretty good she might go ballistic after a second display of energy between her and Brogan.

"Brogan, please take Saari's hand," the Councilor requested.

Brogan glanced quickly at her and winked. Then in a serious tone, at odds with his brief display of lightheartedness, he spoke. "Brogan Vincent."

Just as Dhelis had done before, he raised his left arm straight out, his outstretched palm facing upward. Looking straight ahead at the Council members, he waited patiently for her to follow his gesture.

She had to step forward in order to reach his hand. "Saari Mitchell," she repeated, and placed her right hand in his. His larger hand folded around her smaller hand, securing their connection.

A sonic boom of energy pulsed between them. Another twinge of pain shot through her chest and leg. The moment passed. She knew, without a doubt, she was completely healed. The connection she shared with Brogan created a rhythmic beat in her hand, steady and strong. She looked up at him, wondering if he felt this new sensation as well.

She watched him smile, nodding his head in answer.

Can he read my thoughts?

Startled, she realized the throbbing energy thumping in her hand was her heartbeat—and not just her heartbeat, but his as well.

Their hearts pounded to the same rhythm, creating an energy flow that pulsated farther out into the room with each beat. The first time they'd shared energy had been painful. Now, she basked in the joining of renewed life. This understanding brought enlightenment. The auric meld, the growing strength of its power energized her.

She was simply amazed.

Lost in sensation, she didn't hear the Councilor's command to separate. Only his release of her hand, the break in connection, penetrated the sensory cocoon that wrapped around her so completely.

Josie shrieked in frustration. After being so strongly connected to Brogan, the harsh sound hurt her ears.

"It's not possible. Tueri are mated as *pairs*. Only twins can have more than one mate. This is some kind of trick," she said, her voice dripping with venom.

Several Council members spoke, their rapid hand gestures punctuating the conversation. The Councilor faced the youngest member present. Her white hair and pale skin marked her as albino, making her stand out in an otherwise already noticeable crowd.

The Councilor's hand tapped the tabletop as they discussed in hushed tones what just happened. The word "resonator" was mentioned, again, and she sighed with resignation.

Without saying a word, she stepped forward and, before anybody knew what she intended, she gripped the Councilor's hand.

He turned his head sharply, clearly startled by her interruption. He looked down at their joined hands, and then back up at her. "I did not give you permission to touch me."

She let go of his hand, her forehead creased with confusion. "Isn't this how you discount a resonator theory?"

The albino female answered her. "Just so. However, the Councilor is an empath. If he is unprepared for such contact, being touched could be very harmful."

"That's enough, Tenneile." The Councilor's eyes cut sideways at the woman, effectively silencing any further comment.

With that explanation, she realized her mistake. "I'm sorry. I meant no disrespect. I only wanted to disprove this resonator theory everybody keeps talking about."

The Councilor stared at Saari with hard, unblinking eyes, making her want to squirm with discomfort. She felt like a small child being punished for unruly behavior. In her defense, she hadn't even known she had done anything wrong.

When the Councilor finally spoke, his words were chosen with careful deliberation. "There have been no unjust claims made here today. Saari Mitchell comes before this Council openly. She has employed neither false methods nor projected artificial abilities. She is Tueri, and as such will be recognized and accepted as one of our own."

Dhelis and Brogan both heaved sighs of relief. She hadn't known there would be more involved at this get together than just showing the Council members the energy connection between the three of them. It seemed she was wrong. Again.

To her utter amazement, the Councilor's eyes warmed with genuine affection and he beamed broadly at her. "Welcome home, child."

Then he looked out at the room and spoke to everyone. "A binding ceremony is scheduled two nights from now. Dhelis Guidry, Saari Mitchell, and Brogan Vincent are declared a Trigonal match."

She noticed all of the members smiled as the entire Council stood and answered as one.

"So be it."

Chapter Twenty-Four

Saari watched the council members file out a door at the back of the room, and with that, they were dismissed. It appeared the meeting was over.

Once the door closed, all hell broke loose.

"Is she the reason you've been avoiding me, Dhelis?" Josie accused.

"I've only just met Saari," Dhelis argued.

Josie huffed in disbelief. "Right. You've been here for months, and I haven't heard two words from you."

Dhelis sighed in frustration. "Josie, this is not the time. If you'd called me instead of just showing up, I would have informed you of the situation. It's not as if I knew any of this was going to happen."

Josie laughed bitterly. "*Informed* me? When did we become so formal? You said you needed time. I respected your wishes. I gave you space. I gave you time to decide what you want. And when I come here to surprise you, I discover you've been seeing other people. Sure you would have told me."

"There is no *we*, Josie. *We* are not a couple. We never were. Whatever I do is none of your damn business," Dhelis snapped. "I only told you I was moving and needed time because you cornered me in a public restaurant. And believe me, I needed the time. If I hadn't gotten away from you, I'd have lost my freakin' mind."

Thana touched Saari's elbow. She tilted her head toward the door, indicating they should leave. Though the interplay between Dhelis and Josie fascinated her, she nodded her head in agreement and followed Thana into the hallway. Brogan trailed after them, trying to give Dhelis some privacy.

They made their way back to the front doors without saying a word. The argument between Dhelis and Josie made her feel like she was watching a reality television show—except this was her life. A lot of important, life-changing things had happened in the last twenty-four hours, and now there was an angry ex-girlfriend thrown in on top of everything else.

When the front door closed behind them, the foyer's bright light disappeared. Outside, soft LED lamps chased the night's shadows off the front porch. The full moon hung overhead, its radiant glow a comforting marker in the dark sky.

She stood on the steps with Brogan and Thana, waiting for Dhelis. They were all lost in their own thoughts, occasionally glancing at one another, flashing quick, embarrassed smiles.

"So," she said, trying to decide how to broach the subject of Dhelis and his ex without being too nosy. The situation required a little finesse, though—not her strongest people skill. Better to just throw the question out there. "How is it that Josie and Dhelis were going to be declared a mated pair if there's no energy connection between them?"

Thana smiled but threw her hands up in a "backing off" motion. "Look. Dhelis is family *and* my partner. I'm not going to speak out of turn. He'll share whatever information with you *he* feels you should know. It's not my place to talk about his personal life."

"Since *I'm* also your mate, I'll answer any question you ask." Brogan crossed his arms and leaned a hip against the metal handrail. "If a Tueri has reached the age of thirty-five without being officially mated, then a petition, a request to be mated to another Tueri who has also not been officially mated, can be considered."

"That man, the Councilor, called Josie a chimera. A breeder of lineage. What did he mean by that? And while we're on the subject of Josie, why'd she claim a second match and pick you?" She lifted her chin toward Brogan.

He sighed. "I haven't a clue. Maybe she was pissed at Dhelis and thought a match with me would make him jealous. As for Josie being a chimera, that's a big deal among the Tueri. Her "gift" is the ability to have children with any Tueri male. Their offspring will always possess Tueri psychic traits. Her pregnancies are shorter than a normal woman's, and she can get pregnant again almost immediately after childbirth if she wants to."

"Oh. Wow. That is a big deal. So how come there aren't a lot more Tueri populating the earth?" Her gaze cut to Thana. The woman stood at the bottom of the steps listening, but didn't seem inclined to jump into the conversation.

"Chimeras are very rare. That's why they have their choice in a marriage petition—requesting a match or dissolution, by the way. They get to choose their mates as long as their choice isn't already mated. That's why Dhelis needed you here. Declaring his match with you was the only way Council could deny Josie's petition."

She digested the information, following the thought to its logical conclusion—which lead to a follow-up question. "Can a requested match without an energy connection have children and can only Tueri with an energy connection actually have children with psychic abilities?"

Brogan tilted his head to the side. The emerald flecks in his eyes deepened in color, but he made no comment on what he might be thinking. Instead, he answered her question.

"Any children born from a requested match, if there are any born at all, are less likely to have any real abilities to speak of. Given their genetic predisposition, these children run the entire spectrum. Most children born of such a match will have no psychic abilities at all. For those children that do have limited psychic ability, they have no knowledge of who they really are. It's much safer for them, and us, if they remain ignorant of their heritage."

Her forehead tightened at this last bit of information. She didn't know enough about the Tueri to form any opinion on whether or not she agreed with this practice. She did know what it was like to have no idea who you were and where you came from. The devastating solitude with no family had left her adrift in an isolated sea of existence, floating through life alone, with no connection to anybody or anything.

Brogan's eyes narrowed as he watched her. Several heartbeats passed, his concentrated stare never wavering from her face. Her insides clenched, expecting the inevitable inquiry about her reaction—about her past. Thankfully, he didn't ask any questions.

With his silence, the coil of tightly wound emotions loosened, allowing her to bring her unsettled nerves under control. This subject touched a deep-seated chord within her. She had to hide her emotions better, unless she was ready to spill her guts like an adolescent teenager blogging to the world about every aspect of her turbulent life.

And she was *so* not ready for that kind of purge.

Her thoughts scattered when the front doors slammed open and Josie charged down the steps. She was furious and moving straight for Saari. Brogan had no time to react before Josie barreled right into her, knocking her off her feet and sending her purse flying.

Dhelis raced through the front doors. Before she toppled over, she caught a brief glimpse of him just before the air shimmered, and he disappeared. He immediately reappeared at the bottom of the steps and just managed to catch her and keep her from breaking her neck on the steps.

The instant they touched, light blasted through the black night, blinding in its brilliance. Dhelis gripped her hand, helping her to her feet. She looked for Josie, wanting to make sure another surprise attack wasn't coming her way. To her astonishment, she could see *everything*. Clearly. Everyone else shielded his or her eyes against the bright light.

"I'm okay," she assured Dhelis, patting his arm. "You can let go now. I can stand on my own."

The change was startling when he released her. A velvety cover of blackness enveloped the night once again, the sky appearing even darker after being so brightly lit.

Dhelis stared after Josie. Nostrils flared, chest heaving with each breath. Fury sharpened the angles of his face to chiseled perfection. There was no doubt in Saari's mind Josie had intentionally tried to hurt her. He obviously agreed.

"Enough, Josie." The harsh tone deepened Dhelis's voice. "This is finished." He punctuated his order with a chopping motion of his hand.

Standing at the bottom of the steps looking at Dhelis, Josie smiled maliciously. She made a *tsking* sound. "Now you know me better than that. I don't give up so easily."

Josie stepped toward her. Brogan tensed and Dhelis moved in close, blocking Josie from touching her again.

Josie laughed at their reaction. "This isn't finished. In fact, I'm just getting started." She blew a kiss in Saari's direction. "See you real soon."

She watched Josie walk into the night, feeling a cold spot gather between her shoulder blades and wrap around her spine. That woman was dangerous. She would definitely have to watch her back.

Brogan rushed to her side, his forehead wrinkled and lips set in a thin, grim line. "Are you all right? Did she reopen your wound?"

"I'm fine." Wanting to reassure everybody she wasn't hurt, she pulled the top of her blouse down, exposing the upper half of the left side of her chest. Both Dhelis and Brogan stood gaping at her exposed flesh.

"You're healed," Dhelis said in disbelief.

"It's gone," Brogan echoed in amazement.

Thana just looked on in curious observation. She wasn't sure if Thana knew what the flashy display was about, but the woman wasn't hiding her curiosity. She stood on the tips of her toes, her chin lifted to get a better look at Saari over Brogan's shoulder.

She let go of her blouse, covering herself again. "The cut was mostly healed at the clinic, but when Brogan and I touched in the council meeting, it healed completely."

"I saw your injury, Saari!" Dhelis exclaimed. "Tueri people heal faster than normal humans, but healing *this* fast, that's nothing short of a miracle."

She just shrugged. It was a miracle all right.

"So," Dhelis began, the side of his mouth lifting, "I thought you might have a few questions about what just happened."

Like that wasn't an obvious change of subjects.

She raised an eyebrow. "You mean about your ex trying to kill me?"

"What makes you think she's my ex?" Dhelis responded, not missing a beat. "Because we were never a couple. Not really. I told her I needed time to adjust to having a new job in a new city before working on a relationship. I didn't want her going to Council with a marriage petition. Fat lot of good that did me," he grumbled under his breath.

She smiled. Unaccustomed to the emotion, some of the jealous ache in her heart eased. "I know."

"Who told you?" Dhelis's eyes narrowed, his gaze sliding from Thana to Brogan.

"You did." She answered immediately. "Twice as a matter of fact. The first time was during the council meeting, and the second time when you caught me. The minute you touched me, I knew what you were feeling."

She chewed on her lower lip for a couple of seconds, deciding to change the subject herself. "By the way, did you notice the energy connection seemed brighter this time?"

Dhelis nodded his head.

"I'm not sure," she said, "but I think it was because we were both seriously pissed off. Our emotions made the energy flare, like our link had more power or something."

"I think you're right," Brogan agreed. "When we touched in the meeting, there was no pain. Our joining felt amazing. And once you were healed, the energy grew, feeding on our emotions."

"Exactly."

She looked behind Brogan and saw Thana quietly watching the interplay between Brogan, Dhelis and herself. Too bad she couldn't read the expression on her face. She wondered if Thana felt like a third—well, *fourth,* wheel. She could check, though. Her senses opened a crack, allowing a whiff of Thana's aura in. Anxiety hovered, but no serious jealousy or dislike flared. Not wanting to lose her opportunity for answers, she closed the connection and turned her attention back to the men.

Brogan and Dhelis stood even closer. Her skin tingled. Heat flared in the pit of her stomach, spreading through her body. Now that she was healed, their combined energies upped the attraction factor. She wanted to climb inside them and roll in their strength. She wondered if they felt the same way.

Focus, she told herself, as she tried to control her raging hormones. She felt like a teenager with her first crush. Her thoughts flashed to Miko, and she realized this magnetic pull drawing her toward Dhelis and Brogan was stronger than the first time she'd touched Miko. Now she had *two* different sets of emotions, auric strength, and psychic energies to deal with.

And fighting her physiologic reaction wasn't easy with both of them standing so close to her. The tingling of Saari's skin promised the sweet release of pleasure-filled endorphins if she'd just reach out to them. *Enough.* She shoved her hands in her pockets to keep from touching either Dhelis or Brogan again.

"Okay," she began, pulling her thoughts together. "I think I get it. This energy thing between you and Brogan and I, that's only supposed to happen between two people, right?"

"Uh-huh." Dhelis and Brogan grunted their answers simultaneously.

"I thought so. But there's a name for there being three of us, so this must have happened before," she reasoned.

"Our situation is called a Trigonal match," Dhelis explained. "Trigonal means three sided. The word is a term of art used in connection with gems or crystals. We use the same terminology, obviously, with our Tueri stones."

"Then this has definitely happened before?"

"Yes," Dhelis answered, "though not very often in this type of group formation. There have been several Trigonal matches in the last couple centuries, more so now with the use of fertility drugs—but they always include a pair of twins."

"You and Brogan aren't twins."

Brogan laughed. "We're not even related."

"We are now," Dhelis said with solemn finality.

"Or will be in two nights, right?" She didn't wait for an answer, but continued speaking, thinking out loud. "This binding ceremony, is it a joining of abilities or is it a marriage?"

Brogan started to answer, but Dhelis spoke over him. "The ceremony is a joining of abilities. Once bound—and the Tueri couple learn to direct and project their psychic energy—no one else sees or feels the match's connection. Eventually, the mated pair should be able to use some measure of their partner's ability, though such an achievement takes time and practice to develop the skill."

Saari stared hard at Dhelis. Without looking away from him, she spoke. "Brogan, the term 'mate' connotes 'breed': the procreation of a species. The word also means 'partner.' Is this binding ceremony also a marriage?"

He didn't hesitate. "Yes."

Dhelis swore. "This is a tricky situation, Saari. I hoped to ease you into the Tueri customs."

She continued to stare at Dhelis but, again, deliberately did not address him. "Brogan, do the two ceremonies occur concurrently?"

He answered immediately. "Only at the mated pair's request."

"But the Tueri never have to force marriages. Our physiological reactions guarantee the match," Dhelis rushed to assure her.

She nodded. "Has there ever been a time a pair has been through a binding ceremony, but not married?"

Brogan smiled. "No."

"Well, I guess there's always a first time."

Saari grinned, enjoying the startled look on Dhelis's face.

Chapter Twenty-Five

Saari took a deep breath. "Look, you guys have lived your whole lives understanding what it means to be Tueri and how these matches are formed. I've only known about the Tueri for a few hours. This is going to take a bit of getting used to."

Dhelis crossed his arms over his chest. "Are you saying you don't want to go through the binding ceremony with us?"

Brogan's humor faded behind a mask of caution.

Well crap. I'm not even technically dating them, and I've already stepped on their feelings.

"No, that's not what I'm saying." She laced her fingers on top of her head, struggling to find the right words. "I just met you—both of you. Going from, 'Hi, my name is…' to 'until death do us part' is a huge leap."

Brogan's head tilted to the side. "There will always be a connection between us. Our energies made that choice for us. What Dhelis and I need to know is, are you interested is pursuing a relationship beyond the physiological aspect?"

Energy thrummed in the air between Dhelis, her and Brogan. She yearned to soak up each vibrating molecule and absorb everything there was to know about each of them. That could only happen by spending time with them, under normal circumstances. If she couldn't even touch their skin without some form of psychic pyrotechnics occurring, could they ever develop a relationship?

But dammit, she wanted to see if they had a shot.

So the binding ceremony was her only chance to find out.

She glanced at both men. The vulnerable look in their eyes told her they did, too.

"I would very much like an opportunity to get to know both of you. So, yes, I'll go through the binding ceremony. The rest will have to come with time."

Dhelis's jaw unclenched.

Brogan's shoulders relaxed.

A cell phone rang, the unexpected noise interrupting their discussion.

"Damned phone. It always rings at the worst possible moments." Dhelis stepped away from them and answered. He waved Brogan over to him.

Saari looked for Thana and saw her gathering up the last of the contents that had fallen out of Saari's purse. She'd forgotten she had the bag with her. "You didn't have to do that."

Thana stood and offered a pensive smile. "No problem. The three of you had a lot to talk about."

Shame at being so rude and insensitive poked her between the eyes. "I'm sorry we ignored you."

"You weren't excluding me on purpose. All of you are in this unusual match, and I'm more like an ineligible member of the hottest new group on the Hollywood 'it' list."

"Thana—" she began.

"It's okay. That's the way Tueri pairing—connections work. We're taught from birth each Tueri has a mate somewhere in the world, the other half of their incomplete soul. So even though *I* don't have a mate, I'm truly happy you've all found each other."

"Thanks." She couldn't help feeling a little sad about Dhelis's cousin not having her own mated bond.

Thana stepped toward her. Something bounced off her shoe, and they heard the sound of metal roll across the cement. Thana picked up the object and gasped. "This is the same brand of makeup as the lipstick tube I audited earlier at the morgue."

"Audited?"

"Here's your purse." She handed the bag over but kept hold of the lipstick. "Can I ask you something?"

"Sure."

Thana held up the silver tube. "Where did you buy this lipstick?"

She took the shiny cylinder from her and looked at the casing. "I got it at the Uptown Mall, but I can't remember the name of the store. I'd know the store if I saw it. It's one of those specialty shops that sell mineral makeup. The whole line is perfume-free and hypoallergenic."

"Do you think you could take me to the store tomorrow? I know you have a lot going on, and I wouldn't normally ask, but this is important. The makeup might relate to the case Dhelis and I are working right now, and I need to follow up on this lead."

"Of course," Saari agreed. "We'll have to get together after my shift at the hospital, though. I wasn't there today, so I really need to be there first thing tomorrow morning."

"Great. What time should we meet, and where should I wait for you?" Thana asked.

She looked at her watch. "Is 8:00 in the evening okay? I work 12-hour shifts a couple days a week, 7:00 to 7:00, and tomorrow's one of my long days."

"That's perfect." Thana sighed. "Thanks. Maybe we'll get lucky."

Dhelis palmed his phone shut and looked at Thana. "We've got a missing woman. Her name is Elizabeth Foster. She was supposed to work the closing shift at The Corner Restaurant, but she never showed up. A call came in from one of her neighbors. The witness had gone outside to dump some trash and saw a man abducting a woman matching Elizabeth Foster's description near the Hartford Building."

"That's just a few blocks from the restaurant," Thana confirmed.

"That can't be a coincidence," Brogan said.

Dhelis turned to Saari. "I'm sorry, but we have to get back to the station. Now."

Saari waved her hand, shooing Dhelis on his way. "Not a problem. Go." She turned to Brogan. "Can I use your cell phone? I'll call Alarico and ask how long it will be before a driver arrives with your car."

Brogan pointed over her shoulder. "My car's already here."

"Good. We won't have to wait." Saari rocked back and forth on the balls of her feet.

"I'll call you both tomorrow," Dhelis promised. He stepped next to Thana and wrapped his hand around her forearm. The air flickered for a moment, and then they were gone.

Saari stood at the bottom of the steps, wondering how her life had spun so out of control. She'd gone from not knowing anything about her past to discovering she's Tueri and being mated with two different men, after dying *and* suffering a broken leg. What a crazy week.

"Earth to Saari." Brogan snapped a finger in front of her.

"Sorry, did you say something?"

"Do you mind if I ask you something?" He stood next to her, his hands shoved deep into the front pockets of his jeans.

"Go ahead." Anxiety nipped at her self-control, but she wasn't about to avoid his questions. They had agreed to honesty. He'd held up his end of the bargain. She would do no less.

His words exploded into the silence. "How did you get away with slapping one of the highest ruling vampires? Are you crazy? In fact, how the hell did you just stroll into that place, let alone have access to *his* office?"

Startled by the outburst, a moment's irritation struck her at his condescending questions. Then his tone registered in her brain. He was concerned. For *her*. She wasn't used to someone caring about her—in a relationship kind of way. A warm feeling suffused her body, making her realize how much she missed caring about someone and being cared about.

Lifting her arm, she showed her tattoo to Brogan. "It's complicated, but the immediate answer is I bear his mark." The intricate pattern wound around her wrist, glinting under the outside lights.

"I noticed the tattoo before, but I didn't pay attention to the design," he murmured, studying her arm. "It's beautiful. I've never seen such color and detail. This actually looks like a piece of jewelry on your wrist." He wrapped an arm around her shoulders and walked her toward his car. "So how'd you come to bear his mark?"

She sagged against him with fatigue. "It's a long story. Honestly, I'm too tired to think right now. Will you be working at the clinic tomorrow?"

"Yeah." He nodded his head.

She chewed on her lower lip for a couple seconds. "I have a 12-hour shift at the hospital, and after that I promised Thana I would meet her at the Uptown Mall to show her a store she's interested in. Can we meet up, have a drink, and talk after that?"

"Absolutely. Just call the clinic when you know what time and where you want me to meet you. I'll be around all day."

As they approached his car, headlights came on and lit up the night. She shielded her eyes. The lights blinked off. A door opened, and a tall figure stepped out of the car. She mentally groaned. Now what?

"Saari, Alarico asked me to give you a ride home," a familiar voice called out.

Brogan stepped toward the car.

She grabbed a fistful of his shirt. "It's okay. I know him. Mag's a friend."

He turned, shielding her from Mag. "I'll give you a ride home."

She looked up at him. This had been one hell of a night, and she still had so many questions. It was a miracle she hadn't developed a splitting headache. "You know, I think I'd like some breathing space before I process everything that's happened. I appreciate the offer, but I'm going to have Mag take me home."

A look of quiet acceptance softened his features, his reaction again taking her by surprise. She'd expected jealousy or anger. Instead, he'd put her first and gave her the space she'd asked for.

"Thank you for understanding."

He kissed the top of her head. "I'll be waiting for your call."

She was tempted to change her mind. Call him back and ply him with a thousand questions.

Be patient. She'd have plenty of time to learn everything there is to know about the Tueri. In fact, now that she knew where she came from—and they'd reached an agreement of sorts—she had all the time in the world.

She watched the taillights of Brogan's car until they disappeared in the distance. How odd that she'd known the man for only a few hours, but now that he wasn't beside her, she didn't sense as much of the night around her. She felt like a lamp with a dimmer switch turned down, making room for shadows under the faded glow.

The passenger door of Mag's car opened. "Are you coming?"

He sat behind the wheel of his 1968 Mustang Bullitt. She slid into the seat and smiled. He had on a pointed birthday hat with a party horn between his lips. An ear-splitting grin lifted her cheeks. Without warning, he threw a handful of confetti at her. Most of it landed in her hair. He blew the horn, and the tube unrolled with a snap, echoing in the small space.

"Happy Birthday, Saari."

She laughed at the comical sight, taken by surprise. "It's not my birthday anymore."

"I know. But you slept all day yesterday, and then you had company, so it just didn't seem like the right time…"

"What-ever. You just forgot, and now you're trying to make up for being a lousy friend."

"I'm here, aren't I?" He dropped the party favors onto the seat and flashed a sad face. "Forgiven?"

She couldn't stay mad at him when he turned his "I'm your faithful friend" puppy-dog eyes her way. "Yes."

He winked at her and grinned, seemingly pleased with himself for having avoided her wrath earlier and now managing to get back on her good side—all in the same night.

"I have a question," she said.

He snorted. "Only one? I'm amazed."

"Okay, maybe a few," she amended. "Do you know Brogan Vincent?"

His eyebrows scrunched together as he concentrated, searching his memory. "I've heard the name, but I don't know who he is."

"He's the Tueri healer Dhelis took me to see—the man I was just standing next to."

"Right. I remember," he said, nodding his head.

"Brogan healed me completely."

He whistled. "Now that's something."

"It is cool, but that's not all. Brogan and I—we're mated, too."

He did a double take. "Is that possible?"

"I guess it is. They have a name for our kind of bonding." She rubbed the bottom of her chin, thinking. "Have you heard about anything like this happening among the Tueri?"

He sighed. "I know the basics: who they are, where they come from, varying abilities. But I'll be honest. I don't know all that much about their mating rituals. Those kinds of details aren't discussed with outsiders."

"Well, if you had to guess, based on what you do know, why do you think this happened—me being connected to both of these men at the same time I mean?"

"Who knows," his hand lifted and dropped back on the steering wheel. "My best guess would be your being immortal has somehow thrown a monkey wrench into the way their system usually works. You're a lot older than any of their people, so you probably have the potential to have stronger abilities than any of them. Maybe that's affected this energy connection."

She lowered her hand and ran her fingertips back and forth across the leather arm rest, considering what he said. If she followed the logic behind his thoughts, the theory made sense. It's not like she had any other reason for why their three-way match happened, and the Council didn't give her a reason at all. They all just jumped for joy and accepted the situation for what it was.

Maybe that's what she needed to do.

Just accept their connection for the match it was.

He turned toward her, a worried look on his face. "Are you okay with all of this? I mean, can they force you to be with these guys?"

Her skin tingled at the thought of being with Brogan or Dhelis. The energy connection they shared was much too strong to ignore. Now that she'd felt the power of each, she itched to touch them again—to feel her energy joined with theirs.

She smiled. "No, they can't force me, but that's not an issue. The energy connection chooses the match. I don't mind that part at all. The fact that there are two men—and they both appeal to me—*that's* awkward. There are issues in that whole discussion I'm not even ready to think about yet."

He suppressed a smile. "For someone who's been alive as long as you have, you still hold some pretty conservative beliefs."

"Don't go there," she warned.

"Take monogamy, for instance," he continued, ignoring her tone. "I can see how you would be conflicted if you're permanently involved with two men at the same time."

"I told you not to go there," she grumbled, a traitorous blush warming her cheeks.

"Does Alarico know about you being mated to two different Tueri men?"

"I don't know. Maybe. We weren't able to talk freely about the whole Tueri situation, though. Brogan was with me, so Alarico kept other issues to himself," she answered.

"You'll have to tell them about your immortality, Saari," he said quietly, zeroing in on another issue she really didn't want to deal with. "Sooner is better than later."

"I know." She agreed.

Her being immortal was as big an issue as there being three of them in a relationship. Both men expected more than a "partnering" of abilities. They wanted a life with her. She accepted that. She had even admitted she wanted to go forward with the joining ceremony. She just wasn't sure if she was strong enough to tell them her secret.

"I'd just like to get to know them a little better. It's been so long since I felt like I belonged to anybody, in that way, and I don't know how Brogan or Dhelis will react. If they decided they didn't want a relationship with me, I don't think I could take the rejection after finally allowing somebody to get close to me."

Other than Alarico and Nisa, Mag was the only other person she'd told about the night she became immortal. She'd lost the only man she'd ever loved as a partner the night Heika cursed her. Over the decades, the gulf of solitude and uncertainty about relationships had grown within her isolated existence.

God, she was tired. Even though she had physically healed, the emotional upheaval had left her drained. She leaned against the door, her head touching the window. Her mind jumped from one piece of information to the next, her brain buzzing like a bee searching flowers for nectar.

"A plate of homemade fries for your thoughts?" Mag bribed.

"I was actually thinking about something Alarico said."

"Oh, and that would be?"

She turned her head and looked at him. "Actually," she began, "I was thinking more of *how* he spoke than what he said."

"What do you mean?" he responded, flipping on the blinker.

"I told him if he ever kept something from me again, I'd kill him."

He pulled into her driveway. After punching in the code to her private gate, he watched it open. "What did he say to that threat?"

"See, here's the crazy part I don't understand." She drummed her fingers on the dash, searching for the right words to explain what happened. "I watched his face when he answered, wanting him to know I meant what I said, but his lips didn't move. It was like he spoke in my head, and only I heard his answer."

His head turned sharply toward her, a shocked look on his face. "I didn't know you two had shared blood."

She gawked at him, wondering if he'd sprout a second head. "We haven't. I mean, he's fed from me, but that's all. And the last time was a couple centuries ago when that idiot doctor tried to bleed him, thinking he could drain the evil out of him." She shuddered. "I hate leeches."

"You're sure—about Alarico, I mean?"

"Believe me, the blood sharing has always been a one-way street."

"Did this happen *after* you had already discovered your connection with both men?"

"Uh-huh, why?"

"Well, then the same logic applies. Maybe this new mind-sharing talent is because you're a Tueri and cursed. Maybe this connection has enhanced your abilities. And since you and Alarico are both so old, now he can talk to you in your head," he finished, grinning.

"You know, you're a jerk for reminding me of my birthday, my age, and all the other crap that goes with it," she joked.

"You're immortal, *Nefer Ka*, not inhuman. Don't dwell on what was. Always look forward, anticipating what will be."

She gave him a genuine smile. "Don't get sappy on me. You're the only one who truly gets my warped sense of humor." Leaning forward, she hugged him, tightening the embrace with reassuring familiarity. "Thanks for listening," she whispered, before letting him go and getting out of the car.

He waited in the driveway, she knew, watching over her while she punched in the security code on the hidden keypad. After climbing the front steps, she turned and waved before going inside and closing the door. At the window, she watched him pull onto the street and head home.

Finally, she was able to breathe a sigh of relief.

Nothing had changed between them. Mag had been her best friend for nearly four decades, becoming her chosen family. She was the light to his dark. The healing balm to the stains on his heart. She would always be his *Nefer Ka*, his beautiful soul—and that meant a part of him was still human.

She accepted that she selfishly relied on their friendship.

Immortality really did mean forever.

And no matter what else happened in her life, Mag would always need her.

Chapter Twenty-Six

Dawn, Saturday, May 24, 2032

Clayton turned off his cell phone as he left his house. The high desert spread in front of him, across the Horse Heaven Hills. No people, no noise, his idea of heaven. He jogged slowly, loosening kinked muscles.

Brilliant orange hues exploded against the horizon, brandishing spikes of purples and reds to chase away the darkness. The lightening sky revealed few clouds, allowing the brightest stars to sparkle a little longer.

The suppressing drugs he'd taken had worn off again and his senses stretched, as if waking from a long nap. Frogs and crickets croaked in the distance. A cat meowed, clawing on somebody's back door. Sprinklers kicked on, the soothing *tick-tick-tick-tick-tick-tick-whoosh* accompanying his pounding strides across the dew-covered ground.

Last night's hunting success buoyed his mood. No reports of a missing woman had been on the morning news or plastered across the front page of the newspaper. In the beginning Clayton had left murdered women for the police to find in order to establish Quinn's killing pattern. After that, he didn't leave a trace. Elizabeth's death—and the others—would come to light, but not today. Not before he was ready.

I just need one more night.

Two more victims and one phone call were all that stood between him and becoming Maurika's dominant. After that, he'd be alpha of his chosen werepack.

Well, one victim really.

He already had a woman on his list—Saari.

And he'd been right—she was a threat to him.

Her canceling an appointment with him last night was out of character—would have been out of character if he hadn't spotted her in the bar with Jordan Stevens. Maurika being connected to the psychic explained everything—including Saari's motivation for coming to him.

He considered the logical sequence as he ran over the highest hill in the chain. When Maurika found that mauled camper a couple of months ago, he'd known she would recognize his scent. Clayton hadn't expected the stupid man to be in a private section of the reserve. He'd had no choice but to kill him. With the victim clearly killed by a wolf, though, the camper's death put the entire pack in danger of discovery.

Because of the timing of the camper's murder, she must have made the intuitive leap he was involved with the women disappearing during the full-moon cycles. But she had no proof that could tie the murder to his human existence or she'd have already talked to the cops. Instead, she'd sent Saari to him.

The day Saari had walked into his office, he'd sensed something different about her—smelled the secrecy. She must be some kind of psychic, hoping to ferret out damaging information against him.

As if he'd ever make such an amateur mistake.

Since Saari hadn't gotten anything on him, Maurika had turned to Jordan Stevens—another psychic. Maurika hadn't been confused about who she left the bar with. She'd gone to Jordan's hotel room on purpose. Once she'd smelled Clayton in the bar, she'd intended to lure him after her.

And he had followed her.

If the authorities had caught Clayton with the same drugs on him that were in Maurika's system, combined with the cocktail waitress making a positive I.D., he'd have been screwed. The bitches had followed him from his office and set him up.

Tick-tick-tick-tick-tick-tick-whoosh. The sprinkler's rhythmic pattern pulsed in time with his footsteps. Actions blunted the edge of his anger. Listening to the sprinkler's rhythmic pattern helped him control his anger. He could reason this out.

The only rational assumption for why their plan didn't work was the interaction between the drugs he'd given Maurika and the ones she'd already taken. She must have felt her change coming on and left the psychic's room to protect him. The fact she didn't remember leaving the hotel and thought *she* killed Jordan Stevens tallied a bonus for him.

By taking Stevens out of the equation, Clayton had severely handicapped Maurika's ability to corner him. Saari was her last hope. And after tonight, Saari wouldn't be in the picture either.

Now he just had to guarantee Saari came in to the office this afternoon. He'd capitalize on the *breakthrough* she had regarding The Dream. She'd been playing him the whole time—a fact that pissed him off but good—about her problem. Now he'd use it to lure her to him.

When Saari left his office tonight, he planned to follow her. At the first opportunity, he'd grab her and take her to the reserve. If he didn't get his last victim, he could live with that. This ended tonight.

The sun's rays finally burned the last of the bright colors from the sky, gifting the morning with a pale blue vault that promised a beautiful summer day. He reached the base of Garfield Hill and turned around.

He needed to shower and head to his office.

Even with a plan in place to run his prey to ground, there was a lot to get done during the daylight hours, and the clock was ticking.

Tonight he'd face another evening sky transformed by an infamous blue moon. Now that he knew Maurika was on to him, involving others to actively keep him from becoming her dominant, he had to step up his game.

The stakes had just gotten higher.

Chapter Twenty-Seven

Noon, May 24, 2032

Dhelis watched Thana over their lunch plates. He'd showered and shaved at the station. They'd both caught a few hours of sleep, but the nap didn't soften the edge that always started to show in her emotions the longer they worked a case.

"So, you never told me how you met Saari."

He sighed. "You knew I'd eventually talk to you about what happened. I just hadn't planned on having this conversation so soon."

"If you'd rather not, I understand," she said, giving him an out.

Now was as good a time as any to broach the subject of his mate.

Thana had always been his partner. She'd never really had to share him with anyone. His past girlfriends never counted because girlfriends were different than a mate. Now he had a mate, and some things would change between him and his cousin.

"It's all right," he waved a hand dismissively. "Night before last, I got a call from Alarico—an order of execution for a rogue vampire—and the vampire had been seen in the area. They needed my help bringing him down. Said only a Stone Rider could get close enough to the maniac to dust him. After I tracked the blood-sucking giant to Sacred Heart Hospital, I understood why."

"Was anybody hurt?"

"Other than the couple Donnie had to burn to hide the vampire's trail, just Saari." He took another bite of his Rueben sandwich.

"You're kidding, right?"

"No," he shook his head. "The vampire stabbed her right before I killed him, and Mag—that's the tracker's name—he grabbed her." He set the sandwich down. "You should have seen her, Thana. There was so much blood. God, I thought she was dead."

"Why didn't you take her into the hospital? You were already there."

He shrugged. "Mag said she'd be okay. I mean, he knew her, and he knew where he was going. I just followed his lead. When we got to her place, he went straight to her bedroom. I grabbed some towels out of the bathroom, but by the time I got to the bedroom he already had her stripped and dressed in a nightshirt. After that, we just sat there, watching her and waiting."

He reached for his soda and took several large gulps. His hand shook, rattling the ice cubes, the tremor a visible indication of how badly the memory of what happened troubled him.

Thana's eyes softened. Her lips parted to speak.

Before she could say anything, he continued. "It was only after she woke up that I knew she was a Tueri. I felt this low hum of energy vibrating in the room. You know how...I mean, you saw us at Council. Then she looked at me, and I couldn't breathe. Her eyes...Can you imagine? I'd discovered a Predecessor. I grabbed her hand and—and that's when it happened. Our energies rolled, and then merged, and it was the most amazing thing I've ever experienced."

His fingertips tingled with the memory of touching her. Heat warmed his body, reminding him how his energy had slid into hers, filling the space opened to him, as her energy wrapped itself around him. His senses had burned her energy signature into his brain and he ached with the need to touch her again.

She smiled. "I am so thrilled for you. You've waited for a very long time. How many petitions of marriage have you turned down? I'm glad you did because you were right. Your mate was out there—you just hadn't found her until yesterday."

"Talk about in the nick of time." He rubbed the back of his neck, trying to smooth the hairs raised from Josie's petition and subsequent threat against Saari.

Thana rubbed a hand down her arm. Apparently she wasn't immune to Josie's chilling effect, either. "Council sure set Josie straight."

"Yes, they did." Picturing the outraged look on Josie's face when Council declared his match with Saari gave him a moment's satisfaction. After months of dodging Josie's marital noose, the crazy chick had been served with some karmic justice.

"For an Unknown, Saari seems to be taking all of this Tueri upheaval in stride. Does Saari know she's a Predecessor?"

"No." He took another bite of his sandwich. "Council hasn't given me permission to tell her, and I'm not planning on mentioning it any time soon. We have enough to figure out and deal with as it is."

"So how does Brogan figure into all this," she asked in a carefully neutral tone.

Dhelis tried not to grit his teeth. "The same way I do, I guess." He sighed. "I can't be upset with Saari. She doesn't have any more control over what happened than Brogan or I do. Our connections just happened."

"I suppose," she said, drawing circles in the salad dressing left on her empty plate. "Maybe she's connected to both of you because she's a Predecessor."

He finished chewing the last bite of his sandwich before he answered her. "I thought about that for a long time last night, and I think you could be right. There hasn't been a Predecessor in centuries, so what information we do have about their abilities is as much myth as fact. We don't know what she's capable of."

"At least Saari's not a resonator," she offered.

"Amen to that. I don't think I could deal if our link went beyond just Brogan and me. Hey, I'm sorry I didn't say anything about what was going on right away. Investigating Jordan Stevens' murder has taken every spare brain cell I've got. Honestly, I just haven't had time to really think through everything that's happened."

She squirmed in her seat. Her eyes lowered as a guilty flush colored her face. "I'm sorry. I shouldn't have pushed you for answers about Saari. Your personal life is none of my business. My curiosity got the better of me this time."

He reached out and placed his hand over hers. "I knew you'd talk to me about what was bothering you when you were ready."

She wrinkled her nose at him. "You know me so well. I guess my questions made it obvious I've been worried about how your being mated would affect us—our partnership. I mean, I know it will on some level."

"My relationship with Saari will affect our partnership, but it won't change that we're partners. We're family. Even if we don't know *what's* happening with the other person, we know when something *is* going on, and that won't ever change."

She rotated her hand under his and squeezed it affectionately. "So next time, I won't push. You talk to me when *you're* ready."

"Fair enough," he agreed, pulling his hand back and reaching for his drink.

Thana squirmed in her chair—again. "I can't stand the guilt another minute. My conscience keeps attacking me from behind an unexpected door to my past."

"What are you talking about?" He leaned back in his chair and tilted his head.

"You haven't intentionally been keeping secrets from me. I, on the other hand, have kept one from you."

"This sounds serious."

"Do you remember when I went to my aunt's after high school graduation?" she asked.

The jump in topics confused him. "Yeah."

"I didn't really go to my aunt's. I came to New Angeles to meet Jordan Stevens," she admitted.

He leaned forward and folded his arms on the table. "Okay, I'm curious. Why would you do something crazy like that?"

"A friend at school won an autographed picture of Jordan from the radio station." Her eyes misted over. "When I touched his signature, I knew."

"Knew what?"

She took a shuddering breath and met his eyes. "Jordan was my mate."

His jaw dropped. "What?" he whispered.

"I spent one incredibly passionate night with him, but he didn't know what our energy connection meant. I requested a meeting with Council when I got home. They told me Jordan didn't know he was Tueri, and they were never going to tell him. Connecting him with the Tueri would be too risky because he was so publicly known."

"Oh, man." Dhelis ran a hand down his face. "Thana, you should never have audited that hotel room. Why didn't you tell me?"

Pursing her lips, she shook her head. "It wasn't relevant. Not in what we do as Tueri. I only told you about Jordan because of Saari. Even though I was denied my mate, I've been connected to him for the last twenty years. I *know* what it feels like to find the other half of your soul."

His shoulders dropped as he absorbed her words. How did she survive, day in and day out, knowing she couldn't be with her mate?

"I know you aren't happy about Brogan's connection with Saari, but I also know the hollow feeling of mere existence when part of you is missing. I didn't have a choice. You do. Don't walk away from the miracle you've been given."

They sat in silence for several minutes.

"I'm sorry. I pushed—again. Look, I could have picked a better time to talk to you about Jordan. Truthfully, if it wasn't for your issue with Saari, I would have never said anything. But you tend to overanalyze everything, and I don't want you to make a terrible mistake you'll regret for the rest of your life."

"I don't think I could walk away from Saari even if I wanted to," he finally spoke. "I'm so drawn to her, Thana. The attraction scares the hell out of me. I guess if our match was just her and me, that'd be okay. But it's not. I have to share her with Brogan."

She leaned forward, staring at him. "I would have shared Jordan with ten women if the concession meant I could be with him. I've spent twenty years alone because nobody else could take his place. Believe me, you don't want to live like that."

"I'm sorry," he offered.

"Just think about what I said."

The man at the next table gathered up his briefcase and headed for the door. Before he'd folded his newspaper and shoved it in the side pocket, Dhelis caught a glimpse of the front page headlining the latest disappearance.

His stomach took a quick turn, and he knew the woman was already dead. Looking up at Thana, he said as much. "I don't think we're going to find her alive, do you?" he asked, changing the subject. Thankfully, she took the hint.

"No," she shook her head. "Things are definitely escalating. We haven't had anything to go on for months, and now we've got a witness. I think we're getting close, and that means he's making mistakes. When that starts to happen, it means things are unraveling."

"I know," he sighed. "I was just hoping we were wrong for once."

"That'd be nice," she mumbled.

"Make sure and let me know the day that happens."

Her color brightened a little. "Hey, I forgot to tell you. I'm meeting Saari at the Uptown Mall tonight. Last night, when I helped her pick up her purse, I saw a lipstick tube like the one the Full-Moon Killer is using. She told me the makeup is from a store she goes to, and she's going to take me through it. Hopefully I'll pick up on something."

"If you think you'll need me I can meet you there," he said, reaching into his pocket for his wallet.

"I don't think you need to be there...unless of course you want to be," she teased.

He grinned. "I think this is the perfect chance for you and Saari to start getting to know each other. A couple of women hanging out at the mall? Nah, I think I'll pass. You're not going to need my help." He dropped a tip on the table before they headed for the door. "What's the worst that could happen, you guys end up shopping and talking about me for a couple of hours?"

Chapter Twenty-Eight

Late Afternoon, May 24, 2032

Saari stood in line in the cafeteria at work, waiting her turn to order. Lunchtime had been hours ago, but she hadn't had time for a break until now. A hospital the size of Sacred Heart didn't have non-peak dining hours—more like lulls between each storm.

Despite what some scientists said about the full moon having no effect on people's behavior, she believed otherwise. She'd suggest those scientists park themselves in an emergency room during a full-moon cycle, compare that experience to any other given month, and *then* publish their study.

Her stomach growled, complaining the line wasn't moving fast enough. Even standing on her tip toes, she wasn't close enough to read the specials on the board. A woman carrying a tray walked past her, and Saari smelled the sugary tang of sweet-n-sour chicken. Her stomach voiced its longing.

She grabbed a free newspaper off the magazine rack, hoping to distract her rumbling stomach with brain food. As she scanned the front page, her eyes were drawn to the bold-printed heading *Candlelight Vigil for Murdered Psychic*. An article followed, detailing the murder on May 22 of the famous psychic Jordan Stevens.

Oh. My. God.

Though he'd been killed late Thursday evening in his hotel room, his body hadn't been discovered by the maid until

Friday morning. Police were investigating several leads, including reports Stevens had been seen in the Zinful Bar Thursday night. Her stomach cramped with anxiety instead of hunger. Dhelis worked as a homicide detective. What if he was on this case? He hadn't mentioned Jordan last night—though the opportunity never presented itself since Council issues had dominated their attention.

What if Dhelis wasn't working the case? Should she just wait and see if someone asked her about being there with Jordan? She hadn't done anything wrong. Waiting, though, when she had information, might look bad. Worse, with her new connection to Dhelis, it might look bad for him—like he was hiding information to protect her. She didn't want Dhelis to think she had anything to hide either—from him or about the case.

She searched her purse for the card with Dhelis's number. He picked up after two rings.

"Guidry."

"Dhelis, its Saari."

"Hey. I didn't expect you to call—so soon. I mean, you said you'd be working late." He sounded distracted.

"Is this a bad time?"

"No. I'd hoped to hear from you. I just thought you'd be too busy."

A tingle of pleasure warmed her body at Dhelis's admission. It had been a long time since somebody expressed an interest in her—especially one that she returned. As much as she would enjoy a leisurely chat though, now wasn't the time. This call had a purpose.

"Will you have some free time today? I need to talk to you."

A smile colored his voice. "Sure. I think I can get away for a bit."

"How about five o'clock at the Jittery Bean on Olympia Drive?" She suggested. "They have the best African Rooibos red tea in town."

"Sounds great. I'll see you then."

She dropped her phone into her purse and looked over the specials she was now close enough to read. Before she could decide on a dish, a message played over the PA system, paging her to the emergency room. She sighed and stepped out of line.

So much for lunch.

~ ☾ ~

Saari entered the coffee shop. She searched for Dhelis, nerves speeding her heartbeat.

The invisible link that connected them snapped into place. Every hair on her arms lifted with the frisson of energy.

The connection she shared with Brogan, while intense, grounded her with its strength. Dhelis's energy set her senses on fire, driving their connection to a fevered pitch. She already knew the two of them would create an emotional firestorm.

And oh, how she wanted to burn.

"Saari." Dhelis's voice came from her right.

She made her way to him through the maze of tables. "Hi."

He stood behind an empty chair and gestured for her to sit. A gentleman. Nice.

She slid into the seat and he pushed her chair in. His warm breath grazed her neck as he brought his head next to hers. "Mmmm, you smell good."

Warmth heated her cheeks.

She'd taken a quick shower before she left the hospital, washing away the antiseptic smell that always clung to her after a shift. The fact that he'd noticed the body spray made the effort worthwhile.

He pressed a soft kiss to her shoulder. A delicious shiver gripped her—and he hadn't even touched her skin.

"I already ordered you a red tea, but it should still be hot." The large cup sat on the table in front of her, packets of sugar and honey next to the cup on a napkin. She noted the small, telling gesture. He'd listened to what she said, hearing what she hadn't.

Sizzle *and* perception.

He took the seat across from her. "I'm sorry I had to leave so quickly last night."

"You were needed at work. I understand."

"Those kind of emergencies will come up—both in my job with the police department and with The Council. I just don't want you to think I'll make a habit of running out on you."

"Wow." She tore open a packet of honey and squeezed the sweetener into her tea. "You Tueri are serious about your mated relationships right off the bat."

Dhelis shook his head once. "Sorry. I didn't mean to push. It's just last night you said you wanted to get to know me, and I didn't want you to think I would purposefully put work before you."

"Okay. How about we start something a little more mundane?"

"What do you mean?"

She tapped the stir stick against her cup. "Do you prefer coffee or tea?"

"Oh." His features relaxed into a smile. "Coffee."

"Yuck. I'll stick with hot chocolate or tea, thanks."

"I'll remember that." He chuckled. "My turn. What's your favorite color?"

"Green. Yours?"

"Red."

She smiled. "See how easy this is?"

They discussed various topics, each asking the other questions. Turns out they had very different tastes in music, liked some of the same fiction authors, and shared a love for horror movies with warped humor in the dialogue.

Their conversation turned toward food.

Dhelis's eyes narrowed with calculation. "Breakfast is my favorite meal of the day. You?"

"Depends on my mood. Do you like eggs?"

"Yes."

She twirled her index finger—"Scrambled?"—lifted both hands palm up—"Sunny side up"—turned her hands palm down—"Or over easy?"

He raised an eyebrow. "I'll answer that question the first morning I wake up next to you."

Her hands dropped to the tabletop.

The timbre of his voice had deepened, the husky tone shooting straight to her brain. Pleasure-filled endorphins raced through her body at the mental image of him lying in bed next to her.

"I look forward to your answer."

His other eyebrow lifted. "As do I."

"I cannot believe I said that out loud." She shook her head. "Okay. Time to put the physiology thing between us back in its box."

Dhelis stuck out his lower lip in an exaggerated pout.

"I'm serious." She wagged a finger at him. "There's something important I need to talk to you about.

"I'm listening."

"I met with Jordan Stevens the night he died."

Silence greeted her admission.

Worry over his response—or lack thereof—made her shift in her seat. "Well, say something."

"You didn't kill him." He lifted his hand in a "what else do you want me to say?" gesture.

"Well *I* know that. How do you know?"

"I reviewed the videotape surveillance from both the bar and the hotel. Jordan was seen entering the bar. Sometime later, I saw the woman he left the bar with—and it wasn't you. She appeared later on the hotel video as well."

She laced her shaking fingers together. "So a woman killed Jordan Stevens?"

"Possibly, but I don't think so. Jordan Stevens was alive when the woman from the bar left his hotel room. There's evidence of a man appearing in the hotel, roaming from floor to floor as if looking for someone. When Jordan stepped out of his room, that unknown male forced him back into his hotel room. Neither Jordan nor the male ever left the room. Jordan's time of death fits with the unidentified male's appearance."

She took a deep breath and forced her clenched hands to loosen. "I would have mentioned seeing Jordan sooner, but I didn't know he had died until this afternoon when I read a newspaper. The article mentioned the Zinful Bar. I wanted to tell you I was there because I didn't want you to think I was keeping information from you."

"You showed up on the video entering and exiting the bar, though not at the same time as Jordan—but I'm glad you told me. It means you care what I think of you. It also means you're concerned enough about me to want to protect *my* professional reputation."

Seriously perceptive.

"So, do I need to fill out a witness statement or something?"

He lifted a shoulder. "Depends on your answers to my next few questions. Did you leave before Jordan Stevens or after?"

"After."

"Did you go to Jordan Stevens' hotel room?"

"No." She shook her head. "I went home and went to bed."

His mouth tightened slightly. "Alone?"

She tilted her head to the side. "Who's asking, Dhelis—you or Detective Guidry?"

"Both."

He was jealous. Wow.

"I was alone, but I have a security system that will show when I got home and then reactivated my alarm. Do you need a report from the company?"

He shook his head. "I doubt we'll need it, since there's no reason for you to give a written statement."

We—not you. Did he mean "we" as in the police department or "we" as in him and Saari?

"Whatever you think is best." She sipped her tea and tried not to overanalyze his last statement.

"I am curious about something you said."

"Oh?"

He leaned forward and wrapped his hands around his coffee cup. "I know Jordan Stevens was a reminiscence psychic. Did the meeting you had with him have anything to do with your being an Unknown?"

"What's an Unknown?"

"A Tueri that Council has no knowledge of or written record of his or her existence."

An instinctive warning whispered in the back of her mind.

Her fake identity detailed an upbringing in multiple foster homes—and it was solid. But despite what her driver's license, birth certificate, and other documents read—he was a cop. If he dug deep enough, he might find out it was a complete invention. Then she'd have to tell him about her immortality, whether she was ready to or not.

And she would tell him—everything—as soon as the time was right.

Today, she just needed to give him enough facts to satisfy him. He'd sense the truth behind her words and let the situation be.

"Sort of, I guess. I was raised by strangers with no idea who my parents were. A friend of mine arranged the reading with Jordan as my birthday present. I had hoped to find some information about a half-remembered memory that might help me discover who I really am."

He squeezed her arm, careful to touch only the sleeve-covered portion. "Did it work?"

She resisted the urge to close her eyes and hide her disappointment at the lack of success. Dhelis was a part of her life now. Getting to know someone meant sharing things with each other—good and bad. "No. Some things just aren't meant to be."

"I'm sorry." His thumb traced a path along her arm. "My family's big enough for the both of us. They'll adore you—you'll see."

"That's sweet of you to say."

His thumb stopped moving. "Wait a minute. The reading was a present? When is your birthday?"

She lifted her chin. "Does your mind ever just focus on one thing?"

"Of course. I'm completely focused on you." He put his other elbow on the table and dropped his chin on his hand. "Now answer the question."

"Yesterday was my birthday."

"Happy belated birthday. And just how old—young are you?"

"Twenty-five."

"Oh, Christ." The arm under his chin dropped to the table. "I'm a decade older than you. I can hear the 'you robbed the cradle' comments already."

A giggle escaped.

He's worried about a decade? I'm looking at a half a freakin' millennium.

"When Thana hears about this, I'll never hear the end of it."

"Oh, speaking of Thana, I'm supposed to meet her at the Uptown Mall at 8:00."

She glanced at her phone, checking the time. "It's 6:00. I can't believe we've been talking for an hour already."

"You still have another hour or so. How about we go get some dinner?"

She wanted to stay with Dhelis and keep talking. They had this *connection* that went beyond the physiological attraction. Like when someone meets somebody new, and they know right away they're going to be really good friends—they just click.

If Saari hadn't already agreed to meet Dr. Lytton at his office, she'd have said yes to Dhelis. Her conscience wouldn't let her cancel two appointments in a row. Especially since the doctor had kept his evenings open and stayed late at work to see her.

"I wish I could say yes." She sighed in resignation. "I have another appointment I can't get out of, and I have to leave now so I'm not late."

Acceptance quickly chased the regret from his expression. "Come on. I'll walk out with you."

He put his arm around her shoulder and guided her through the parking lot.

"This is me." She leaned against her beige Explorer.

"You know, tomorrow night is our binding ceremony. If you're having second thoughts, or just feel like talking, call me. It doesn't matter what time, day or night."

"I'm not going to change my mind, Dhelis. I meant it when I said I wanted to get to know you. The only way we can pursue a relationship is if we get this—" she flopped her hand back and forth—"thing between us under control."

"I agree. The sooner I can touch your skin or kiss you whenever I want, the better."

He leaned forward and brushed her lips with his. Heat sparked between them. Light flared—and disappeared as he broke their contact.

Streams of energy swirled against her skin. His nearness amplified the effect.

She brought her fingertips to her lips, pressing against the tingle he'd left. "Tomorrow. Tomorrow night's good."

Chapter Twenty-Nine

Evening, May 24, 2032

A knock rattled the door of Clayton's office. It was well after 5:00, when his secretary always locked everything up for the night and left. He checked the clock. 6:30.

Saari had arrived.

Once she's under hypnosis, I'll find out what she and Maurika planned for me.

He walked up front and saw her through the glass door. A small burst of pleasure warmed him at her appearance.

Usually, Saari showed up at his office dressed in hospitals scrubs, her hair scraped back in a ponytail. Not today. A pair of trendy jeans and a bell-sleeved, pastel-colored blouse replaced her drab work clothes. Her hair hung past her shoulders in loose waves. Even the sweet, vanilla smell of her shampoo complemented the spicy, exotic scent of her body wash.

She's dressed to impress—for someone else or as part of a plan involving me?

He opened the door. "Saari, I'm glad you could make it. I hope you're feeling better?"

"Much, thank you."

He led her back to his office and gestured toward her normal chair. After she sat, he took his place behind his desk. His notebook already lay open, waiting to be filled with detailed notes of their session. "Why don't we jump right in, shall we?"

"Okay."

"Yesterday, May 23, was the big date. By the way, happy birthday." He made sure to smile.

"It turned out to be a really good day."

"In your message last evening you mentioned taking some sleeping pills in order to rest, and apparently they worked because you didn't have The Dream before you called me, correct?"

Her chin dipped in acknowledgment.

"Did you take any sleeping pills last night?"

"Actually, no, I did not." As she sat back in her chair, a 100-watt smile lit up her face.

He noted her use of formal language, as well as the gestural retreat. Both responses pointed to secrecy. *She's hiding something all right. How did I miss the tells before? The bitch should have been an actress.*

"And I didn't have The Dream last night." She lifted both her hands in a "can you believe it?" gesture. "That's got to mean I'm making progress, right?"

"That's a definite possibility." He added her remarks to his file notes.

"Then do you think I'm just following my normal pattern? I mean, I generally stop having The Dream once my birthday passes. This year's been different though. Since I began seeing you, every time I slept I had the nightmare. Do you think I'm going to start having it again?"

He pictured Saari's naked, dead body, posed on the stone altar at the wolf reserve. Long, raven-colored locks framed her face, the soft curls kissing her shoulders. Her empty, tri-colored eyes stared through him.

None of the other *human* women were like her. Her connection to Maurika made his choice to use her as the centerpiece of his work even more special. Saari would be his *pièce de résistance.*

I promise, you'll never dream again.

"That depends, I suppose." He set his pencil down and lowered his hands to his desktop. "Let's break this down. You've had this recurring dream every year since your fiancé died. As I mentioned at our last session, the fact you kept having The Dream over and over meant you were subconsciously working out *why* you were having this dream in the first place."

She nodded. "That makes sense, but it doesn't explain why the last two times I've slept I haven't had The Dream. I don't understand why it stopped."

"Something has occurred in your life recently that changed the reason you usually have The Dream." He picked up the crystal orb he used when hypnotizing his patients. With practiced ease, he rolled it back and forth across his palm, creating swirling prisms of light.

"I don't know of—any change..." Her eyes, following the orb's path, widened.

She's mine now.

He smiled with vicious satisfaction.

"Let me in. *Tell me everything.*" His voice resonated with a deeper inflection, delivering the trigger phrase in a soft but commanding tone.

Her gaze shot to his face. "Tell you everything about what?"

The orb slid off his hand and bounced onto the desk. He managed to catch the rolling piece of crystal before it fell off the edge and shattered on the floor. *Why didn't the trigger work?*

And he'd misinterpreted her physical response.

He had to be more careful. Nothing about Saari was as it seemed.

"You never finished your sentence, and your eyes widened as if you'd thought of something. Any information could help explain the change in your habitual pattern. The smallest detail could be vital."

Her lips closed and her eyes narrowed with hesitation.

Clayton set the orb on its pedestal and rested his chin on his folded hands. "You've had a tremendous breakthrough, Saari. Now is the time to push forward. You said you came to me because you needed to know why you kept having The Dream. You may have already discovered the answer and just haven't realized it yet."

"Well, I did meet someone." She tugged at her ear.

Indecision. It's a man, and she's unsettled about his role in her life.

"Is this person merely a friend or has a romantic involvement developed?" He waited for her to work through her thoughts.

"We're sort of dating. It's just he reminds me so much of Mi—Michael. His touch is familiar, but so different at the same time. Does that make any sense?" Her head tilted slightly, as if she was truly interested in his opinion.

Damn she's good, imparting just enough truth to make her story plausible. But I'm better. I'll beat her at her game.

"How long have you been dating?"

"Not long." She hedged.

He nodded once. "If the man truly reminds you of Michael, you'd have a natural attraction already grounded in familiar emotions. Because the man can't be Michael, the differences in personality will be more evident. That fact you've just started seeing this man accounts for your uncertainty."

"So you're saying I should stop comparing one man against the other?"

"Well, only in the sense that it hinders your ability to be objective."

Her eyebrows scrunched in confusion. "I don't understand."

"We are all attracted to individuals for different reasons: physical attributes, personality traits, intellectual acuity. Some men like blondes. Some women prefer tall men. Whatever the preference, an overlap of traits will occur in every relationship a person has. Just make sure you're seeing each person as they are, not who you want them to be."

"I see how that could become a negative obstacle that damages a relationship—or in my case sabotages the mere possibility of even having one." She leaned forward in her chair and rested her forearms on her knees. "That still doesn't explain why I keep having The Dream."

Maurika was smart to send someone with a real problem. That's why Saari initially fooled me. Her recurring dream is real.

"When was the last time you allowed yourself to love someone—let them become a part of every facet of your life without holding back any part of yourself?"

She inhaled sharply and straightened. "Not since Mi— Michael. Not since Michael died."

"And why is that?"

"Because I didn't believe I'd ever find real love again. Not after what happened." A tear slipped down her cheek. "Is it really that simple?"

He chuckled softly. "Nothing is ever simple. Look how long you've been working toward a resolution. So many hurdles stood in your way: grief over Michael's death, the pain of his loss, the fear of being alone. All of those emotions prevented you from looking forward—from moving on."

"You're right, and the point is so obvious. How did I not see all this before?"

"You weren't ready to face these issues. Now that you've moved past them, looking behind always seems easier than looking forward."

Saari stood and grinned at him. "I feel lighter. Like some burden I didn't even know I carried has lifted. Thank you for that."

"My pleasure."

She turned to leave. When she reached his office doorway, she looked back over her shoulder. "At our first session, I didn't believe you could help me. Kind of ironic isn't it, this power of belief?"

He watched her disappear into the hallway, heard the front door close behind her. Professional pride buoyed his mood. His notes would detail Saari's breakthrough, her personal realizations, and positive attitude toward her new relationship. When he had time tomorrow, he'd finish his visit report.

After placing her file into the drawer, he locked the cabinet and hustled downstairs to the parking lot. Saari's tan SUV pulled onto the street and stopped for a red light. He slid behind the wheel of his car and tailed her.

His thoughts jumped ahead, working out how things would go once Saari's body was found. Her last days would be investigated. That path would lead to *his* door. His subpoenaed files would provide the press with a beautiful tragedy.

Saari's emotional issues over the death of her fiancé brought her to his office. Their subsequent sessions helped her overcome her fears, allowing her to meet someone and begin a new relationship.

Another young, vibrant woman killed before she had a chance to live.

The press would crucify Quinn, the public finding him guilty of Saari's murder before he ever sets foot inside a courtroom.

The light turned green.

Maurika and the pack were his.

All I have to do is kill Saari.

Chapter Thirty

Saari pulled into an empty space and threw the Explorer into park. She glared at the dashboard clock in frustration. It had taken her almost an hour to get across town. She'd left Dr. Lytton's office in plenty of time to meet Thana at the Uptown Mall. But traffic had been a mess. A wreck on 395 took out two of the five lanes, snarling the exit for the other highway she needed.

She sprinted for the mall's parking lot elevator. The slim hope of catching the lift before its doors closed increased her stride like a runner's last burst of speed during a fifty-yard dash. She squeezed between the doors just before they shut. Leaning against the side rail, she muttered between each panting breath about lousy drivers, the need for better highways, and general frustration at being late.

She'd told Thana she would meet her in the food court at the Uptown Mall at eight o'clock. It was 8:40, and she didn't have a number to try to reach her. Dhelis's phone had gone straight to voice mail when she'd tried calling him.

"Late and impolite" was not the kind of first impression she wanted to make on Dhelis's cousin.

The elevator doors opened. A harassed-looking mother tried to wrestle her exhausted toddler into a package-laden stroller, nearly crashing into Saari as she passed. Stepping around the frustrated parent, she moved through the crowd, walking at a brisk pace. She scanned the groups of people seated at tables in the center of the food court, searching for Thana's bright red hair.

Since she was more than half an hour late, maybe Thana had already left. No. She had said the makeup was somehow connected to a case the police were working on. This was an important lead. Thana wouldn't have left.

She kept looking. She'd almost given up, when a rather large man rose and left the table where he'd been eating. There Thana was, seated at a small table for two, her hands folded in her lap. A half-empty bottle of water sat on the table before her. Thana faced the opposite entrance to the food court when Saari approached the table.

"I am so sorry. I hate being late. I didn't have your number. There was a pileup on the highway, and I couldn't get a hold of Dhelis to get a message to you." She blew a strand of hair away from her face and dropped into the chair opposite Thana. Her forehead wrinkled, "Did I already say how sorry I am?"

"Yeah, you did." Thana smiled. "It's okay. I hadn't thought to give you my number either, so I share the blame."

A couple carrying plates heaped with piles of marinara spaghetti topped with spicy meatballs sat down at the table next to them. The garlic and sweet basil scent from their dinner wafted over Saari. Her stomach growled—loudly—causing both the man and woman, along with Thana, to stare at her.

"Excuse me," she mumbled. "The emergency room never emptied, so I didn't get a lunch break."

Thana looked at her watch. "The stores don't close 'til 10:00. We have plenty of time. Why don't you get something to eat?"

"You're sure? You don't mind?" she asked, praying Thana wasn't just being polite.

"Go ahead."

She didn't waste another second. After heading straight to the Thai food counter, she ordered a combination plate with pad Thai noodles, and a large water bottle.

When she got to the register to pay, she reached for her purse and felt nothing but air. She'd been in such a hurry to get inside the mall, she'd left the suitcase she normally carried as a handbag stuffed under the seat in her Explorer. Patting her front pockets revealed her keys and a piece of gum. With a triumphant smile, she remembered the cash she'd meant to buy lunch with lay folded in her back pocket. She had just enough to cover dinner.

The instant she got back to the table, she picked up her chopsticks and ate as fast as she could shovel the food into her mouth. Her stomach rumbled in constant complaint, and she tried to fill it so it would stop making noise.

Thana sat patiently, not saying a word.

Less than ten minutes later, she finished her food, leaned back in her chair and heaved a large sigh. "Much better. I was so hungry, I was starting to get a headache."

She glanced around the food court. Though there were several empty tables, theirs was still surrounded by people close enough to overhear their conversation. She leaned forward in her chair. "If you're ready, I can take you through the store."

"Perfect."

Saari left the table and dumped her garbage. Thana finished her water and followed her. She held the trash flap open for Thana to toss her empty container.

Although the mall closed in an hour, she was surprised at how many people milled around, drifting in and out of stores. She waited for a break in the traffic, and spoke quietly to Thana.

"You said this makeup store might relate to a case you and Dhelis are working on. Are you allowed to talk about it?"

Thana looked sideways for a minute before answering. Saari figured she was deciding how much she could tell her. "Thank you for understanding the need to be discrete. This is an active investigation, and I don't want any leaks to be attributed to any of my—" her fingers made quote marks in the air "—*unorthodox* methods."

She wasn't sure how to respond to the statement laced with emotional undertones.

"Look, you're Tueri. And you're mated to both Dhelis and Brogan. I have no idea how that kind of match happened—we're all still trying to figure that out—but since I'm Dhelis's partner, and his only local family, you and I should get to know each other."

She breathed an internal sigh of relief.

Thana's admission bridged the gulf between the Tueri world and her mostly solitude existence. A soft flutter of happiness settled in her heart at Thana's offered branch of friendship. And since she knew virtually nothing about the Tueri, having a Tueri friend—one not ruled by testosterone—to help her understand where she came from would be a blessing.

Thana took a deep breath. "Trust has to start somewhere, so here goes. Have you been following the news about the Full-Moon Killer?"

She nodded her head, not wanting to interrupt Thana now that she was sharing information with her.

"Well, the bodies we found several months ago had a particular characteristic unique to this killer. There is always a tube of lipstick found with the victim, always the same color, and the lipstick has only been used once—worn by the woman killed. Until now, we haven't been able to figure out where the makeup came from."

She considered this information. "My lipstick tube was the same kind then?"

Thana's forehead creased. "Well, your lipstick tube was very similar. It had an identical feel. I think it's the same manufacturer. I'm hoping to get information about the tube I'm looking for. This store is probably a long shot, but I'll take any help I can get at this point."

Both women lapsed into silence as they walked toward the west wing of the mall. Most of the people on their side of the walkway moved in one direction like a centipede on an escalator, and they followed along the same general path behind them.

Sooner than expected, they reached their destination.

Saari stopped in front of some open glass doors. "This is Splendor, the store I told you about last night. Do you want me to show you where the lipsticks are, or do you just want to wander through on your own so I don't interfere with your work?"

Thana smiled. "I think it would be better if I looked around alone. If you could stay close by, though, in case I have any questions, I'd appreciate it."

"Sure." She waited until the other woman passed her and entered the store before she went inside. She knew Thana was a psychic, but she wondered just what kind of psychic she was. The whole time they had been together, she noticed Thana kept her hands in her pockets or on her arms crossed over her chest. She hadn't touched anybody or anything all night.

Now, Thana touched everything. Her fingers trailed along the items of makeup on display. She moved around the front counter, finally stopping before the lipstick case. All of the tubes were testers. A cup full of Q-tips perched on the display case for would-be customers to use in order to find just the right shade.

One by one Thana lifted the tubes, opening them to look at the color hidden inside. She took more time when she came across a bright red shade of lipstick. She ran her fingers over the entire cylinder, inside and out, finally smearing some of the shade onto her skin.

Saari looked at the saleswoman, wondering if she would admonish Thana for not following the rules about only using the Q-tips. The clerk was busy helping a man at the front register, oblivious to Thana's etiquette *faux pas*.

A low, feminine chuckle told her the clerk had more than a commissioned interest in her customer. She leaned forward over the counter—and Saari did a double take. Doctor Lytton, the head shrink she'd been seeing, smiled politely at the clerk.

What is he doing here?

Saari stepped behind the tall makeup display. She *so* did not want to have a conversation with him in front of Thana. How was she supposed to explain her reason for seeing a therapist?

"Well you see, Thana, it's like this. I told my doctor I was having dreams about an ex-fiancé killed during a robbery. Michael and I were engaged. But I've really been having recurring dreams about Miko, the only man I've ever loved— who is not the fiancé I told the doctor about—and the night Miko died.

Since she had just been declared Dhelis's—and Brogan's— mate, that would be an awkward moment.

Not to mention the whole "I'm immortal" issue.

Better not to take any chances.

She kept a wary eye on the front counter while following Thana's progress from behind the display. As long as she kept the barrier between herself and the front counter, Doctor Lytton wouldn't see her. She had enough on her plate to deal with, without having to discuss some very private details of her life.

Thana put another lipstick back and slowly worked her way around to the last display, this one holding colored lip glosses. She shook her head, and Saari assumed nothing had caught her attention. With a determined expression, Thana headed for the front counter where the saleswoman stood.

Thankfully, Dr. Lytton had already walked out the front doors. The clerk watched him with an appreciative gleam in her eyes that made Saari want to gag.

When he rounded the corner and moved out of sight, the clerk glanced across the counter at Thana. "Can I help you?"

"Are those two displays the only lipsticks you have in stock?"

The saleswoman pasted her best friend "I work on commission" smile on her face. "We carry over 100 different shades. I'm sure we can find something that flatters your beautiful complexion."

Thana read the woman's nametag. "I'm sorry, Ellen, I didn't make myself clear. I meant to ask if those are the only displays that hold testers for the general public to try."

"Oh," Ellen said, now understanding what she meant. "Yes, they are. But we also carry an extended-wear line of lipsticks. Those are kept up here at the counter where we do scheduled beauty appointments."

"I see."

She interpreted the frustrated look on the psychic's face as "this trip is a bust." Too bad Thana hadn't found the lipstick she was looking for. The makeup lead might have broken her case wide open.

"The extended wear lipsticks are from a different line than the ones we have out on display."

"They are?" Thana's voice rose with interest.

Saari noted the change in Thana's tone. A small burst of excitement sparked in the back of her mind. They might find some helpful information about the lipstick manufacturer after all.

"I'm looking for a specific shade of red, and I was hoping your store carried this color," Thana mused.

"Do you know the name of the shade you're trying to find?" Ellen asked, her tone politely helpful.

"No." The psychic shook her head. "But I'd know the color if I saw it. Could you show me whatever reds you carry in the extended-wear line?"

Ellen reached under the counter and pulled out a tray of lipstick tubes. After picking out three, she handed them to Thana.

Thana returned the first two, indicating they weren't the right shade. When she opened the third tube, her grip tightened on the cylinder. Thana nodded once in her direction, letting her know she'd found an exact match. She looked at the bottom of the cylinder and read the name given to that particular color aloud. "Dramatic Red."

Of course it is. She almost snorted.

"I love this color," Thana gushed to Ellen. "It's just so sexy, you know?"

Ellen laughed, eyes rounded with astonished camaraderie. "That's exactly what the man that was just here said. He bought two tubes for his wife."

Dr. Lytton was married? Saari hadn't noticed a ring. Of course, she wasn't looking for one.

"You mean the guy that was at the register as I came in?" Thana leaned against the counter, testing its surface. Her lips tightened.

"Yep," Ellen responded.

"Did he buy anything else? I mean, anything that might go with this shade of red?" She asked easily, as her fingertips skimmed across the credit card pad.

The other woman looked at her funny for a couple of seconds. Saari figured Ellen must be a commissioned employee because she answered, shooting for an up-sell. "No. I gave him our newest perfume tester to smell, but he said his wife didn't wear perfume."

Thana traced the lettering on the perfume bottle sitting on the counter. When she picked it up to smell its fragrance, her eyes rounded with surprise. Thana stared at her, tilted her head towards the door, and then quickly put the bottle down.

Bingo.

Thana flashed her badge. "Ellen, I'm Detective Brunges, and I need to know if that man gave you his name or paid with a credit card?"

Ellen's eyes widened and she stepped back from the counter. "No. I don't know who he is, and he paid in cash. Why?"

"Thank you for your time, Ellen. I'm sure I'll be back." Thana walked out of the store without looking back.

"You're welcome. Have a nice evening." Ellen called after her.

Saari exited right behind her. Once they reached the middle of the walkway, her new friend turned and faced her.

"Did you see the man at the counter when we went into the store?" she asked abruptly.

A sick feeling grew in the pit of her stomach. "Yeah. Why?"

"Because I need to find him. *Now*. He's the Full-Moon Killer, and I have to stop him before he kills again tonight."

Her jaw dropped.

Thana took off, darting around people in her way, missing Saari's response.

Doctor Lytton was the Full-Moon Killer?

She raced after Thana, alternately looking for her shrink's sandy, blond-colored hair or the psychic's bright red among the crowd. The east wing of the mall emptied into another section. She spotted Thana heading for the east exit at the other end of the stores. Lytton must have already left the mall.

When she got to the parking lot, Thana's hair floated behind her as she chased Lytton at a dead run.

Saari had realized what Thana was going to do the instant her own feet hit the pavement, and veered off to her right. Her Explorer was only parked two rows away. Keys in hand, she clicked the button on her remote and started the engine.

"Stop. Police." Thana shouted over and over.

He turned his head in Thana's direction. When he saw her running toward him, he ran in the opposite direction. Car lights flashed from the very end of the last row, adjacent to the street exit facing the highway onramp.

Thana poured on speed, trying to get closer to the car. His brake lights came on. He'd started the car. There was no way Thana was going to catch him.

Speeding through the parking lot, she turned into the row next to Thana less than 30 seconds later. Thana turned to the side sharply, obviously hearing a vehicle approaching fast. When Thana realized it was her, she smiled and dashed over to the Explorer. Opening the passenger door, she dropped into the seat.

"He just made the light, heading for the highway. I think we can catch him."

Saari stepped on the gas, squealing the tires. "I know we can, because if we lose him, I know where to find the bastard."

"*What?*"

She turned toward Thana. "He's a..."

"Look out!"

A car turned into the parking lot in front of them. She swerved toward the pedestrian-free sidewalk, bounced over the curb, swung the Explorer into the on-ramp lane and kept moving.

Though the light was red, she didn't slow down. A quick look in both directions was all she needed to find a hole in traffic. She jerked the steering wheel to the left, avoiding a turning Jeep. A hard pull to the right took them out of the oncoming-traffic lane. The quick maneuvers made the Explorer fishtail to the left, between two more turning cars.

With a determined smile, she corrected their drift and roared onto the highway.

Chapter Thirty-One

Saari risked a quick look at Thana. Her seatbelt was already buckled. She held the handrail with her right hand and her cell phone open in her left. Her head turned toward Saari, her mouth tight with anxiety.

"He's only ahead of us by a mile or two. When you're within a quarter mile, just pace him. I don't want to spook him."

She nodded, holding the steering wheel in a white-knuckled grip. "I won't lose him."

They'd only been driving for a couple of minutes, trying to get close enough to make sure they tracked Dr. Lytton's car. The gods of justice had smiled on them, aiding their pursuit. Lights from buildings flanking both sides of the highway lit the roadway. Rays of moonlight illuminated the night sky.

She spotted the white Honda up ahead. Thana was still on the phone with Dhelis, urgently updating him on their situation.

Not wanting to startle her, she reached over and tapped Thana on the knee. Once she had her attention, she pointed out the front windshield toward the tail lights up ahead. Thana's head nodded, letting her know she'd seen the car.

"Tell him your killer's name is Doctor Clayton Bishop Lytton."

Thana's eyes narrowed in speculation. "And you know this how?"

She stared out the window, eyes glued to the doctor's car. They'd reached the outskirts of the city. The fruit plant marked the last bit of industry before the highway meandered past acres of rolling hills out toward Nowhere's Ville.

She managed to keep from sighing with resignation. "I've been seeing the therapist about some recurring dreams. I recognized him in the store, but didn't know he was your bad guy until you told me."

"Did you hear all that, Dhelis?" Thana asked. "Serious? How am I supposed to know where he's going?" Her eyebrow lifted. "Saari, Dhelis asked if *you* know where he's going?"

"No, I have no clue where he's headed."

Thana checked her wristwatch. "We've been driving for less than five minutes. We're heading out of town, moving east on I-50."

She saw Thana shake her head no. Then apparently realizing Dhelis couldn't see her, she answered his question out loud.

"There is no place for me to drop her off. We're moving out toward the middle of nowhere."

Dhelis's voice crackled through the phone. Once she'd told them the killer's name, he nearly shouted everything he said after that.

So much for the gods smiling on her.

They'd merely been toying with her. The Full-Moon Killer was her shrink.

"Look, I think you should get Brogan just to be on the safe side. You can bring him with you. Start heading our direction, and I'll call you as soon as I know where we're going."

Thana snapped her phone shut and tapped it on her knee. She didn't have to be a genius to realize the sharp, staccato beat telegraphed Thana's suspicion. She snuck a quick glance. Thana gazed out the front window, watching the car up ahead. She spoke without turning her head.

"How long have you been seeing this doctor?"

Her fingers tightened on the steering wheel. "Three weeks."

"I don't mean to be insensitive, but I need to know why you were seeing him. If we can't keep you out of this, the police department will be all over your connection." Thana's head tilted to the side, giving her the full weight of her stare.

She hated lying to her new friend, but she couldn't tell her the truth—the *whole* truth anyway. But she could give her enough. A legitimate reason the police could verify. "A few years ago I was engaged to a man named Michael Cohen. We were eating at an outdoor café when the bank at the end of the block was robbed. Michael was killed during a shootout between the police and the robbery suspect. Yesterday was the anniversary of Michael's death. For weeks now, I've been dreaming of that day, watching him die."

Thana's fingertips brushed her arm with a feather-light touch. "I heard about that tragedy. I'm sorry—sorry for your loss, and sorry that I had to ask."

She nodded—then shoved aside a heaping dose of guilt for using Michael's death as a diversionary tactic. This was not the time to dwell. They had other issues to deal with. "I understand. My therapy worked out at the end, but I had my doubts at the beginning of our sessions. They didn't seem to be working."

Thana's forehead creased, a flicker of caution showing in her eyes. "What do you mean?"

"The dreams didn't go away. They got worse and came more often. In fact, every time I slept I had the dream—until last night. Doctor Lytton really helped me tonight, though. I had a session with him before I met you at the mall. He helped me realize it's time for me to move forward."

"Wait a minute. You met with Lytton right before you met me at the mall?"

"Uh-huh. Why is that important?"

"Because it's too coincidental that I 'stumbled' across your psych, the Full-Moon Killer, right after he had a session with you. Jesus, Saari. He was probably following you, planning to target you as his next victim. Now you're in a vehicle with me following him. I might as well hand you over trussed in a red bow." Thana shook her head. "Dhelis was right. This is too dangerous. Pull over, and we'll wait for backup. They can go after Doctor Lytton."

"No way," she exclaimed. "He bought more lipstick—two tubes. Why would he do that if he was setting me up as his next victim? Especially since he left before we did. He must have already snatched his next victim, and we have no idea where he's going. If he kills another woman while we're twiddling our thumbs on the side of the road, can you live with that guilt? I can't."

When Thana didn't answer, she knew she almost had her convinced to keep following the psychotic shrink. A little more persuasion and there'd be no turning back. She tried her last shot of verbal ammunition.

"You can't use your Tueri position to subvert your duty as an officer to safeguard the public. My connection to Dhelis, and you for that matter, can't be the excuse you use when trading my protection for somebody else's."

"You don't play fair, you know that?" Thana shook her head again. "If something happens to you, I won't have to worry about getting in trouble with the department. Dhelis *and* Brogan will kill me."

"Stop worrying. Nothing's going to happen to me."

Nothing permanent anyway, she amended silently.

Thana gave a rueful laugh. "Even though we know who he is now, if you hadn't gone for your vehicle, I'd have lost him. Thanks."

"You're welcome."

Looking out the window again, she tracked the white car's progress.

They fell into a tension-filled silence. The car's engine hummed along, its powerful whine filling the dead air while she concentrated on the road. She evaluated the tendril of energy she used to monitor Thana's emotions. The farther out of the city they drove, the greater her anxiety became.

Some time later, the phone rang. Both women jumped, startled by the intrusion. Thana flipped open the phone. "Hello?"

She heard Dhelis's voice again, but this time she couldn't make out much of what he said.

"We're almost to the nature reserve about 30 miles out of town," Thana told him. "We just turned off the highway. The sign said the office is 4.6 miles ahead."

Dhelis's tone rose, his words a burst of rapid fire exchange through the phone. Saari heard her name yelled.

"No, I didn't drop her off anywhere—she's driving. I'll have her stay in the vehicle and wait for you and Brogan. You and I can look for the doctor before the other officers arrive."

Up ahead, the white car abruptly turned left, leaving the asphalted road. A plume of dust floated in the air, creating a trail for the two women to follow.

"He just turned off the road, Dhelis. He's following some dirt path into the woods."

Saari had killed the lights when she took the reserve exit so as not to alert the bastard they were following him. The roadway had been okay, the moon throwing enough light she could keep moving safely. Now that they traveled on a dirt road, things were getting dicey. She had to slow down to stay on the path.

They drove for a few more miles until they came upon an open space among the trees. Moonlight reflecting off the parked Honda's back window caught her attention. She stopped the Explorer and turned off the engine.

"We found his car." Thana read off the license plate number.

She still had cell phone coverage? At least something was going their way.

Thana turned in her seat. "I don't see him anywhere. How far out are you?" Her foot tapped the floorboard. "Okay. Saari will stay here. I don't want to lose him, so I'll check the area."

With a sigh, Thana closed her phone and dropped it in her jacket pocket. She reached under her coat and pulled out her department-issued Glock. Saari watched her do a press-check, ensuring a round was chambered.

"Dhelis and Brogan are less than ten minutes away. Knowing Dhelis, he'll be here in five. He started out here right after I called him. I'm sure he's doing over a hundred as it is."

She pointed toward the trees. "Why doesn't he just pop out here?"

"He can't. Half the police department is following him. Just stay here and wait for the guys to get here. You'll be safe in the vehicle until Brogan can stay with you. He's here in case any healing needs to be done tonight, but he can protect you as well as Dhelis or me. He's trained tactical with the Tueri, so you don't have to worry."

She met Thana's stare head on. "I'm worried about you, not me. I think you should wait until Dhelis gets here. Doctor Lytton could have set traps out here. By yourself, you could get hurt."

Red curls bounced as Thana shook her head. "I'm a cop, Saari. This is what I do. Think about this. Even if he had followed you, he had no way of knowing you planned to meet anyone. We caught him by surprise. And I already know about his methods. He plans to use that lipstick he bought. Since he didn't take anyone out of the car with him, he must already have his victims here. And he always puts the lipstick on them *before* they die. That means they're still alive. I'll be careful, but I can't wait any longer."

She sighed. "Okay. Just don't go too far. Dhelis still has to find you out there." She leaned forward and flipped the internal dimmer switch off. No light would shine and give away Thana's position when she opened her door.

"You're beginning to make me think you've done this before," she said with a contemplative look on her face, before getting out of the Explorer. The door closed with a quiet *click*. She made her way into the wooded area using the trees as cover.

Saari watched Thana disappear into the night, her instincts screaming this was a mistake. An uneasy vibe floated on the air. Sweat dampened her palms as the restless pressure increased with each passing moment. Five minutes later, Thana was still somewhere in the woods, and Dhelis and Brogan hadn't arrived.

Where are they?

She should call them. Her purse was stuffed under her seat. She had Dhelis's number. She could call him and find out how far away they were from the reserve. Gripping the steering wheel for balance, she twisted to her right, feeling along the floor for the bag.

A shadow loomed across her window. *Finally.* She looked up, thinking Dhelis or Brogan had arrived.

A startled cry escaped her lips.

Chapter Thirty-Two

His blond hair stood out on his head, frizzed as if he'd been zapped by electricity. The skin on his face blurred in the moonlight. His elongated jaw gave him a slight under bite. Saari blinked, trying to clear her vision. It didn't help.

With a vicious smile, Doctor Lytton raised his fists and stepped toward the Explorer. She turned her face away an instant before he smashed her window. Pieces of shattered safety glass showered her hair and back. He reached under her armpits and yanked her backwards.

Her seat belt held her in place. She grabbed onto the steering wheel and twisted, trying to break his hold. He laughed. The pressure under her right arm lessened. Metal screeched as he ripped out the seatbelt housing anchored to the frame. The seat belt collapsed onto her lap, the loose ends fluttering.

Sharp metallic points cut her arms as he dragged her through the broken window frame. Before her legs dropped free, she struggled. She had to slow him down, give Dhelis time to reach the reserve. Twisting her arms, she clawed at his face. With a snarl, he locked his arms around her, pinning her against his chest.

Her feet dangled above his knees. Wait, he wasn't that much taller than her…

She stared at his hands, hoping to see him cut to shreds after destroying her Explorer. There wasn't even any blood. Her frustration changed to wide-eyed surprise at the shape of his hands—

Not hands.

Claws. Razor-sharp nails tipped the misshapen bones. Coarse, nasty-looking patches of hair covered his discolored skin.

"Hello, Saari." He squeezed her middle. "Hold on tight. You don't want to get lost in the woods. You might get hurt."

He laughed at his own joke.

She kept silent.

Carrying her as if she were a child, he jogged through the woods. After a few minutes, he spoke. "You're going to make a great article in the press. 'Woman overcomes tragic past and meets new love, only to be murdered by a raving lunatic.' Quinn will be convicted as the Full-Moon Killer, ensuring Maurika and the pack will be mine. Plus, can you imagine what your story will do for my therapy practice?"

Her head reeled. What was he talking about? She couldn't *actually* be murdered—of course, he didn't know that. But who were these other people—Quinn, Maurika, and what pack...pack of what?

"Oh, come on now. Don't be shy. You never had a problem talking to me during our sessions. So, tell me what this whole meadow part of your dream was about? I never quite figured out your connection to that."

If he hadn't been holding her, she'd have fallen. Panic raced through her bloodstream. How did he know about Miko? She'd never said Miko's name or anything about the meadow. But he'd somehow learned about her true dream.

Realization curdled in her stomach.

Her suspicion goaded her on.

"You made my dreams worse, didn't you? How did you force me to have the dream every time I slept?" She shoved her fear of being discovered as an immortal into a box in her head and slammed the lid.

"Normally I wouldn't share my trade secrets, but you won't be alive come morning. Why not?" Her body lifted with the shrug of his shoulders. "Regression hypnosis. You were very susceptible to post-hypnotic suggestions. I just told you you'd have the dream every time you slept until you told me your secret. Your subconscious did the rest. Each session you revealed a little more. Another session or two and I'd have learned everything there was to know about the meadow."

Saari reached into herself, opening her extra sense. She touched Lytton's energy, exploring each emotion as a blind person memorizes someone's features. Relief washed over her, soothing the worst of her panic.

He didn't know anything about Miko and her immortality.

"I was so pleased with the resolution to your recurring-dream problem. You worked through your issues despite your true motivation for coming to my office." His tone hardened. "Tell me what you've been hiding about Maurika during our sessions, and I promise you, I'll kill you quickly."

Again with this Maurika. What was he talking about?

And damn, but Thana had been right.

"You followed me to the mall, didn't you?"

"Speaking of the mall, thank you for the convenient stop—I needed to buy more lipstick. And yes, I was following you. I had planned to snatch you somewhere less public. Unfortunately, your friend shouting about being a police officer changed everything. I had to get out of there. Then I saw your SUV fishtail in the intersection and knew *you'd* follow *me* all the way out here." He sighed. "Did you girls call anyone, the police maybe?"

Like hell she was going to say anything else to this whack job.

She wasn't about to make a sound that would draw Thana's attention. He planned on killing them both. Thana would definitely die. Whatever he did to her, Saari would live. *That* was a foregone conclusion.

Lytton's path veered through the trees. To her eyes, nothing in particular marked a trail. Acacia trees grew randomly, shrubs and wild vegetation filling the spaces between the trunks. Her captor never slowed down, telling her he was taking her somewhere specific. Her stomach knotted. She had no idea in what direction her Explorer was parked.

Her skin tingled in warning an instant before his hot breath passed across her ear.

"Your friend is almost to the playground," he taunted. "We should beat her there."

She prayed Thana was nowhere near the place he was talking about. The longer he had to search for her, the better chance Thana had for surviving. Dhelis and Brogan would be at the reserve any minute. They had to be. Someone had to stop this psycho.

Lytton jogged out of the trees into a clearing. The smell hit her first. He stopped running and stood still, making sure she saw each woman he had placed on display like some twisted art exhibit.

"What, no screaming? You surprise me."

She bit her tongue to keep from shrieking in rage.

Ropes and chains held some of the women in specific poses. Others leaned against rocks or each other. She estimated there had to be close to twenty women in the clearing. Her heart ached at the tableau of death. *Someone, somewhere, waited for news of their missing loved one.*

The bastard moved forward slowly. "Let me give you the grand tour."

He turned, forcing her to look at his gruesome handiwork.

The first woman's arm was chained in an upright position, hand open as if waving. Her teeth were missing, the lower jaw disengaged, creating the illusion of a grin-bearing host. The play at joviality offered a horrific welcome.

The next female sat on a flat rock, head tilted to the side, her arm outstretched. All the digits on her hand were missing except her rigid index finger, pointing them on. Another woman lay on a fallen tree trunk: one knee up, an arm thrown over her eyes to block the afternoon sun during a nap.

A pair of women sat on the grass, shoulder to shoulder. Each of them held wilted flowers in their hands. The brown-edged, crumbling petals trailed onto their outspread skirts. The stench of rotting flesh was an overpowering fragrance.

Lytton rotated, and she saw yet another woman sitting on the ground. Her bent knees pointed to the starry sky. Bare, delicate feet touched the earth with pointed toes. Chains secured her ankles to the ground. Heavy metal hoops anchored her arms where they stretched behind her. The palms of her hands pressed against the dirt, poised to support her weight. Her skirt bunched on one side at her hips, showing decomposing flesh. With her closed eyes and head thrown back in wild abandon, the blatant eroticism was not lost in the irony of her death.

It was a grossly provocative presentation.

Nausea rolled through her stomach, threatening to empty at the next horrific sight. She stared at the ground, not wanting to see any more of this man's work. She couldn't help but think of the macabre scene before her as an exhibit of death. The closer they got to the center of the clearing, the more grotesque each woman's pose. He'd meticulously planned the layout.

She realized the women they passed first were most deteriorated, the stages of decay less as they moved forward. What she didn't understand was the women's state as a whole. All of the rotting bodies were intact. They were on a reserve. Wild animals roamed the area. They would surely have been drawn to this site. Why hadn't they chewed on any of the women?

The killer's chest rumbled against her back as he spoke.

"I watched you park your SUV by the trees. No lights or sirens followed. You should have warned your cop friend her gun won't make any difference."

"The police are already here," she bluffed, speaking for the first time since he grabbed her. She had to stall him. Maybe if he believed her, she could buy Thana some time.

"Not yet," he laughed. "But they're coming. Isn't it great when a plan comes together?"

That was the last thing she heard before the back of her head exploded with pain and everything went black.

Chapter Thirty-Three

Brogan gripped the handrail as the car swerved onto the dirt road. Dhelis slowed as the tires skidded on the loose dirt.

"Don't slow down, man."

"Hold on."

The car slid dangerously close to the edge of the path, narrowly missing a tree. A loud roar from the engine filled the car as Dhelis stomped on the accelerator. He cranked hard on the wheel, straightening the car's direction.

"I've had a bad feeling all night. We need to get to Saari and Thana as fast as possible."

"I'm already going faster than I should," Dhelis growled. "If I hadn't already called for backup, I would have just used my stone and *Ridden* us there."

"We have to find them before *he* does." Worry for his mate chewed at Brogan's insides, devouring his patience. He should have driven and made Dhelis Ride straight to Saari.

Rocks pinged against the undercarriage, the only sound breaking the tense silence.

"Look." Brogan pointed.

Up ahead, the lane narrowed and the men spotted two vehicles.

"I don't recognize either of them, do you?"

Dhelis nodded his head. "That white Honda's registered to Doctor Lytton. The plate number Thana gave me matches. The Explorer belongs to Saari. At least she parked where anyone driving from this direction could see her."

Brogan jumped out of the car before Dhelis skidded to a stop, running directly to the driver's side of Saari's Explorer. Dhelis burst from the car, seconds behind him.

"Son of a bitch!"

Brogan's guts knotted. He had known with certainty, even before he reached the door, the Explorer would be empty.

"She's gone." Glass crunched under his feet. "The window's been broken out. That bastard came and got her."

Dhelis ran to his side, his gun in his right hand and a flashlight in the other. The light shone over the interior. Saari's purse lay on its side. Her personal items littered the floorboard like a spilled trash can. The keys dangled in the ignition.

"He caught her by surprise." Worry colored Dhelis's tone.

Brogan noted a piece of fabric stuck on the broken metal frame. Several drops of blood marked the cloth, appearing almost black in the moonlight. He gritted his teeth and slid his crystal dagger into his palm. "If he hurts her, he'd better pray to God I don't catch him."

The flashlight played over the ground. "There's a set of large footprints headed away from the vehicles, into the trees." The light followed the trail. "They've got to be his. Come on."

They followed the prints, moving fast. Neither said a word. The trail continued through the trees, frustrating him. Foliage blocked a good portion of the moonlight. The flashlight only illuminated a small area directly in front of them.

Please let Saari be okay.

Trees and foliage thinned, finally opening onto a clearing. They skidded to a halt at the edge of the trees. Moonlight lit the sky like a halogen lamp, revealing a sickening view.

Women's bodies stood, sat, and lay like grotesque flowers, rotting in a garden of death. No sound reached him, leaving the night eerily silent. The hairs stood straight up on his arms.

The evil intent behind the tableau of dead women, posed for onlookers, thickened the tension in the air.

"There's Saari," Brogan whispered, pointing to the center of the clearing.

His friend took in the scene at a glance—then turned. He pointed at himself and then swung his arm to the right. Another gesture sent Brogan toward the left side of the meadow. They could cover everything in the clearing that way, while still keeping Saari in sight.

They crept forward, moving into the open field. Sweat popped out on his forehead, his nerves stretched taut as a piano wire. Now *they* were moving targets. Leaving the tree line left them with no cover, but he trusted Dhelis. His friend knew what he was doing. Brogan nearly sighed with relief when they pulled even with Saari. She lay yards away, directly between him and Dhelis.

Please let her be alive.

Dhelis signaled to him. He pointed at Brogan, brought two fingers in front of his eyes, and then pointed to Saari.

He got the message. *Brogan, watch her.*

He nodded he understood.

Dhelis thumped his chest, turned and stretched an arm toward the woods.

They'd found Saari. Dhelis wanted to look for Thana.

The air puckered around Dhelis and he disappeared from the clearing.

Chapter Thirty-Four

Dhelis forced thoughts of Saari from his mind.

Seeing her lying so still had nearly stopped his heart. If she'd been hurt, Brogan would heal her—then protect her. If she was already dead, neither of them could do anything for her. He swallowed. His fear over the last possibility cut like shards of glass, but Thana needed him.

He focused on his cousin.

Picturing her standing in front of him, facing him had been a tactical decision. If Lytton had her, the bastard would have to go through him to get to her. Praying she was alone, he didn't want to startle her.

The air settled around him as he registered her location and stepped into the new space. Thana jumped and her arm lifted in his direction. Her finger flexed and then moved off the trigger of her gun.

"Damn it, Dhelis. I nearly shot you!" she hissed.

No one else was in sight. He'd managed to find his cousin before that psychopath had gotten to her. "Sorry. Come on. Let's go back to Saari and Brogan."

She shook her head. "I've been tracking a smaller set of footprints. I think one of his victims got away—or is at least trying to."

He stared at the ground where she pointed. Sure enough, a small set of tracks veered through the trees. His worry over Saari and Thana had been bad enough. Now they had to look for someone else. And the tracks headed toward the meadow filled with dead women.

Anxiety twisted in his gut, the serpentine cramp reminding him lives were at stake. "Let's get moving. Lytton's got to be somewhere close."

They followed the tracks, listening for any sound that would give away the killer's presence. The night remained eerily quiet, devoid of any sign of animal life. Thana guarded their rear against a sneak attack.

A strong odor hung heavy and stagnant on the air. He put a hand over his nose. "Do you smell that?"

She nodded. "Smells like rotting meat to me."

"I agree. I think the stench is coming from over there," he pointed.

They moved toward the shrubs, searching for the source of the odor. The buzzing of flies told them whatever they found was already dead. He pushed the foliage back and spotted a deer. Something big had brought it down, making a meal of it sometime in the last couple of days.

"Keep an eye out for bears. I don't think a wolf did this."

"Great," Thana whispered. "We're tracking a serial killer and possibly a bear. I need a bigger gun."

Leaves rustled to his left. He stopped and scanned the area ahead. The breeze scratched shrubs against tree trunks like eerie fingernails grating on a chalkboard. He couldn't see anyone, but the hairs on the back of his neck lifted. His intuition shouted someone else was near.

He motioned to Thana, and they stepped behind a tree. As they watched, a woman sprinted across their path fifty yards ahead. Moving into the clear, he called out to the woman. "Police. Wait!"

She didn't turn around or give any indication she heard him.

"Crap." He started after her.

"Do you think Lytton's chasing her?" Thana kept her voice low, staying close without blocking their gun hands.

"Maybe. Not sure it matters now, though. We're almost to the place I left Saari. That's where Lytton ultimately wants both women."

They raced into the meadow.

Brogan knelt near Saari. He didn't see the woman anywhere.

Branches and twigs snapped in the underbrush behind him. A loud roar filled the woods and rolled into the clearing.

Dhelis pivoted toward the sound. A large figure crashed through the trees and burst into the clearing. Several gunshots echoed in answer. He caught flashes of Thana's muzzle fire and the loud pops of a semi-automatic. Dhelis lifted his gun and fired, tracking the huge, crazed man out of the woods.

As the figure drew closer, he realized it wasn't a man. Its physical shape closely resembled one, but it was something else entirely. This *creature* was much taller than a man—most likely topping seven feet. It had longer than normal arms. Long, coarse hair covered its entire body. Thana put another round in its chest. It growled with rage, flashing a mouthful of razor-sharp teeth.

Bigfoot. No fucking way.

Whatever the hell it was, he intended to kill it. He slid a new clip home and pulled the trigger.

Bullets tore through the creature's body from both their guns. The impacting force of gunfire twisted the thing like a marionette dancing on strings.

It didn't stop its headlong race toward them.

Dhelis stopped firing just before it reached them. He grabbed Thana and Rode them to the edge of the tree line. The creature slashed empty air, roaring in frustration.

Another large creature barreled out of the trees. The massive beast plowed into the first, wrestling it to the ground. The two rolled in the dirt, each one trying to regain its feet, clawing at the other one as it moved.

Stunned, he stared at Thana. "What the hell are they?"

"I don't know, but I'm not about to stand around and wait for one of them to turn on us." Thana ejected her empty magazine. She slapped in a new one and brought her gun up in one fluid motion, ready to start shooting again. Before she could fire on the pair, the woman they'd seen earlier ran from the woods, screaming at the top of her lungs.

"Don't shoot," she gasped. "You might hit Quinn." She stopped a few feet away, sucking in air, her attention split between him, Thana, and the creatures thrashing before them.

Who was she, and why did she look familiar? More importantly, what did she have to do with the bizarre...whatever they are?

"You can't kill them with your guns anyway. The bullets just stun them. Any wounds heal as soon as they shift. But if you do hurt them, you'll anger them. Then they'll turn on you."

The creatures growled viciously as they tore at each other.

He gaped at the crazed attack. "Jesus, they're trying to kill each other."

They fought like grizzly bears, battling over territory. Both were cut and bleeding, though if he had to guess, he'd say the creature that came out of the woods second was doing considerably more damage.

"Should we try to stop them?"

"How?" Thana's voice cracked with disbelief.

"I don't know." He stared the new woman, but she was completely absorbed in the battle. Her fists clenched like she wanted to jump in, but knew enough to let the monsters fight it out.

As long as Saari was safe, they could kill each other for all he cared.

Dhelis watched the clearing for Lytton.

That bastard *he* planned on killing.

Chapter Thirty-Five

Brogan ignored the fighting and concentrated on Saari. She lay on a large flat rock shaped like an altar. Her milk-white pale skin showed in stark contrast against the pool of blood spreading beneath her head. He placed his ear next to her lips. Her warm breath skimmed across his skin, slow and irregular. His hands shook with relief. She was hurt, but alive.

Thank God Dhelis had brought him along.

She had a severe head injury and moving her was too risky. He'd have to heal her where she lay, trusting Dhelis and Thana to keep them safe. He placed his stone on her forehead, his palms centered over the gem. Heat gathered in his hands.

The moment he touched her skin, a loud boom blasted the night. With their bond already established, their energies immediately merged and rolled. His heart beat in time to hers, irregular at first, before settling into a steady rhythm. With each beat their energy gained power, the growing force pulsating outward.

Pulling back his awareness, Brogan glanced toward Dhelis. He wondered if Dhelis felt his and Saari's connection. Dhelis stood next to Thana, his eyes wide as saucers. An "O" shaped his lips, jaw hanging open in shock.

A woman he'd never seen before stood on the other side of Dhelis. She dropped to her knees, mashing her hands over her ears.

Even more incredible, the two creatures stopped fighting and howled in pain.

~ ☾ ~

Saari came awake instantly, her eyes popping open. Brogan's face loomed above her, calm and reassuring. Their hearts beat as one, steadying and lifting. She smiled, forgetting for a moment where they were. The cold rock at her back and the smell of rotting flesh jolted her memory.

Animals wailed. With each shared heartbeat, their howls grew louder. The proximity of the noise finally registered in her brain. She sat up, dislodging Brogan's hands and breaking the connection. Her gaze searched the meadow, locking onto two large creatures. One collapsed to its knees and swayed. The other shook its head as if trying to clear its senses.

Dhelis stood next to Thana. Both of them had their weapons out, poised to fire.

A stranger stood at the edge of the clearing beside Dhelis and Thana. She slumped on the ground, her body bent over double, hands flattened against the sides of her head. Her body rocked back and forth. Saari heard her moans of pain.

The beast still standing snapped its head up and let loose a horrible scream. It leapt forward, biting at the neck of the creature kneeling in the dirt.

While she stared, horrified but helpless to interfere, the stronger beast flung the creature side to side, like a dog trying to break its prey's neck. When the beast finally let go, the other thing's head had nearly been severed from its body. It fell over, jerking occasionally, as it died.

~ ☾ ~

Dhelis stood perfectly still beside Thana and the kneeling woman, waiting for the remaining creature to turn on them. He watched it spin around, shaking its head back and forth, flinging blood in several directions. It growled ferociously, sniffing the air.

The woman next to them slowly stood. One hand dangled by her side, the other she held behind her back. He squinted, trying to see what she hid. His hand twitched, uncertain whether the beasts or the woman was the bigger threat. The woman's jaws moved, chewing something. She swallowed, closed her eyes and shivered. Her skin rippled, like a wave generated by something swimming just below a lake's surface.

A moment passed, and her eyes opened. She huffed, moving in measured steps toward the beast. The creature tilted its head, feral eyes focused on her. Huffing again, she growled low in the back of her throat. Her sounds seemed to calm the creature. She stopped directly in front of it.

Reaching out with her left hand, she touched the beast, stroking its face. She made an odd noise, a strange mix of mewling growls. The thing mimicked her. In a blur of motion, she brought her other hand around and slammed something against the beast's side. It howled in rage, swinging its arm and knocking the woman aside.

It moved toward her, and he stepped forward, taking aim. He caught movement to his side and realized Thana had also raised her weapon.

Before he could fire, the woman rolled to her feet, screaming. "Don't shoot. Please, don't shoot. He's about to shift."

The beast stopped moving and swayed on its feet.

"What did you do?" Dhelis yelled.

"I drugged him." The woman gasped. "You're seeing it take effect."

The creature toppled. She rushed forward and caught its body to her, slowly lowering it to the ground.

How did the woman manage to hold that enormous creature's weight?

Thana kept her gun trained on the creature. "How did you get close enough to that thing to control it?"

"Just watch," the woman pleaded.

"Watch what?" He had had enough surprises for one night. He wanted answers.

The thing on the ground twitched like an electroshock patient. The coarse hair covering its body disappeared in the blink of an eye. The creature changed, transforming into a very groggy and very naked man.

Thana, Saari, and Brogan gasped. In his peripheral vision, Dhelis saw Brogan step between Saari and the beast, protecting her.

"Oh." Kneeling, Saari studied the woman. "You're both lunates."

He noted her statement was a declaration of fact rather than a question.

The woman's chin shot up. "Yes, we are." She answered in a solemn tone.

A loud groan captured everyone's attention. The naked man's eyelids fluttered several times and opened.

"I feel like I was hit by a train. Christ, Rika, does this stuff always make your head pound like this?" he complained, his voice deep and rough.

"Yes, it does," the woman chuckled, helping him to his feet. Relief rippled through her tone.

Thana and Saari kept their eyes at face level, tactfully ignoring the man's nude form. Dhelis didn't give a damn. They had to deal with more important things. Like who these people were—what these people were—and why they'd been out here with the Full-Moon Killer. Were they in league with him or hunting him? "Who are you?" he demanded.

"I'm Maurika Nichols," the woman announced, "and this is Quinn Holman. We run the reserve. We've been tracking this killer for a couple months now."

He stared at the man introduced as Quinn. Though coherent, the guy seemed a little unsteady on his feet. Not a scratch marred his skin, but he was hard pressed to see anything because of the blood covering Quinn's body. How much of it was his and how much was the other creature's?

He lowered his gun but kept it out. After the fight he just witnessed, and not knowing for sure who was responsible for all the dead bodies in the meadow, he wasn't taking any chances. "Pleasure to meet you and all that, but we've got bigger problems to deal with before the entire police department gets here." He nodded his head toward the area where the other creature had fallen.

Every head turned like a well-rehearsed choreographed moment.

A creature no longer lay in the dirt. Instead, a horribly mangled man sprawled in an undignified heap. Quinn moved forward first, not hesitating as he knelt near the bleeding man. Before he could warn him to be careful, Maurika spoke.

"He's already dead. Quinn killed him. That's why his body shows the injuries. The moon forced a change earlier, so he was unable to shift back and heal himself."

"Saari, is that Lytton?" Dhelis glanced toward her, pointing at the man Quinn had just killed.

Her face tightened in anger. "That's him."

Quinn's chin came up suddenly. His head canted to the left, listening to something nobody else heard. "The police are almost to the reserve. I can hear their sirens."

"I saw you shimmer." Maurika stared at Dhelis. "You're Tueri. Did the Council send you?"

He hesitated. How did they know about the Council and that he was Tueri—when he didn't know anything about them? He had to take their word the police were coming. Too many other lives would be at risk if the public learned about the Tueri *and* that Bigfoot was real.

"I'm not sure how you two fit into all of this, but you need to get out of here. The police can't know about you. The Council will deal with any fallout." He looked at Quinn. "Do you live on the reserve or just work out here?"

Quinn stood. "We live here. We have a jeep parked a few miles from here. We can be back to our cabin in about an hour. Can you give us that long before you send anyone our way?"

"Not a problem," he assured the man.

The pair jogged into the woods without saying another word or looking back even once. Within seconds, the forest swallowed them. They disappeared, almost as if they'd never been in the clearing.

"We're going to need to talk about this later." He shouted after them, positive they heard him.

He turned toward Thana, Brogan and Saari. "We can't keep Saari and Brogan out of this, so we've got to talk fast. Listen up. This is how everything went down."

He quickly outlined how they would explain what happened, without implicating the lunate creatures. After he finished, they all nodded they understood.

Before he could have them repeat what they needed to remember, police officers descended on the clearing in a confusion of lights, shouts and human bodies.

Chapter Thirty-Six

Early Morning May 25, 2032—New Angeles

Saari shivered as a gust of wind blew past the open door of Dhelis's car.

"Cold?" Brogan asked.

"Yes." She clenched her teeth to stop them clacking together.

Floodlights illuminated the dirt road, marking the retrieval team's temporary command post. Brogan vanished into the expanding group of uniformed officers and emergency services medics. She tried to track his progress by following the reflection of light off his bald head, but lost even that advantage when he disappeared around the side of an ambulance.

A small spurt of panic at losing sight of him jolted her system like a splash of cold water. She hadn't seen Dhelis for hours. Having Brogan close, knowing he was safe, had been the only balm to her frayed nerves.

A few minutes later Brogan reappeared with a blanket. Her rigid posture relaxed.

He draped the heated cover around her shoulders. His gaze locked onto hers. "Are you okay? I've been trying to gauge your reaction about all of this, but you haven't said two words to me since the police showed up." Leaning against the open door, his stance clearly indicated he wasn't leaving her side.

How was she supposed to tell him the idea of finding happiness in their new relationship and then losing it scared her more than any physical pain she might suffer? Everything was too new, too uncertain. Only time would make them comfortable around each other, bring them closer.

But she'd promised him honesty.

"I was terrified." Her breath shuddered. "After Clayton grabbed me, I was worried he'd find Thana. But when I saw Quinn fighting Clayton in lunate form, the two of them ripping and tearing at each other, my heart nearly stopped beating. That fight could have turned on the rest of us. Either you or Dhelis or both of you could have been killed." Her voice trailed off, barely above a whisper.

His features relaxed, a small smile pulling at the corner of his mouth. "I was just as concerned about you—and Dhelis and Thana. We all came out of this without a scratch—except for you. Does your head hurt?" He lifted a hand, finger pointing toward the back of her head.

"No. At least not from getting whacked earlier. All the noise and lights from the people behind us might give me a headache, though."

He snorted in agreement.

News reporters and television crews had shown up a couple hours ago. They crowded behind a blockade the police put up fifty yards or so away from where Dhelis's car was parked.

She looked over her shoulder, staring at the throng of onlookers. "Crap, there are more reporters. Why didn't you tell me the crowd had grown?" she asked, turning back to him.

"They've been there all night. It was a pretty large group from the beginning. I didn't think a few more would matter," he shrugged.

"I suppose you're right." She looked back at the group of people clustered together behind a few small barricades and flimsy tape. "What do you think the police would do if they all rushed the barricade at once?"

"I don't know. It's an interesting question, though. Why don't you ask them," he answered, nodding to his left.

She followed his gaze. "Finally," she muttered.

Dhelis and Thana came out of the trees with several uniformed officers and a couple of men wearing suits. As they approached the car, she got out and stood next to Brogan. Left alone for hours, she had no idea what would happen next. Brogan's closed expression bordered on grim.

"I think we've finally fit all of the pieces together." The man wearing the best suit—she assumed he was the Chief since he had spoken first—rubbed a hand over his face. "It's one hell of a story, but the media is gonna love it. The two lead detectives on this case, Dhelis Guidry and Thana Brunges, are going to handle the press conference."

Dhelis and Thana stepped forward out of the crowd of officers, as if on cue.

"After our detectives have given their statement," he continued, "I'm sure there will be questions directed to both of you, Mr. Vincent and Ms. Mitchell, if you feel up to it. If you give them an interview now, the press will be more likely to leave you alone later."

She turned slightly and looked up at Brogan, a questioning look in her eyes.

He slid his arm around her blanket-covered shoulders, pulling her close. "We'd just as soon get this over with, sir. If you think this will keep the media from stalking us, then we're willing to deal with them now."

"Excellent," the Chief responded.

Dhelis and Thana moved past them toward the blockade. Dhelis's features tightened, but he didn't say a word. She wondered if that was a sign of problems to come over their three-sided match. Stifling a groan, she slammed a mental door on the newly occupied relationship room in her mind. *Now is so not the time to think about that issue.*

Brogan urged her forward. She trudged after Dhelis and Thana. Several police officers fell in behind her and Brogan, escorting the group for safety. Her irritation quickly changed to gratitude for the extra protection. The closer they got to the waiting media, the louder their shouted questions became. Lights blazed, blinding the group with their glare.

Officers yelled for the press to quiet down in order for the Chief to make a statement. The Chief stepped in front of the crowd, his stance relaxed and in control. His voice boomed across the artificially lit field. "The people of New Angeles can sleep easier knowing the Full-Moon Killer's murder spree has finally ended."

Light bulbs flashed. Reporters shouted questions over each other, each struggling to gain the Chief's individual attention. The Chief spoke over the reporters, forcing the throng of information seekers to stop talking in order to hear what he said.

"I'd like to introduce Dhelis Guidry and Thana Brunges, the lead detectives on this case." He swept an arm in Dhelis and Thana's direction. "Your individual questions should be directed to them."

"You gonna handle the questions this time?" Dhelis motioned toward the reporters and smiled at Thana.

"Not me," Thana muttered. "You know I prefer to stay out of the press as much as possible."

Dhelis nodded and stepped forward. A few hushed murmurs could be heard as the crowd waited for him to speak.

"Late last night my partner and I received information about the Full-Moon Killer that directed us to the reserve. He has been identified as Doctor Clayton Bishop Lytton."

A ripple of mumbling passed among the group, but no one interrupted his explanation.

"When we arrived at the reserve, we found his car. That led us to believe he and possibly his latest victim were somewhere in the vicinity. Upon searching the woods, we discovered a clearing that contains more than fifteen victims—all of which are yet to be identified."

"As we investigated the scene, we found a victim alive. That victim is Ms. Saari Mitchell. While attempting to ascertain the extent of Ms. Mitchell's injuries,

Mr. Lytton suddenly appeared at the clearing, running out of the trees. We heard growling noises, and observed several wolves chasing Mr. Lytton as he approached our position. Before my partner and I could react, the wolves attacked Mr. Lytton. Though we intervened, Mr. Lytton's injuries were fatal."

Questions and answers volleyed back and forth for several minutes before a reporter in the crowd turned his attention toward her. She was only half paying attention when Brogan nudged her in the side and nodded his head toward the reporters.

"Ms. Mitchell?" Dhelis motioned her forward.

She left Brogan's side and stood next to Dhelis. She needed to know he was all right. She wished he'd put his arm around her, too. The reporter cleared his throat with impatience, pulling her back to the interview. "I'm sorry, could you repeat the question?"

"When were you abducted, and what injuries did you receive, Ms. Mitchell?"

She pulled the blanket tight around her shoulders. Her forehead wrinkled as she thought about her answer. "I think it was sometime between 11:00 and 11:30 last night when he pulled me from my vehicle."

Before she could answer the rest of the question, someone else shouted at her. "Were you alone when Mr. Lytton took you, and if not, what happened to your companion?" Lights and cameras pointed in Brogan's direction. She knew her explanation had to be right on or things would get very complicated very fast.

"Yes, I was alone. I had gone back to the Explorer to get my cell phone. I don't wear a watch, and I wanted to keep track of the time. Brogan was setting up our campsite, so I decided to run back and get it. I was sitting in the driver's seat reaching for my purse when the window behind me shattered. He must have hit me on the back of the head with something because I don't remember anything after that until the detectives found me."

The explanation was convenient but believable.

More questions were shouted, each of the reporters trying to gain her attention. Light bulbs flashed repeatedly, almost blinding her with the swimming black dots crowding her vision. Different voices, male and female, yelled to her, adding to the confusion. "I don't—" she began, trying to answer their questions.

Dhelis stepped in front of her, addressing the crowd. "I believe Ms. Mitchell has answered enough questions for now. She's had a very traumatic night, and I'm sure she could use some rest."

The crowd surged forward. Officers shouted and pushed them back. Brogan wrapped a protective arm around her. Thana and Dhelis moved up on either side of them, and the remaining officers in their escort fell in behind them, creating a buffer between them and the media.

She wasn't sure which beast had sharper teeth: the growling lunates or the frenzied media sharks.

Chapter Thirty-Seven

The road next to the reserve had become the base camp for the investigating police officers. The Chief claimed it was a fine example of organization. Saari thought the chaos looked more like a three-ring circus. After navigating through the mass of people, Thana, Dhelis, Saari and Brogan finally reached Dhelis's car.

"We'll escort you home, Ms. Mitchell," Dhelis told her and Brogan. "Your vehicle can't be released from the crime scene yet. I apologize for the inconvenience." Lowering his voice he added, "On our way out, I think we need to stop by a certain cabin and have a little chat with our new friends."

Brogan nodded his head in agreement. He opened the rear passenger door. She mouthed "thank you" and got in. He climbed in behind her. Thana slid into the front passenger seat, and Dhelis drove.

As the car moved past the mob of reporters, lights flashed while they tried to take as many pictures as possible. She dropped her chin and let her hair hide her face. The car finally moved beyond the reach of the reporters' telephoto lenses, and everyone in the car breathed a sigh of relief.

"Hey, Dhelis?" She leaned forward and tapped his shoulder. "Won't the police be sending some officers over to interview Maurika and Quinn? I'm assuming we shouldn't be there when they drop by."

"We won't stay long, but now's our best shot. It'll take hours for the department to clear the site. What extra manpower they had is controlling that mob of reporters. And I need to know what really happened so I can inform Council," he answered.

"This didn't have anything to do with vampires. So why is the Council involved?" She rested her arms on her knees for balance. With the blanket wrapped around her shoulders and her head shoved between the two front seats, she felt like a turtle coming out of its shell. At least she wasn't talking to the back of his head.

They reached the asphalt road. The car turned at the impromptu intersection and followed the plaques with painted arrows leading to the information center. "The Council has liaisons with many of the different preternatural factions in the city—in the nation, actually. A mutually shared flow of information is necessary to keep the human world from learning of our existence."

"So when you say 'our' existence, you don't just mean vampires and Tueri. You're talking about every other group of beings that are not strictly human, right?" She was just starting to realize how far reaching the Tueri Council's network of information might be.

"Right." Dhelis turned into a small parking lot.

Thana's head swiveled in her direction. "Hey, how come the car didn't light up like a halogen spotlight when you touched Dhelis?"

"There has to be skin to skin contact," she answered, jumping topics without missing a beat. She brushed her fingertips against Dhelis's shirt-clad arm in demonstration. "See, no reaction. Must be a physiological explanation—pheromones, hormones, some Tueri chemical secretion thing."

"Eugh." Thana's lips curled as if she'd bitten into something sour. "That theory does tend to suck the romance right out of a connection, doesn't it?"

Brogan chuckled. "No way. The 'wow' factor is way too cool."

"I think we should look for them here first," Dhelis interrupted, bringing everyone's attention back to the reason for their side trip. "There's a Jeep parked out front. It must be theirs. Plus, a light's on inside." He got out of the car, indicating everyone should follow him.

A sign on the face of the building read *Office*. Brogan looked at the outside of the structure. "I don't think this is the place those werewolves were talking about. They said cabin. This isn't a cabin."

"They aren't werewolves," Saari corrected. "They're lunates."

A small fizzle of excitement jolted her system with a shot of adrenaline, chasing away the night's fatigue. She'd heard about lunates over the last five centuries, but never seen one until last night—or was it morning?

Before Dhelis could knock, the front door opened. The woman who had introduced herself earlier as Maurika smiled. "You're right, we aren't werewolves. I'm a lunate, and so is Quinn—the man you met last night. Sorry about the eavesdropping. I have really good hearing." She held out her arm in a welcoming gesture. "Please, come in."

She wondered if the woman had overheard any of their conversation in the car.

Their group moved into the waiting room, and then fell into step behind Maurika. She led them through the animal clinic, past cages both empty and occupied, to an oversized office at the back of the building. When they entered, Quinn stood next to a large window looking out at the mountains. Even from the doorway, the view through the window was spectacular.

The room's inviting nature pulled her forward. Blended earth tones decorated the room, giving it a relaxed, homey feel. Dark wood floors contrasted with walls the color of warm sand, giving the illusion of peaceful, open space. Burnt orange and rust-colored rugs chased away the floor's cold draft.

Brown leather furniture hinted at a bit of affluence, without losing the comfortable feel the decor created.

She perched on the edge of the couch. Brogan sat down next to her, setting his hand on her knee. Thana chose a matching chair facing the desk. Dhelis stood between the couch and chair, close to both his cousin and his mate. He was ready in case there were any more surprises.

"Would someone please tell me what a lunate is?" Dhelis asked without preamble.

Quinn remained behind Maurika, his hands on her shoulders. Though he faced Dhelis, he remained silent.

"I'm the pack's leader. So it falls to me to explain," Maurika said. "Humans call us Bigfoot. Yeti. Sasquatch."

"I knew Bigfoot was real!" Brogan slapped his other hand against his leg.

Saari couldn't help smiling at his boyish enthusiasm.

"I thought the alpha male ruled the pack," Dhelis interrupted.

"That's true for werewolves, but not in the case of lunates." Maurika answered without hesitation. "We're related to the werewolves—a cousin if you will—but we're much older. Your tri-colored eyes give you away as Tueri, so you know after the change humans evolved in many ways. Lunates are another form of that evolution, though there aren't many of us left. The werewolves greatly outnumber us."

That made sense. Saari had heard of them, but had never seen a lunate before tonight.

"You said you and Quinn are both lunates." Dhelis pointed in their direction.

Maurika nodded in confirmation.

"Wolves mate for life. Is it the same with lunates?" he asked.

"It is," Quinn answered.

"I think I know what happened. Clayton Lytton, a.k.a. psycho head shrink, challenged Quinn as your mate, didn't he?" Saari interrupted.

Dhelis looked sideways at her, but said nothing.

Maybe she shouldn't have said anything. Having prior knowledge of the lunates' existence might work against her. If she said too much, she'd have to explain how she knew of the lunates' existence in the first place. Which would lead to her being immortal—and she wasn't ready to give *that* explanation yet. So that would mean she'd have to lie. Considering the fragility of her new relationships with Brogan and Dhelis, lying was not an option.

Better to keep her thoughts to herself.

"Lytton never challenged Quinn outright," Maurika answered. "He was smart enough to know he couldn't beat Quinn. Instead, he came to our pack nearly a year ago—under a false name we later learned—asking to be accepted as a member. But there was something off about him. The pack turned him down."

Something Lytton had said to her clicked. She looked at Dhelis. "Rather than challenge Quinn directly, Lytton had decided to eliminate him. He told me he planned to set Quinn up for the murders."

"That makes sense." Maurika nodded.

"Was that the last time you heard from Lytton?" Dhelis stepped closer to Saari. She didn't think he was even aware he'd moved toward her.

"Yes. We thought Lytton had left town. Then women started turning up dead. At first, we had no idea the Full-Moon Killer and the lunate who asked to be a member of our pack were the same person. Then, when our pack found a camper killed close to the reserve, we knew Lytton had murdered him. His scent was on the body."

"We're lucky no police dogs were at the scene tonight to track your scent," Dhelis groaned.

Maurika snorted. "I know. We thought Lytton was trying to set the pack up. Expose our existence. Then, a couple days ago, we found a woman's body *on* the reserve. Lytton's scent was all over her body. That's when we were certain he was the Full-Moon Killer."

Thana gasped. "There's another woman's body—that's not in the group at the meadow?"

A tendril of shock swirled in the pit of Saari's stomach. How many women did Lytton kill? And how did he choose them all? Not that it mattered in the end. He'd decided to kill her easily enough. She thanked the gods of fate the man was dead.

"Why didn't you call the police when you found the bodies?" Dhelis asked.

"I was protecting our pack. If I'd called the police, they would have been crawling all over the reserve. The lunate was only killing on nights with a full moon. Our pack, most of which are werewolves, runs on the reserve. That increased the risk of exposing the werewolves exponentially," Maurika pointed out.

"True. That's a good point. Why didn't you report it to your liaison instead?" Dhelis lifted a shoulder.

"Our liaison disappeared six months ago. We haven't heard a word from Council—or anyone else for that matter. That's why I tried to stop Lytton myself. I've hunted for him every full moon," Maurika responded.

Dhelis's eyes narrowed. "Hunted how?"

"Lunates are different than werewolves in physical shape as well as compulsory changes. Werewolves are forced to shift for three nights every month. Lunates are only forced to shift on the nights of a blue moon, that being a *second* full moon in the same month. It doesn't occur often, only every couple of years usually, but it does happen. Any lunate can change at will, just as Quinn and I can, except for those three nights of a blue moon. Those nights, we have no control. No memory."

"Except you didn't change when you came screaming out of the woods." Thana pointed at Quinn. "Only him and that other one changed."

"We've been working on a way to keep from changing. The valerian herb works on all lupines. Holding back a change is not as imperative for us as it is for the werewolves, though. Werewolves change more often, and sometimes they can't get somewhere safe. Then it's dangerous for everybody," Quinn answered quietly.

No kidding. Saari didn't want to run into another changed lunate, let alone a werewolf. Her only defense against that kind of strength was immortality. Lytton's killing spree had proved the general population had no defense whatsoever.

"That's what you were chewing on when I saw your skin ripple," Dhelis muttered. "You'd been in the woods hunting him, and Quinn actually found him."

"Exactly," Maurika said eagerly. "Now you understand." She reached in her pocket and pulled out a small, clear bottle filled with tablets. She handed them to Thana, who was closest to her, gesturing for her to pass them to Dhelis.

The moment Thana touched the container, her demeanor changed. Her chin shot up. "I recognize your signature. You're the woman who was in the hotel room with Jordan Stevens the night he was killed."

"That's why you look familiar." Dhelis's eyes rounded at the shocking announcement. "I saw you on the hotel's security footage."

Maurika froze. A shiver racked her body before she heaved a great sigh. "There's something you need to know," she began. Her voice broke, and Quinn tightened his grip on her shoulders, as if silently cautioning her. She reached up and patted one of his hands.

"I killed Jordan Stevens," she said in a rush. "It was an accident. I didn't mean to, I swear. I was in a bar downtown looking for Lytton. Of course, I didn't know his real name then, but I'd actually found him. I didn't think he'd seen me. I'd been taking my pills to keep from changing, but he put something in my drink that made me really groggy. I don't recall going back to Stevens' hotel room. The last thing I do remember is telling him to run," she finished, tears rolling down her cheeks.

Oh, man. Saari hadn't seen that coming. The image of Jordan Stevens with his arm wrapped around a woman—this woman—popped into her head. Maurika had been talking to Jordan Stevens at the bar when she and Nisa left.

Thana's spine straightened, as she glanced in Dhelis's direction.

Dhelis and Thana's reactions toward Maurika made Saari wonder how the Council would sanction Maurika over Jordan's death. She reached out toward Maurika, running her extra sense over the woman's aura like an x-ray machine capturing an internal image. Guilt warred with obligation. Horror circled fear. Not a trace of deception or dishonesty threaded itself through her senses.

Placing her palm against the inside of the blanket, she pressed the extra barrier of fabric against Dhelis's leg and squeezed. His gaze jerked her way. An eyebrow lifted in surprise at her contact.

"Let it go, Dhelis," she said, her words barely above a whisper. "She's telling you the truth. I can feel her emotions."

She pleaded with her eyes for him not to ask any questions. His lips parted, and she shook her head, cutting him off.

"I'm filing that information away for later inquiry," Dhelis warned her, matching her quiet tone. He turned back to Maurika.

"You didn't kill Jordan, Maurika." Dhelis's voice softened.

Saari mentally groaned, remembering something else Dhelis had said. He thought the killer was male. If she kept opening her mouth like this, Dhelis was going to figure out she had a few mind-numbing secrets of her own.

"Of course I did. I was in his hotel room. The next morning, I woke up at the reserve, covered in blood. The paper said the man had been torn to pieces. That's the only explanation."

"No, it's not. Jordan was alive *after* you went tearing out of his hotel room. The security tapes also show Lytton showed up, checking several floors of the hotel. It appeared he was looking for someone. He caught Jordan in the hallway, shoved him back into his room, and neither came out again." Dhelis shook his head for emphasis. "You did *not* kill the psychic. Lytton did."

Maurika swallowed. "But I was covered in blood. How do you explain that?"

"We found a mauled deer near the clearing. It looked like it had been killed a couple of days ago. If you check the carcass, I bet you'll find your scent all over it," Thana told her.

"It's still my fault he killed Jordan. Lytton must have been following my scent. He probably figured he could overpower me while I was drugged and become my dominant. One way or another, he wanted control of our pack."

"Does that mean it's your fault Lytton kidnapped me?" Saari asked. The woman seemed determined to share responsibility for Lytton's actions.

Maurika turned to her. "I don't understand?"

"How's this for a string of coincidences? I'd been seeing Lytton as his patient for a few weeks. The only thing I can figure is he saw me in the bar talking to Jordan. Then he saw you in the bar and tracked you to Jordan's room. Lytton must have figured you and I had some kind of connection. That explains why he kept asking me at the reserve what you had planned."

"But I've never met you before tonight." Maurika protested.

"You and Saari know that, but he believed otherwise. And that's Saari's point. You're not responsible for the things Lytton did. He chose to hurt and kill those people. You tried to stop him."

A flash of unexpected pleasure warmed her heart at Dhelis's effort to reassure Maurika. Dhelis was truly a champion of justice. Even though they'd caught the killer, his moral compass wouldn't allow anyone else to suffer if he could help it—and that apparently included transference of guilt.

Dhelis ran a hand through his hair. "You won't be questioned. As it stands now, the police assume Lytton killed Stevens because he saw or, being the kind of psychic he was, knew something. As for the Council, I'll talk with them. There was no liaison to work with, so you were pretty much on your own. But you protected your pack, and others, from exposure. No one can ask for more than that."

Maurika took a few shuddered breaths and nodded her head. "Thank you," she said quietly, her shoulders sagging in relief. Quinn wrapped his arms around her, holding her while she leaned against him for support. He dipped his chin gratefully toward Dhelis, silently communicating his thanks.

Brogan stood up. He helped Saari to her feet, his motion a not-too-subtle hint it was time they left.

Thana slid out of the chair gracefully. She handed the bottle of pills back to Maurika. "You have to promise not to hunt like that again—at least not without talking to us first. Let us handle the riskier aspects of bringing down a suspect. We don't change under a full moon."

Maurika laughed, hiccupping. "You've got a deal. I don't think I could live with myself if something like this happened again."

Dhelis smiled. "We'll see ourselves out. I have a feeling we're going to need to learn our way around this place."

Once outside the room, Dhelis put his finger to his lips to remind them not to speak. Maurika had overheard their discussion on the way into the building. They had no idea how far the lunate's hearing reached, so the four of them made their way to the car in silence. No one spoke until Dhelis pulled onto the highway.

"Wow. That wrapped up your case in a pretty red bow." Brogan thumped the back of Dhelis's seat. "No more Full-Moon Killer *and* you get to call the Council out for being negligent. They weren't handling local pack matters, and our training didn't include knowledge of lunates."

"Should be an interesting meeting." Dhelis tapped the steering wheel. "Maybe I'll wait and bring that up next week. We've got bigger issues on our plate where Council's concerned."

That was putting things mildly. Their joining ceremony was not item one on her personal list of things to worry about. She planned to go through with it—she just couldn't keep the butterflies in her stomach from fluttering anxiously every time she thought too long about their triple-sided match. Thankfully, she was too tired to concentrate on one thought for long.

"I suppose we do," Brogan agreed, putting his arm behind his head and relaxing in his seat.

"So," she said to no one in particular, "I assume somebody will pick me up tonight since my Explorer needs some serious body work—after the police are through with it?"

"I will," Brogan volunteered. "I'm sure Dhelis will be doing paperwork on this case all day."

She caught Dhelis's stare in the rearview mirror. He looked as tired as she felt. She leaned her head back against the seat and closed her eyes. Exhaustion crept at her edge of consciousness. Her arms slid to the seat, muscles heavy and relaxed.

"Do either of you know where Saari lives?" Brogan asked.

Saari tried to respond. Numb lips refused to form coherent words. Her thoughts stalled, mired in a thick bog of fatigue.

"I do." Dhelis answered.

Wonder colored her drowsy mind.

She had not one but *two* men that wanted to take care of her.

Chapter Thirty-Eight

Dhelis watched the foliage fly by, the vibrant colors merging into a blurred palate of green and yellow hues. The tree-lined highway gave way to industrial plants on the outskirts of the city. In a few more miles, commercial buildings would flank the road. Heat shimmered on the pavement ahead. He wished he had his sunglasses to shade his eyes from the sun's mid-morning glare.

"Why don't you drop me off at the station, and I'll start the paperwork," Thana suggested, interrupting the silence. "You can take Saari and Brogan home. I'm sure the three of you could use a little time to yourselves."

A quick glimpse at his cousin showed tight lines around her eyes. He wondered how she was holding up. Even though Jordan and Thana had spent their lives apart, his death had affected her deeply. Knowing he'd died in a senseless tragedy—even though his killer was dead—couldn't be easy for her. He figured her offer of privacy was as much for herself as it was for everybody else.

He glanced in the rearview mirror. Brogan raised his eyebrows as if to say "it's up to you."

"You're sure?" he asked, cutting his gaze toward Thana.

"Of course I'm sure. Really, I don't mind."

Changing lanes, he jumped in the right-hand lane to switch highways. The police station was only ten minutes away. Once he'd made the decision, a curious feeling of anxiety settled in the pit of his stomach. He wondered at his sudden nervousness.

He glanced in the rearview mirror again, studying Saari while she slept. She sat curled against Brogan's side, her arm resting on his chest over the blanket. Brogan's head lay against the back of the seat, his arms wrapped around her.

His fingers tightened around the steering wheel as he realized what that feeling was: jealousy.

Thankfully, Brogan's eyes were closed. He'd missed his reaction. Pulling his emotions under control, he was forced to admit the idea of sharing Saari wasn't going to be as easy to accept as he hoped. His head told him one thing, while his testosterone-ladened heart told him another.

A red light drew his attention. Startled, he realized they were a block away from the police station. He'd driven for the last ten minutes on autopilot. He stopped in front of the station's front door.

"I should be back in an hour or so. I won't be long," he promised Thana.

"No problem. Take your time. I plan on doing my own report first anyway," she teased. "See you later, Brogan. Hey, one of you tell Saari I'm glad she's okay. I'll talk to her in a couple of days."

"I will—and thanks."

Thana closed the door and tapped the roof. Though it was broad daylight, he waited until she was in the station before he pulled away. He'd watched her back since they were kids, the gesture now second nature.

"How long will it take to get to Saari's place?" Brogan asked, keeping his voice low.

"Not long." He wasn't surprised that Brogan assumed Saari would be dropped off first. The two of them needed to talk, and obviously they both preferred to keep her out of their discussion. "She's actually not too far from either one of us—just in a much better neighborhood."

He took the overpass, heading toward the ocean. They rode in silence, allowing Saari to sleep. The drive gave him a chance to think about how he could explain his feelings to Brogan.

Much sooner than he wanted, they pulled up in front of Saari's place.

"This is where she lives?" Brogan murmured, surprise clear in his voice.

"Home sweet home."

"You weren't kidding when you said she lived in a better neighborhood. Her house sits on a huge lot!" Brogan exclaimed. "How'd she afford such a great piece of property?"

"Terrific. So now you're just interested in me for my money?" Saari popped off, her voice gravelly from sleep.

He turned toward the back seat just as Brogan's head came around.

"Of course not," Brogan replied, his voice rising on an indignant tone.

"Relax. I'm just kidding," she chuckled.

Dhelis reached over the seat and handed Saari her purse. "I made sure they took photographs of everything they needed so you could have your things back. Your vehicle will take a few more days. Sorry."

"That was thoughtful of you. Thanks." She took the bag from him with one hand, her other lingering on his arm.

He noticed the gesture, and a measure of calm acceptance rolled through him. Whatever the connection to Brogan, Saari was his mate, and she felt the energy connection between them as keenly as he did. No matter how long it took, they'd manage to work things out.

She pulled her hand back with a sigh, glancing at her watch. "I can't believe I slept for over an hour. You should have woken me."

"Why?" Brogan asked. "You're tired and need sleep."

"I am tired, but you two must be dead on your feet. When was the last time you slept, Dhelis?"

"I caught some sleep at the station yesterday. I'm good for a few more hours. After I finish my report, I'll take a nap."

"I'm going to bed as soon as I get home," Brogan said.

"So who's picking me up tonight?" she asked, her head swiveling between Brogan and himself.

Dhelis looked toward Brogan, but Brogan remained silent. He settled on a vague lack of knowledge. "I'm not exactly sure how this works, so I'll call you later and let you know." The excuse sounded like a copout even to his ears.

"Do you have my number?"

"It's in the witness statement you gave last night," Dhelis confirmed. He counted himself lucky she hadn't pointed out he was stalling.

"Oh, right. I forgot. Very clever, Detective." Opening the door, she stepped out of the car. He popped his seatbelt, intending to walk her up the front steps. She pressed a hand against his door, stopping him. "The security gate runs the perimeter of the property. I'll be fine."

"All right," he gave in, settling behind the wheel.

She leaned her head through the window, looking around him. "See you tonight, Brogan."

"Absolutely. Sweet dreams."

He watched her punch in a code at the gate and hurry through. She approached the wall on the other side, and the gate closed behind her. A quick jog brought her to the front door. She turned and waved goodbye, before disappearing inside.

The passenger door opened and closed as Brogan moved to the front seat. After buckling his seatbelt, he pointed at the front windshield. "She's safely inside. We can go now."

He pulled away from the curb and headed toward Brogan's place. As he navigated the residential streets, Dhelis mulled over the best way to approach Brogan. His emotional insecurity had his insides tied in knots of anxiety. Their friendship was relatively new, making the conversation difficult to begin.

"I won't apologize for being mated to Saari," Brogan said, keeping his tone mellow and even. "I had no control over that happening." Brogan turned toward him. "But I am sorry this is tearing you up, man. You were moon-eyed over the thought of a soul mate—your one and only. And now when you've found her, she's not your mate exclusively. That's a tough pill to swallow."

Brogan's words hit home. Dhelis' stomach clenched as his emotions twisted faster than a kid's spinning top. He had to guard his words. The three of them were in a Trigonal match, and he didn't want to hurt Brogan through heedless cruelty.

"I didn't mean to make you feel responsible. I *know* this isn't your fault. This match is nobody's fault. I think that pisses me off more than anything. I don't have anyone to blame. There's no target for my anger."

"I won't walk away from her, Dhelis. I can't."

"I didn't ask you to," he shot back, his anger flaring. Gritting his teeth, he took a deep breath and blew it out. "I want us to work this out."

Brogan scrubbed his hands down his face. "Then we will. What's it gonna take to make you comfortable about our three-sided relationship?"

He took a moment to really think about Brogan's question. He wanted their match to be healthy and successful—like any other relationship. After accepting that jealousy was at the core of his initial reaction, he prayed a solution would be easier to find.

"I need some time to get used to the idea that you and I are both Saari's mates. We each need to build a relationship with her, but I want us to do it equally and with respect," he said. "And not just with her, but between us as well."

"That's fair. We already know the chemical attraction is there. Now we need to create a solid connection with her."

Brogan grinned. "And I agree not to seduce her before you've grown accustomed to our match."

Dhelis snorted. "Who says she'd go for you first?"

"I don't think we should make Saari chose."

"You're right. She won't have to choose." He turned onto Brogan's block.

"So neither of us will sleep with her until you've said you're okay with this. The question is, how to get Saari to agree without telling her why?"

He pulled into the circular driveway that fronted Brogan's house and smiled, feeling in control of his emotions once again. "We let her think it's her idea."

Chapter Thirty-Nine

Evening, May 25, 2032—New Angeles

Saari inspected the large room at the Roullier Estate. The walls were painted in soothing pastels, their muted shades cleverly blended together to create a soft, flowing palette of calm. A dense, butter-cream carpet covered the floor, a perfect complement to the relaxing theme.

In the middle of the room stood three, intricately-carved pillars made from Tueri stone. A different-colored crystal sat atop each column, like a gem decorating the end of a scepter. Light not only reflected off the crystals, it seemed to also pass through them.

The room contained only three chairs, currently occupied by Brogan, Dhelis and herself. They sat in ordered silence. The three of them had traveled to the estate separately, at the direction of their hired drivers. She gave her mates a nervous glance. There hadn't been a chance to discuss the ceremony and its significance with either of them.

Maybe that was the Council's plan all along.

The enormity of their situation hit her. She hadn't been nervous until this very moment—until she *really* considered what she was about to do. Now her stomach felt like it was full of tiny butterflies beating their wings frantically, trying to escape.

She wondered if her reaction was a Freudian analogy.

Was she trying to find a way out of this? More decades than she could remember had passed since she last belonged with or to anybody. It felt strange starting again now. Especially with all the emotional and logistical issues the three of them needed to work out.

Did she really want to be bound to these two men forever? Well, forever was a relative term for her. But it was a reality for them, and they weren't showing any doubt.

What was she so afraid of anyway?

She couldn't imagine not being with them. Her energy connection with each man felt as natural to her as breathing. *Theirs* was the kind of chemistry poets heralded finding "once in a lifetime." So, yeah, she wanted a relationship with Dhelis and Brogan. Absolutely. Everything would sort itself out once they spent some time together and got to know each other.

The liberating sense of relief she'd experienced yesterday filled her spirit. Here, right now was where she was meant to be. Her knotted heartstrings unwound, finally freeing her from her ties to the past. Miko had shown her what a soul match should be, but he was gone. Dhelis and Brogan were her future.

Now she could move on.

She smiled. The butterflies in her stomach settled into a swirling hum of anticipation.

A door opened and several Council members came toward them. Her back straightened with a shiver of nervous excitement. Dhelis and Brogan stood, their hands clasped behind them in a show of respect. She followed their example.

The members took their places around the stone pillars. Each of them wore shimmering white robes, as opposed to the black gowns they had worn during her first contact with them. In contrast, Saari, Dhelis, and Brogan were garbed in different-colored robes. She had been instructed to wear nothing underneath her ceremonial dress, as it was an integral part of the ritual. She assumed the guys received the same direction.

The oldest Councilor spoke, commanding everyone's attention. "Brogan, Dhelis and Saari, if you would each stand behind the pillar whose colored crystal corresponds to your robe. Please stay outside the Trigonal space."

Trigonal space? He must mean between the pillars.

The three of them moved toward the center of the room, careful to stay outside the triangle-shaped area created by the positioned columns. Each stopped behind their designated pillar.

Brogan was dressed in a beautiful dark-green material that seemed to move and breathe on its own, almost as if the cloth were a living thing. Dhelis wore a rich purple robe, shot through with gold flecks that caught the light and shimmered every time he moved. She had been given a clear robe that was opaque in places—fortunately the most important ones.

All of the council members joined hands, bringing the members a few steps closer. They tightened their circle around not just the pillars, but Brogan, Dhelis, and her as well.

"Please disrobe and step within the Trigonal space," the Councilor directed.

Saari blinked with surprise. "Do what?"

Several of the male Council members smothered smiles at her reaction.

"This ceremony requires you to stand exposed before each other, stripped of all worldly influences. You are offering everything that you are, everything you have to give—your body, your abilities, your very soul—to your partners for safe keeping," the Councilor explained.

She looked at Brogan and Dhelis, gauging their reaction. Dhelis chuckled with his usual insouciance. Brogan winked with playful acceptance. Both men dropped their robes and moved into the open space.

"Bunch of perverts," she mumbled, letting her robe drop to the floor. She took a deep breath and stepped into the triangle. Brogan and Dhelis politely kept their eyes trained on her face. Their effort not to embarrass her was sweet. It didn't stop her from staring openly at both of them—*all* of them.

Brogan was all muscle. Not overly bulky like some body builders, but thick and ripped. Dhelis had a wide chest but a lankier build. Lean and mean came to mind. Things tightened below her stomach.

Dhelis rolled his shoulders, a devilish twinkle lighting his eyes.

Brogan puckered his lips in a kiss.

Shrugging, she gave a lopsided grin. "Just figured it was my turn to look—you know, one for all and all for one, right?"

The Councilor cleared his throat.

"Tueri aptitude for psychic potential grounds itself in the use of our stones. Therefore, the most important capabilities are receiving, directing and repelling energy in every form. Each Tueri match must choose for themselves whether to accept this extraordinary bond of sensory connection through our crystal medium."

She met the Councilor's gaze.

The old man's eyes shone with quiet dignity and his spine straightened with pride. "Do you, Dhelis, Brogan and Saari, accept this bonded connection as a permanent union?"

"I do." Brogan and Dhelis answered simultaneously.

Saari looked first at Dhelis, then Brogan. "I do."

A glimmer of warmth flared deep within her center, like the sun's first rays after a bitter winter. Never before had those two words meant so much. With these two men, she would share the secret part of herself she hadn't shared with anyone.

"So be it." As a group, every Council member had sanctioned their decision.

The Councilor continued, his sonorous tone echoing through the room.

"The three of you model a pyramid, each point an equal distance within the triangle. This Trigonal shape is a precise arrangement of stone and crystal, creating a specific boundary around a highly influenced space. It is within this space that the spectrum of your abilities will be received and united."

The room quieted, and a mood of serious formality settled over them.

"Brogan," he continued, "You are a healer with unlimited potential. Your ability is represented by green tourmaline. This crystal enables you not only to project but also absorb energy from the universe. No matter the circumstance, your therapeutic ability will modify itself to accomplish the healing of an individual's particular needs."

He moved on.

"Dhelis, your ability is represented through bi-colored fluorite. As a Stone Rider, you have the ability to recognize other dimensions of consciousness. This allows you to have an awareness of everything, without losing your own place in existence. Such an expansion of perception enables you to see the doorways within reality. Traveling anywhere you wish, at any given moment, is possible simply by focusing your mind and willing it."

She glanced at Brogan. Her skills would be defined next. A cramp of nervousness tightened her stomach. Brogan grinned, reassuring her. She shook her head, almost embarrassed by her insecurity.

"Saari, your ability is represented by smoky quartz. This crystal allows you to contain or project the highest amount of energy. Because of its grounding ability, it is one of the most powerful stones to use in a healing. The energy vibration enables others to accept their physical presence, follow their heart's direction, and understand their purpose in life."

The Councilor paused, giving her a moment to reflect on his summation of their abilities. A quiet sense of peace settled over her. She had never been able to define who or even what she was. Now she had a connection. She knew where she came from. There was a purpose behind her unique gift.

The Council members stepped forward again, each of them touching the imaginary lines that delineated the shape of their pyramid.

"Brogan, Dhelis, and Saari, join hands. Know that your stones serve as a bridge between each other, your energies equally balanced, forever connecting your abilities."

Dhelis and Brogan each reached for her. The three of them grasped hands. Their fingers locked, forming an unbreakable bond within the protective triangle of Council members, crystals, and stones.

Light exploded, illuminating the inner triangle they'd created. Those outside of the Trigonal center shielded their eyes, blinded by the light's brilliance. Her skin rippled under a hot wave of heavy energy. Sound pulsated through the room, pouring into and combining with the shimmers of heat.

Inside the joined shield, three individual energies roared to life. The energy soared, seeking an outlet. Those standing outside the shield amplified the expanding intensity, reflecting it back into the triangular space.

Each of their separate energies was forced to roll together within their immediate connection, sliding and undulating against and around each other. The furor heightened her consciousness, making her aware of every nerve ending in her body. Their shifting energies created a delicious friction as their "other" senses brushed against one another. The sensation flared, sending a direct shot to her cortex. Desire rippled through her body, flowing outward, adding to the pulsing sensation. Her energy throbbed with pleasure, as it writhed like an erotic belly dancer against Dhelis and Brogan's energies.

Space quickly became limited in the small triangular-shaped boundary. Their individual strengths fought for supremacy, like caged lions searching for an opening. There was no quarter given; no angle to be found. Finding no place of authority in the equal space, the energy flowed inward, finally merging in one powerful burst that sent the Council members staggering backward. Some lost their footing and fell to the floor. The final surge of power caused Saari, Dhelis, and Brogan to break their connection. They stood staring at each other, panting. Her euphoric state made it hard to focus on understanding the magnitude of what just happened.

Brogan broke the silence. "Damn. Was that as good for you as it was for me?" He laughed, the deep male sound filled with pleasure.

Dhelis just smiled and shook his head.

Her brain function, on the other hand, had returned with a vengeance. She turned to the Councilor. "Will the connection always be like that between the three of us?"

The old man smiled. "I don't know. Based on what we felt *outside* the pyramid, I'd guess each time you connect, the three of you will always experience what you all felt *inside* the pyramid."

Tenneile, the same council member who had spoken to her last time, helped one of the older members stand up before answering. "That was the official binding of your energies. Now you three will have to work together to learn how to control as well as project your merged abilities outward. When you go to Las Vegas in a few months for training, you'll receive tutoring that will help teach you how to work together."

"Cool," she said, grateful their "super powers" came with a manual. Another thought wrinkled her forehead as the woman's explanation replayed in her head. "Hey, do we have to do this binding thing again, naked, in front of other people?"

Tenneile laughed. "No. That's only required for the official binding. Your energies were exposed and joined with each other, and nothing can change that now. Your appearance in Vegas will just be for instruction."

Dhelis draped her robe over her shoulders, leaving his arm around her. She'd managed to miss him covering up. He made up for it by dancing his fingers lightly along her neck. Brogan, having already put his robe on, reached out and held her hand. The three of them stood like that, feeling energy rolling through them once again. She felt it build, nearly overwhelming her senses.

"All right, boys, that's enough for today," she chuckled, pulling out of their grasp. They both looked like children who'd had their favorite toy taken away. This private thought caused her to blush after realizing *she* was that toy.

Dhelis crossed his arms over his chest, smiling despite his stern stance. "So, where do we go from here?"

Brogan looked to her for her answer.

"Well," she began, "I'm going to get dressed. Then, I suggest we go get something to eat. I don't know about you guys, but I'm starving. After that, we'll trade phone numbers. You call me, I'll call you—" she shrugged.

Dhelis put his hand on the back of her neck and stepped toward her. His lips slanted over hers, soft and demanding. Heat filled her, curling her toes. She gripped his elbows to keep her knees from buckling.

He pulled back far enough to look into her eyes. "I think we're beyond that stage."

"I'll have extra house keys made."

Satisfaction lit his eyes.

She lowered her arms with a sigh and gripped his hand. Her fingers threaded with his. They had each chosen to be bound together. Her insecurities melted away. She faced the door and saw Brogan holding it open for her and Dhelis.

He stretched a hand toward her. "We'll all have extra house keys made."

She smiled and reached for Brogan.

ACKNOWLEDGMENTS

My sincerest thanks to Cathy Perkins; my friend, critique partner and fellow writer—without you, there'd be no Moonlight. Each of the amazing gals at Crescent Moon Press: Hannah Karol, Marlene Castricato and Steph Murray—thank you for believing in my story and taking a chance on an Unknown. My remarkable editor Heather Howland, whose freakin' yellow highlighter of doom helped me see past the words on the page and become a better writer. Ash Arceneaux for Moonlight Bleu's gorgeous cover. Lisa Lang for my beautiful photographs. Cheryl Pelletier, Karen Kirk and Patricia Yonkers for reading chapters of this manuscript and offering brutally honest opinions. Alex Ekstrom, who read the entire first draft (I'm *so* sorry, my friend).

Tori, Amanda, Alyssa and Brenna—for not complaining (too loudly) when mom closed
the office door to write.

ABOUT THE AUTHOR

Renee Rearden had such a passion for the written word, she changed her major in college and received a Court Reporting degree. Now, instead of *writing* down what everybody else says, she spends her time writing paranormal romance and urban fantasy. She lives in the Pacific Northwest with her family, where she is currently working on her latest novel.

Visit Renee Rearden at her website www.reneerearden.com.

LaVergne, TN USA
24 August 2010
194449LV00002B/4/P